The
Cinema Murder

" Can't you take my parole? Can't you leave me alone until
they come from England? " FRONTISPIECE. *See page 300.*

The Cinema Murder

E. PHILLIPS OPPENHEIM

WILDSIDE PRESS

INTRODUCTION

Meet E. Phillips Oppenheim

Edward Phillips Oppenheim (1866-1946) was an Englishman, born in London, the son of a leather merchant. For twenty years he worked in his father's business, while beginning to publish novels. His first, subsidized by his father, barely broke even, but before long he was successful, enough so that a rich admirer, also in the leather business, bought out the firm and put Oppenheim on salary to support his writing career. Oppenheim soon hit his stride and became a bestseller, one of the most popular writers of his generation. He produced one hundred and sixteen novels and thirty-nine collections of short stories. At least twenty-one films were produced from his work, mostly in the silent era, including three versions of his most popular work, *The Great Impersonation*.

Oppenheim's specialty was the fast-moving, glamorous suspense thriller, written in a breezy, easy-to-read style. He was the epitome of the "entertainment" writer of his day, without any pretensions of literature. His stories are filled with high society people, spies, diplomats, and political intrigue, without much actual detection, so, it has been remarked, his relationship to the formal mystery story is slight. One difference between Oppenheim and many other writers who described glamorous high society was that he had actually been there. Once he was successful, he had a yacht and a villa on the French Riviera, where he spent his winters and moved in elite circles.

In his most famous work, *The Great Impersonation,* a German and an Englishman, who could be identical twins, meet together in Africa and note their uncanny resemblance. Then the German plots to make the Englishman disappear and steal his identity in order to carry on an espionage mission. The trick of the book is that the reader follows the man's return to England without ever knowing *which* man has returned. Is it the Englishman or the German impostor? Even those closest to him don't know.

Oppenheim was widely admired in his day. John Buchan, the author of *The Thirty-Nine Steps* called him "My master in fiction."

—Darrell Schweitzer
Philadelphia, Pennsylvania

BOOK I

CHAPTER I

With a somewhat prolonged grinding of the brakes and an unnecessary amount of fuss in the way of letting off steam, the afternoon train from London came to a standstill in the station at Detton Magna. An elderly porter, putting on his coat as he came, issued, with the dogged aid of one bound by custom to perform a hopeless mission, from the small, red-brick lamp room. The station master, occupying a position of vantage in front of the shed which enclosed the booking office, looked up and down the lifeless row of closed and streaming windows, with an expectancy dulled by daily disappointment, for the passengers who seldom alighted. On this occasion no records were broken. A solitary young man stepped out on to the wet and flinty platform, handed over the half of a third-class return ticket from London, passed through the two open doors and commenced to climb the long ascent which led into the town.

He wore no overcoat, and for protection against the inclement weather he was able only to turn up the collar of his well-worn blue serge coat. The damp of a ceaselessly wet day seemed to have laid its cheerless pall upon the whole exceedingly ugly landscape. The hedges, blackened with smuts from the colliery on the other side of the slope, were dripping also with raindrops. The road, flinty and light grey in colour, was greasy with repellent-looking mud — there were puddles even in the asphalt-covered pathway which he trod. On either side of him stretched the shrunken, unpastoral-looking fields of an industrial neighbourhood. The town-village which stretched up the hillside before him presented scarcely a single redeeming feature. The small, grey stone houses, hard and unadorned, were interrupted at intervals by rows of brand-new, red-brick cottages. In the background were the tall chimneys of several factories; on the left, a colliery shaft raised its smoke-blackened finger to the lowering clouds.

After his first glance around at these familiar and unlovely objects, Philip Romilly walked with his head a little thrown back, his eyes lifted as though with intent to the melancholy and watery skies. He was a young man well above medium height, slim, almost inclined to be angular, yet with a good carriage notwithstanding a stoop which seemed more the result of an habitual depression than occasioned by any physical weakness. His features were large, his mouth querulous, a little discontented, his eyes filled with the light of a silent and rebellious bitterness which seemed, somehow, to have found a more or less permanent abode in his face. His clothes, although they were neat, had seen better days. He was ungloved, and he carried under his arm a small parcel, which appeared to contain a book, carefully done up in brown paper.

As he reached the outskirts of the village he slackened his pace. Standing a little way back from the road, from which they were separated by an ugly, gravelled playground, were the familiar school buildings, with the usual inscription carved in stone above the door. He laid his hand upon the wooden gate and paused. From inside he could catch the drone of children's voices. He glanced at his watch. It was barely twenty minutes past four. For a moment he hesitated. Then he strolled on, and, turning at the gate of an adjoining cottage, the nearest to the schools of a little unlovely row, he tried the latch, found it yield to his touch, and stepped inside. He closed the door behind him and turned, with a little weary sigh of content, towards a large easy-chair drawn up in front of the fire. For a single moment he seemed about to throw himself into its depths — his long fingers, indeed, a little blue with the cold, seemed already on their way towards the genial warmth of the flames. Then he stopped short. He stood perfectly still in an attitude of arrested motion, his eyes, wonderingly at first, and then with a strange, unanalysable expression, seeming to embark upon a lengthened, a scrupulous, an almost horrified estimate of his surroundings.

To the ordinary observer there would have been nothing remarkable in the appearance of the little room, save its entirely unexpected air of luxury and refinement. There was a small Chippendale sideboard against the wall, a round, gate-legged table on which stood a blue china bowl filled with pink roses, a couple of luxurious easy-chairs, some old prints upon the wall. On the sideboard was a basket, as yet unpacked, filled with hothouse fruit, and on a low settee by the side of one of the easy-chairs were a little pile of reviews, several volumes of poetry, and a couple of library books. In the centre of the mantelpiece was a photograph, the photograph of a man a little older, perhaps, than this newly-arrived visitor, with rounder face, dressed in country tweeds, a flower in his buttonhole, the picture of a prosperous man, yet with a curious, almost disturbing likeness to the pale, over-nervous, loose-framed youth whose eye had been attracted by its presence, and who was gazing at it, spellbound.

"Douglas!" he muttered. "Douglas!"

He flung his hat upon the table and for a moment his hand rested upon his forehead. He was confronted with a mystery which baffled him, a mystery whose sinister possibilities were slowly framing themselves in his mind. While he stood there he was suddenly conscious of the sound of the opening gate, brisk footsteps up the tiled way, the soft swirl of a woman's skirt. The latch was raised, the door opened and closed. The newcomer stood upon the threshold, gazing at him.

"Philip!" she exclaimed. "Why, Philip!"

There was a curious change in the girl's tone, from almost glad welcome to a note of abrupt fear in that last pronouncement of his name. She stood looking at him, the victim, apparently, of so many emotions that there was nothing definite to be drawn either from her tone or expression. She was a young woman of medium height and slim, delicate figure, attractive, with large, discontented mouth, full, clear eyes and a wealth of dark brown hair. She was very simply dressed and yet in a manner which scarcely suggested the school-teacher. To the man who confronted her, his left hand gripping the mantelpiece, his eyes filled with a flaming jealousy, there was something entirely new in the hang of her well-cut skirt, the soft colouring of her low-necked blouse, the greater animation of her piquant face with its somewhat dazzling complexion. His hand flashed out towards her as he asked his question.

" What does it mean, Beatrice? "

She showed signs of recovering herself. With a little shrug of the shoulders she turned towards the door which led into an inner room.

" Let me get you some tea, Philip," she begged. " You look so cold and wet."

" Stay here, please," he insisted.

She paused reluctantly. There was a curious lack of anything peremptory in his manner, yet somehow, although she would have given the world to have passed for a few moments into the shelter of the little kitchen beyond, she was impelled to do as he bade her.

" Don't be silly, Philip," she said petulantly. " You know you want some tea, and so do I. Sit down, please, and make yourself comfortable. Why didn't you let me know you were coming? "

" Perhaps it would have been better," he agreed quietly. " However, since I am here, answer my question."

She drew a little breath. After all, although she was lacking in any real strength of character, she was filled with a certain compensatory doggedness. His challenge was there to be faced. There was no way out of it. She would have lied willingly enough but for the sheer futility of falsehood. She commenced the task of bracing herself for the struggle.

" You had better," she said, " frame your question

a little more exactly. I will then try to answer it."

He was stung by her altered demeanour, embarrassed by an avalanche of words. A hundred questions were burning upon his lips. It was by a great effort of self-control that he remained coherent.

"The last time I visited you," he began, "was three months ago. Your cottage then was furnished as one would expect it to be furnished. You had a deal dresser, a deal table, one rather hard easy-chair and a very old wicker one. You had, if I remember rightly, a strip of linoleum upon the floor, and a single rug. Your flowers were from the hedges and your fruit from the one apple tree in the garden behind. Your clothes — am I mistaken about your clothes or are you dressed more expensively?"

"I am dressed more expensively," she admitted.

"You and I both know the value of these things," he went on, with a little sweep of the hand. "We know the value of them because we were once accustomed to them, because we have both since experienced the passionate craving for them or the things they represent. Chippendale furniture, a Turkey carpet, roses in January, hothouse fruit, Bartolozzi prints, do not march with an income of fifty pounds a year."

"They do not," she assented equably. "All the things which you see here and which you have mentioned, are presents."

His forefinger shot out with a sudden vigour towards the photograph.

"From him?"

"From Douglas," she admitted, "from your cousin."

He took the photograph into his hand, looked at it for a moment, and dashed it into the grate. The glass of the frame was shivered into a hundred pieces. The girl only shrugged her shoulders. She was holding herself in reserve. As for him, his eyes were hot, there was a dry choking in his throat. He had passed through many weary and depressed days, struggling always against the grinding monotony of life and his surroundings. Now for the first time he felt that there was something worse.

" What does it mean? " he asked once more.

She seemed almost to dilate as she answered him. Her feet were firmly planted upon the ground. There was a new look in her face, a look of decision. She was more or less a coward but she felt no fear. She even leaned a little towards him and looked him in the face.

" It means," she pronounced slowly, " exactly what it seems to mean."

The words conveyed horrible things to him, but he was spechless. He could only wait.

" You and I, Philip," she continued, " have been — well, I suppose we should call it engaged — for three years. During those three years I have earned, by disgusting and wearisome labour, just enough to keep me alive in a world which has had nothing to offer me but ugliness and discomfort and misery. You, as you admitted last time we met, have done no better. You have lived in a garret and gone often hungry to bed. For three years this has been going on. All that time I have waited for you to bring something human, something reasonable, something warm into my life, and you have failed. I have passed, in those three years, from twenty-three to twenty-six. In three more I shall be in my thirtieth year — that is to say, the best time of my life will have passed. You see, I have been thinking, and I have had enough."

He stood quite dumb. The girl's newly-revealed personality seemed to fill the room. He felt crowded out. She was, at that stage, absolutely mistress of the situation. . . . She passed him carelessly by, flung herself into the easy-chair and crossed her legs. As though he were looking at some person in another world, he realized that she was wearing shoes of shapely cut, and silk stockings.

" Our engagement," she went on, " was at first the dearest thing in life to me. It could have been the most wonderful thing in life. I am only an ordinary person with an ordinary character, but I have the capacity to love unselfishly, and I am at heart as faithful and as good as any other woman. But there is my birthright. I have had three years of sordid and utterly miserable life, teaching squalid, dirty, unlovable children things they had much better not know. I have lived here, here in Detton Magna, among the smuts and the mists, where the flowers seem withered and even the meadows are stony, where the people are hard and coarse as their ugly houses, where virtue is ugly, and vice is ugly, and living is ugly, and death is fearsome. And now you see what I have chosen — not in a moment's folly, mind, because I am not foolish; not in a moment's passion, either, because until now the only real feeling I have had in life was for you. But I have chosen, and I hold to my choice."

" They won't let you stay here," he muttered.

" They needn't," she answered calmly. " There are other ways in which I can at least earn as much as the miserable pittance doled out to me here. I have avoided even considering them before. Shall I tell you why? Because I didn't want to face the temptation they might bring with them. I always knew what would happen if escape became hopeless. It's the ugliness I can't stand — the ugliness of cheap food, cheap clothes, uncomfortable furniture, coarse voices, coarse friends if I would have them. How do you suppose I have lived here these last three years, a teacher in the national schools? Look up and down this long, dreary street, at the names above the shops, at the villas in which the trades-people live, and ask yourself where my friends were to come from? The clergyman, perhaps? He is over seventy, a widower, and he never comes near the place. Why, I'd have been content to have been patronized if there had been anyone here to do it, who wore the right sort of clothes and said the right sort of thing in the right tone. But the others — well, that's done with."

He remained curiously dumb. His eyes were fixed upon the fragments of the photograph in the grate. In a corner of the room an old-fashioned clock ticked wheezily. A lump of coal fell out on the hearth, which she replaced mechanically with her foot. His silence seemed to irritate and perplex her. She looked away from him, drew her chair a little closer to the fire, and sat with her head resting upon her hands. Her tone had become almost meditative.

" I knew that this would come one day," she went

on. "Why don't you speak and get it over? Are you waiting to clothe your phrases? Are you afraid of the naked words? I'm not. Let me hear them. Don't be more melodramatic than you can help because, as you know, I am cursed with a sense of humour, but don't stand there saying nothing."

He raised his eyes and looked at her in silence, an alternative which she found it hard to endure. Then, after a moment's shivering recoil into her chair, she sprang to her feet.

"Listen," she cried passionately, "I don't care what you think! I tell you that if you were really a man, if you had a man's heart in your body, you'd have sinned yourself before now — robbed some one, murdered them, torn the things that make life from the fate that refuses to give them. What is it they pay you," she went on contemptuously, "at that miserable art school of yours? Sixty pounds a year! How much do you get to eat and drink out of that? What sort of clothes have you to wear? Are you content? Yet even you have been better off than I. You have always your chance. Your play may be accepted or your stories published. I haven't even had that forlorn hope. But even you, Philip, may wait too long. There are too many laws, nowadays, for life to be lived naturally. If I were a man, a man like you, I'd break them."

Her taunts apparently moved him no more than the inner tragedy which her words had revealed. He did not for one moment give any sign of abandoning the unnatural calm which seemed to have descended upon him. He took up his hat from the table, and thrust the little brown paper parcel which he had been carrying, into his pocket. His eyes for a single moment met the challenge of hers, and again she was conscious of some nameless, inexplicable fear.

" Perhaps," he said, as he turned away, " I may do that."

His hand was upon the latch before she realized that he was actually going. She sprang to her feet. Abuse, scorn, upbraidings, even violence — she had been prepared for all of these. There was something about this self-restraint, however, this strange, brooding silence, which terrified her more than anything she could have imagined.

" Philip!" she shrieked. " You're not going? You're not going like this? You haven't said anything!"

He closed the door with firm fingers. Her knees trembled, she was conscious of an unexpected weakness. She abandoned her first intention of following him, and stood before the window, holding tightly to the sash. He had reached the gate now and paused for a moment, looking up the long, windy street. Then he crossed to the other side of the road, stepped over a stile and disappeared, walking without haste, with firm footsteps, along a cindered path which bordered the sluggish-looking canal. He had come and gone, and she knew what fear was!

CHAPTER II

The railway station at Detton Magna presented, if possible, an even more dreary appearance than earlier in the day, as the time drew near that night for the departure of the last train northwards. Its long strip of flinty platform was utterly deserted. Around the three flickering gas-lamps the drizzling rain fell continuously. The weary porter came yawning out of his lamp room into the booking office, where the station master sat alone, his chair turned away from the open wicket window to the smouldering embers of the smoky fire.

" No passengers to-night, seemingly," the latter remarked to his subordinate.

" Not a sign of one," was the reply. " That young chap who came down from London on a one-day return excursion, hasn't gone back, either. That'll do his ticket in."

The outside door was suddenly opened and closed. The sound of footsteps approaching the ticket window was heard. A long, white hand was thrust through the aperture, a voice was heard from the invisible outside.

" Third to Detton Junction, please."

The station-master took the ticket from a little rack, received the exact sum he demanded, swept it into the till, and resumed his place before the fire. The porter, with the lamp in his hand, lounged out into the booking-hall. The prospective passenger, however, was nowhere in sight. He looked back into the office.

" Was that Jim Spender going up to see his barmaid again? " he asked his superior.

The station master yawned drowsily.

" Didn't notice," he answered. " What an old woman you're getting, George! Want to know everybody's business, don't you? "

The porter withdrew, a little huffed. When, a few minutes later, the train drew in, he even avoided ostentatiously a journey to the far end of the platform to open the door for the solitary passenger who was standing there. He passed up the train and slammed the door without even glancing in at the window. Then he stood and watched the red lights disappear.

" Was it Jim? " the station master asked him, on their way out.

" Didn't notice," his subordinate replied, a little curtly. " Maybe it was and maybe it wasn't. Good night! "

Philip Romilly sat back in the corner of his empty third-class carriage, peering out of the window, in which he could see only the reflection of the feeble gas-lamp. There was no doubt about it, however — they were moving. The first stage of his journey had commenced. The blessed sense of motion, after so long waiting, at first soothed and then exhilarated him. In a few moments he became restless. He let down the rain-blurred window and leaned out. The cool dampness of the night was immensely refreshing, the rain softened his hot cheeks. He sat there, peering away into the shadows, struggling for the sight of definite objects — a tree, a house, the outline of a field — anything to keep the other thoughts away, the thoughts that came sometimes like the aftermath of a grisly, unrealisable nightmare. Then he felt chilly, drew up the window, thrust his hands into his pockets from which he drew out a handsome cigarette case, struck a match, and smoked with vivid appreciation of the quality of the tobacco, examined the crest on the case as he put it away, and finally patted with surreptitious eagerness the flat morocco letter case in his inside pocket.

At the Junction, he made his way into the refreshment room and ordered a long whisky and soda, which he drank in a couple of gulps. Then he hastened to the booking office and took a first-class ticket to Liverpool, and a few minutes later secured a seat in the long, north-bound express which came gliding up to the side of the platform. He spent some time in the lavatory, washing, arranging his hair, straightening his tie, after which he made his way into the elaborate dining-car and found a comfortable corner seat. The luxury of his surroundings soothed his jagged nerves. The car was comfortably warmed, the electric light upon his table was softly shaded. The steward who waited upon him was swift-footed and obsequious, and seemed entirely oblivious of Philip's shabby, half-soaked clothes. He ordered champagne a little vaguely, and the wine ran through his veins with a curious potency. He ate and drank now and then mechanically, now and then with the keenest appetite. Afterwards he smoked a cigar, drank coffee, and sipped a liqueur with the appreciation of a connoisseur. A fellow passenger passed him an evening paper, which he glanced through with apparent interest. Before he reached his journey's end he had ordered and drunk another liqueur. He tipped the steward handsomely. It was the first well-cooked meal which he had eaten for many months.

Arrived at Liverpool, he entered a cab and drove to the Adelphi Hotel. He made his way at once to the office. His clothes were dry now and the rest and warmth had given him more confidence.

" You have a room engaged for me, I think," he said, " Mr. Douglas Romilly. I sent some luggage on."

The man merely glanced at him and handed him a ticket.

" Number sixty-seven, sir, on the second floor," he announced.

A porter conducted him up-stairs into a large, well-furnished bedroom. A fire was blazing in the grate; a dressing-case, a steamer trunk and a hatbox were set out at the foot of the bedstead.

" The heavier luggage, labelled for the hold, sir," the man told him, " is down-stairs, and will go direct to the steamer to-morrow morning. That was according to your instructions, I believe."

" Quite right," Philip assented. " What time does the boat sail? "

" Three o'clock, sir."

Philip frowned. This was his first disappointment. He had fancied himself on board early in the day. The prospect of a long morning's inaction seemed already to terrify him.

"Not till the afternoon," he muttered.

"Matter of tide, sir," the man explained. "You can go on board any time after eleven o'clock in the morning, though. Very much obliged to you, sir."

The porter withdrew, entirely satisfied with his tip. Philip Romilly locked the door after him carefully. Then he drew a bunch of keys from his pocket and, after several attempts, opened both the steamer trunk and the dressing-case. He surveyed their carefully packed contents with a certain grim and fantastic amusement, handled the silver brushes, shook out a purple brocaded dressing-gown, laid out a suit of clothes for the morrow, even selected a shirt and put the links in it. Finally he wandered into the adjoining bathroom, took a hot bath, packed away at the bottom of the steamer trunk the clothes which he had been wearing, went to bed — and slept.

CHAPTER III

The sun was shining into his bedroom when Philip Romilly was awakened the next morning by a discreet tapping at the door. He sat up in bed and shouted " Come in." He had no occasion to hesitate for a moment. He knew perfectly well where he was, he remembered exactly everything that had happened. The knocking at the door was disquieting but he faced it without a tremor. The floor waiter appeared and bowed deferentially.

" There is a gentleman on the telephone wishes to speak to you, sir," he announced. " I have connected him with the instrument by your side."

" To speak with me? " Philip repeated. " Are you quite sure? "

" Yes, sir. Mr. Douglas Romilly he asked for. He said that his name was Mr. Gayes, I believe."

The man left the room and Philip took up the receiver. For a moment he sat and thought. The situation was perplexing, in a sense ominous, yet it had to be faced. He held the instrument to his ear.

" Hullo? Who's that? " he enquired.

" That Mr. Romilly? " was the reply, in a man's pleasant voice. " Mr. Douglas Romilly? "

" Yes! "

" Good! I'm Gayes — Mr. Gayes of Gayes

Brothers. My people wrote me last night **from** Leicester that you would be here this morning. **You** are crossing, aren't you, on the *Elletania?* "

Philip remained monosyllabic.

" Yes," he admitted cautiously.

" Can't you come round and see us this morning? " Mr. Gayes invited. " And look here, Mr. Romilly, in any case I want you to lunch with me at the club. My car shall come round and fetch you at any time you say."

" Sorry," Philip replied. " I am very busy this morning, and I am engaged for lunch."

" Oh, come, that's too bad," the other protested, " I really want to have a chat with you on business matters, Mr. Romilly. Will you spare me half an hour if I come round? "

" Tell me exactly what it is you want? " Philip insisted.

" Oh! just the usual thing," was the cheerful answer. " We hear you are off to America on a buying tour. Our last advices don't indicate a very easy market over there. I am not at all sure that we couldn't do better for you here, and give you better terms."

Philip began to feel more sure of himself. The situation, after all, he realized, was not exactly alarming.

" Very kind of you," he said. " My arrangements are all made now, though, and I can't interfere with them."

" Well, I'm going to bother you with a few quotations, anyway. See here, I'll just run round to see you. My car is waiting at the door now. I won't keep you more than a few minutes."

"Don't come before twelve," Philip begged. "I shall be busy until then."

"At twelve o'clock precisely, then," was the reply. "I shall hope to induce you to change your mind about luncheon. It's quite a long time since we had you at the club. Good-by!"

Philip set down the telephone. He was still in his pajamas and the morning was cold, but he suddenly felt a great drop of perspiration on his forehead. It was the sort of thing, this, which he had expected — had been prepared for, in fact — but it was none the less, in its way, gruesome. There was a further knock at the door, and the waiter reappeared.

"Can I bring you any breakfast, sir?" he enquired.

"What time is it?"

"Half-past nine, sir."

"Bring me some coffee and rolls and butter," Philip ordered.

He sprang out of bed, bathed, dressed, and ate his breakfast. Then he lit a cigarette, repacked his dressing-case, and descended into the hall. He made his way to the hall porter's enquiry office.

"I am going to pay some calls in the city," he announced — "Mr. Romilly is my name — and I may not be able to get back here before my boat sails. I am going on the *Elletania*. Can I have my luggage sent there direct?"

"By all means, sir."

"Every article is properly labelled," Philip continued. "Those in my bedroom — number sixty-seven — are for the cabin, and those you have in your charge are for the hold."

"That will be quite all right, sir," the man assured him pocketing his liberal tip. "I will see to the matter myself."

Philip paid his bill at the office and breathed a little more freely as he left the hotel. Passing a large, plate-glass window he stopped suddenly and stared at his own reflection. There was something unfamiliar in the hang of his well-cut clothes and fashionable Homburg hat. It was like the shadow of some one else passing — some one to whom those clothes belonged. Then he remembered, remembered with a cold shiver which blanched his cheeks and brought a little agonised murmur to his lips. The moment passed, however, crushed down, stifled as he had sworn that he would stifle all such memories. He turned in at a barber's shop, had his hair cut, and yielded to the solicitations of a fluffy-haired young lady who was dying to go to America if only somebody would take her, and who was sure that he ought to have a manicure before his voyage. Afterwards he entered a call office and rang up the hotel on the telephone.

"Mr. Romilly speaking," he announced. "Will you kindly tell Mr. Gayes, if he calls to see me, that I have been detained in the city, and shall not be back."

The man took down the message. Philip strolled out once more into the streets, wandering aimlessly about for an hour or more. By this time it was nearly one o'clock, and, selecting a restaurant, he entered and ordered luncheon. Once more it came over him, as he looked around the place, that he had, after all, only a very imperfect hold upon his own identity. It seemed impossible that he, Philip Romilly, should be there, ordering precisely what appealed to him most, without thought or care of the cost. He ate and drank slowly and with discrimination, and when he left the place he felt stronger. He sought out a first-class tobacconist's, bought some cigarettes, and enquired his way to the dock. At a few minutes after two, he passed up the gangway and boarded the great steamer. One of the little army of linen-coated stewards enquired the number of his room and conducted him below.

"Anything I can do for you, sir, before your luggage comes on?" the man asked civilly.

Philip shook his head and wandered up on deck again, where there were already a fair number of passengers in evidence. He leaned over the side, watching the constant stream of porters bearing supplies, and the steerage passengers passing into the forepart of the ship. With every moment his impatience grew. He looked at his watch sometimes half a dozen times in ten minutes, changed his position continually, started violently whenever he heard an unexpected footstep behind him. Finally he broke a promise he had made to himself. He bought newspapers, took them into a sheltered corner, and tore them open. Column by column he searched them through feverishly, running his finger down one side and up the next. It seemed impossible to find nowhere the heading he dreaded to see, to realize that they were entirely empty of any exciting incident. He satisfied himself at last, however. The

disappearance of a half-starved art teacher had not
yet blazoned out to a sympathetic world. It was
so much to the good. . . . There was a touch upon
his shoulder, and he felt a chill of horror. When
he turned around, it was the steward who had conducted him below, holding out a telegram.

"I beg your pardon, sir," he said. "Telegram
just arrived for you."

He passed on almost at once, in search of some
one else. Philip stood for several moments perfectly
still. He looked at the inscription — *Douglas Romilly* — set his teeth and tore open the envelope:

Understood you were returning to factory before leaving. Am posting a few final particulars to Waldorf
Hotel, New York. Staff joins me in wishing you bon
voyage.

Philip felt his heart cease its pounding, felt an
immense sense of relief. It was a wonderful thing,
this message. It cleared up one point on which he had
been anxious and unsettled. It was taken for granted at the Works, then, that he had come straight to
Liverpool. He walked up and down the deck on the
side remote from the dock, driving this into his mind.

Everything was wonderfully simplified. If only he
could get across, once reach New York! Meanwhile,
he looked at his watch again and discovered that it
wanted but ten minutes to three. He made his way
back down to his stateroom, which was already filled
with his luggage. He shook out an ulster from a
bundle of wraps, and selected a tweed cap. Already
there was a faint touch of the sea in the river breeze,
and he was impatient for the immeasurable open

spaces, the salt wind, the rise and fall of the great ship. Then, as he stood on the threshold of his cabin, he heard voices.

" Down in number 110, eh? "

" Yes, sir," he heard his steward's voice reply. " Mr. Romilly has just gone down. You've only a minute, sir, before the last call for passengers."

" That's all right," the voice which had spoken to him over the telephone that morning replied. " I'd just like to shake hands with him and wish him bon voyage."

Philip's teeth came together in a little fury of anger. It was maddening, this, to be trapped when only a few minutes remained between him and safety! His brain worked swiftly. He took his chance of finding the next stateroom empty, as it happened to be, and stepped quickly inside. He kept his back to the door until the footsteps had passed. He heard the knock at his stateroom, stepped back into the corridor, and passed along a little gangway to the other side of the ship. He hurried up the stairs and into the smoking-room. The bugle was sounding now, and hoarse voices were shouting:

" Every one for the shore! Last call for the shore! "

" Give me a brandy and soda," he begged the steward, who was just opening the bar.

The man glanced at the clock and obeyed. Philip swallowed half of it at a gulp, then sat down with the tumbler in his hand. All of a sudden something disappeared from in front of one of the portholes. His heart gave a little jump. They were moving! He sprang up and hurried to the doorway. Slowly but unmistakably they were gliding away from the dock. Already a lengthening line of people were waving their handkerchiefs and shouting farewells. Around them in the river little tugs were screaming, and the ropes from the dock had been thrown loose. Philip stepped to the rail, his heart growing lighter at every moment. His ubiquitous steward, laden with hand luggage, paused for a moment.

"I sent a gentleman down to your stateroom just before the steamer started, sir," he announced, "gentleman of the name of Gayes, who wanted to say good-by to you."

"Bad luck!" Philip answered. "I must have just missed him."

The steward turned around and pointed to the quay.

"There he is, sir — elderly gentleman in a grey suit, and a bunch of violets in his buttonhole. He's looking straight at you."

Philip raised his cap and waved it with enthusiasm. After a moment's hesitation, the other man did the same. The steward collected his belongings and shuffled off.

"He picked you out, sir, all right," he remarked as he disappeared in the companionway.

Philip turned away with a little final wave of the hand.

"Glad I didn't miss him altogether," he observed cheerfully. "Good-afternoon, Mr. Gayes! Good-by, England!"

CHAPTER IV

Mr. Raymond Greene, very soon after the bugle had sounded for dinner that evening, took his place at the head of one of the small tables in the saloon and wished every one good evening. It was perfectly apparent that he meant to enjoy the trip, that he was prepared to like his fellow passengers and that he wished them to know it. Even the somewhat melancholy-looking steward, who had been waiting for his arrival, cheered up at the sight of his beaming face, and the other four occupants of the table returned his salutation according to their lights.

"Two vacant places, I am sorry to see," Mr. Greene observed. "One of them I can answer for, though. The young lady who is to sit on my right will be down directly — Miss Elizabeth Dalstan, the great actress, you know. She is by way of being under my charge. Very charming and talented young lady she is. Let us see who our other absentee is."

He stretched across and glanced at the name upon the card.

"Mr. Douglas Romilly," he read out. "Quite a good name — English, without a doubt. I have crossed with you before, haven't I, sir?" he went on affably, turning to his nearest neighbour on the left.

A burly, many-chinned American signified his assent.

"Why, I should say so," he admitted, "and I'd like a five-dollar bill, Mr. Greene, for every film I've seen of yours in the United States."

Mr. Greene beamed with satisfaction.

"Well, I am glad to hear you've come across my stuff," he declared. "I've made some name for myself on the films and I am proud of it. Raymond Greene it is, at your service."

"Joseph P. Hyam's mine," the large American announced, watching the disappearance of his soup plate with an air of regret. "I'm in the clothing business. If my wife were here, she'd say you wouldn't think it to look at me. Never was faddy about myself, though," he added, with a glance at Mr. Greene's very correct dinner attire.

"You ought to remember me, Mr. Greene," one of the two men remarked from the right-hand side of the table. "I've played golf with you at Baltusrol more than once."

Mr. Greene glanced surreptitiously at the card and smiled.

"Why, it's James P. Busby, of course!" he exclaimed. "Your father's the Busby Iron Works, isn't he?"

The young man nodded.

"And this is Mr. Caroll, one of our engineers," he said, indicating a rather rough-looking personage by his side.

"Delighted to meet you both," Mr. Greene assured them. "Say, I remember your golf, Mr. Busby! You're some driver, eh? And those long

putts of yours — you never took three on any green
that I can remember!"

"Been playing in England?" the young man
asked.

Mr. Raymond Greene shook his head.

"When I am on business," he explained, "I don't
carry my sticks about with me, and I tell you this
last fortnight has been a giddy whirl for me. I was
in Berlin Wednesday night, and I did business in
Vienna last Monday. Ah! here comes Miss Dalstan."

He rose ceremoniously to his feet. A young lady
who was still wearing her travelling clothes smiled
at him delightfully and sank into the chair by his
side. During the little stir caused by her arrival,
no one paid any attention to the man who had
slipped into the other vacant place opposite. Mr.
Greene, however, when he had finished making known
his companion's wants to the steward, welcomed
Philip Romilly genially.

"Now we're a full table," he declared. "That's
what I like. I only hope we'll keep it up all the
voyage. Mind, there'll be a forfeit for the first one
that misses a meal. Mr. Romilly, isn't it?" he went
on, glancing at his left-hand neighbour's card once
more. "My name's Raymond Greene. I am an old
traveller and there's nothing I enjoy more, outside
my business, than these little ocean trips, especially
when they come after a pretty strenuous time on
shore. Crossed many times, sir?"

"Never before," Philip answered.

"First trip, eh?" Mr. Greene remarked, mildly
interested. "Well, well, you've some surprises in

store for you, then. Let me make you acquainted
with your opposite neighbour, Miss Elizabeth Dalstan. I dare say, even if you haven't been in the
States, you know some of our principal actresses by
name."

Philip raised his head and caught a glimpse of a
rather pale face, a mass of deep brown hair, a pleasant smile from a very shapely mouth, and the rather
intense regard of a pair of wonderfully soft eyes,
whose colour at that moment he was not able to de-
termine.

"I have had the pleasure of seeing Miss Dalstan
on the stage," he observed.

"Capital!" Mr. Raymond Greene exclaimed.
"We haven't met before, have we, Mr. Romilly?
Something kind of familiar in your face. You are
not by way of being in the Profession, are you?"

Romilly shook his head.

"I am a manufacturer," he acknowledged.

"That so?" his neighbour remarked, a trifle surprised. "Queer! I had a fancy that we'd met, and
quite lately, too. I am in the cinema business. You
may have heard of me — Raymond Greene?"

"I have seen some of your films," Philip told him.
"Very excellent productions, if you will allow me
to say so."

"That's pleasant hearing at any time," Mr.
Greene admitted, with a gratified smile. "Well, I
can see that we are going to be quite a friendly party.
That's Mr. Busby on your right, Mr. Romilly —
some golfer, I can tell you! — and his friend Mr.
Caroll alongside. The lady next you —"

"My name is Miss Pinsent," the elderly lady indicated declared pleasantly, replying to Mr. Greene's interrogative glance. "It is my first trip to America, too. I am going out to see a nephew who has settled in Chicago."

"Capital!" Mr. Raymond Greene repeated. "Now we are all more or less a family party. What did you say your line of business was, Mr. Romilly?"

"I don't remember mentioning it," Philip observed, "but I am a manufacturer of boots and shoes."

Elizabeth Dalstan looked across at him a little curiously. One might have surmised that she was in some way disappointed.

"Coming over to learn a thing or two from us, eh?" Mr. Greene went on. "You use all our machinery, don't you? Well, there's Paul Lawton on board, from Brockton. I should think he has one of the biggest plants in Massachusetts. I must make you acquainted with him."

Philip frowned slightly.

"That is very kind of you, Mr. Greene," he acknowledged, "but do you know I would very much rather not talk business with any one while I am on the steamer? I am a little overworked and I need the rest."

Elizabeth Dalstan looked at her vis-à-vis with some renewal of her former interest. She saw a young man who was, without doubt, good-looking, although he certainly had an over-tired and somewhat depressed appearance. His cheeks were colourless, and there were little dark lines under his eyes as though he suffered from sleeplessness. He was clean-shaven and he had the sensitive mouth of an artist.

His forehead was high and exceptionally good. His air of breeding was unmistakable.

"You do look a little fagged," Mr. Raymond Greene observed sympathetically. "Well, these are strenuous days in business. We all have to stretch out as far as we can go, and keep stretched out, or else some one else will get ahead of us. Business been good with you this fall, Mr. Romilly?"

"Very fair, thank you," Philip answered a little vaguely. "Tell me, Miss Dalstan," he went on, leaning slightly towards her, and with a note of curiosity in his tone, "I want to know your candid opinion of the last act of the play I saw you in — 'Henderson's Second Wife'? I made up my mind that if ever I had the privilege of meeting you, I would ask you that question."

"I know exactly why," she declared, with a quick little nod of appreciation. "Listen."

They talked together for some time, earnestly. Mr. Greene addressed his conversation to his neighbours lower down the table. It was not until the arrival of dessert that Philip and his vis-à-vis abandoned their discussion.

"Tell me, have you written yourself, Mr. Romilly?" Elizabeth Dalstan asked him with interest.

"I have made an attempt at it," he confessed.

"Most difficult thing in the whole world to write a play," Mr. Raymond Greene intervened, seeing an opportunity to join once more in the conversation. "Most difficult thing in the world, I should say. Now with pictures it's entirely different. The slightest little happening in everyday life may give you the

start, and then, there you are — the whole thing un-
ravels itself.   Now let me give you an example," he
went on, helping himself to a little more whisky and
soda.   " Only yesterday afternoon, on our way up to
Liverpool, the train got pulled up somewhere in
Derbyshire, and I sat looking out of the window.   It
was a dreary neighbourhood, a miserable afternoon,
and we happened to be crossing a rather high viaduct.
Down below were some meadows and a canal, and by
the side of the canal, a path.   At a certain point — I
should think about half a mile from where the train
was standing — this path went underneath a rude
bridge, built of bricks and covered over with turf.
Well, as I sat there I could see two men, both approaching the bridge along the path from opposite
directions.   One was tall, dressed in light tweeds, a
good-looking fellow — looked like one of your country squires except that he was a little on the thin
side.   The other was a sombre-looking person,
dressed in dark clothes, about your height and build,
I should say, Mr. Romilly.   Well, they both disappeared under that bridge at the same moment, and
I don't know why, but I leaned forward to see them
come out.   The train was there for quite another two
minutes, perhaps more.   There wasn't another soul
anywhere in sight, and it was raining as it only can
rain in England."

Mr. Raymond Greene paused.   Every one at the
table had been listening intently.   He glanced around
at their rapt faces with satisfaction.   He was conscious of the artist's dramatic touch.   Once more it
had not failed him.   He had excited interest.   In
Philip Romilly's eyes there was something even more

than interest. It seemed almost as though he were trying to project his thoughts back and conjure up for himself the very scene which was being described to him. The young man was certainly in a very delicate state of health, Mr. Greene decided.

"You are keeping us in suspense, sir," the elderly lady complained, leaning forward in her place. "Please go on. What happened when they came out?"

"That," Mr. Raymond Greene said impressively, "is the point of the story. The train remained standing there, as I have said, for several minutes — as many minutes, in fact, as it would have taken them seconds to have traversed that tunnel. Notwithstanding that, they neither of them appeared again. I sat there, believe me, with my eyes fastened upon that path, and when the train started I leaned out of the window until we had rounded the curve and we were out of sight, but I never saw either of those two men again. Now there's the beginning of a film story for you! What do you want more than that? There's dramatic interest, surprise, an original situation."

"After all, I suppose the explanation was quite a simple one," Mr. Busby remarked. "They were probably acquaintances, and they stayed to have a chat."

Mr. Raymond Greene shook his head doubtfully.

"All I can say to that is that it was a queer place to choose for a little friendly conversation," he pronounced. "They were both tall men — about the same height, I should say — and it would have been impossible for them to have even stood upright."

" You mentioned the fact, did you not," the lady who called herself Miss Pinsent observed, " that it was raining heavily at the time? Perhaps they stayed under the bridge to shelter."

" That's something I never thought of," Mr. Greene admitted, " perhaps for the reason that they both of them seemed quite indifferent to the rain. The young man in the dark clothes hadn't even an umbrella. I must admit that I allowed my thoughts to travel in another direction. Professional instinct, you see. It was a fairly broad canal, and the water was nearly up to the towing-path. I'd lay a wager it was twelve or fifteen feet deep. Supposing those two men had met on that narrow path and quarrelled! Supposing —"

" Don't! "

Mr. Raymond Greene stopped short. He gazed in amazement at Elizabeth Dalstan, who had suddenly clutched his hand. There was something in her face which puzzled as well as startled him. She had been looking at her opposite neighbour but she turned back towards the narrator of this thrilling story as the monosyllable broke from her lips.

" Please stop," she begged. " You are too dramatic, Mr. Greene. You really frighten me."

" Frighten you ? " he repeated. " My dear Miss Dalstan! "

" I suppose it is very absurd of me," she went on, smiling appealingly at him, " but your words were altogether too graphic. I can't bear to think of what might have taken place underneath that tunnel! You must remember that I saw it, too. Don't go on. Don't talk about it any more. I am going up-

stairs for my cigarette.   Are you coming to get my
chair for me, Mr. Greene, or must I rely upon the
deck steward? "

Mr. Raymond Greene was a very gallant man, and
he did not hesitate for a moment.   He sprang to
his feet and escorted the young lady from the saloon.
He glanced back, as he left the table, to nod his
adieux to the little company whom he had taken
under his charge.   Philip Romilly was gazing steadfastly out of the porthole.

" Kind of delicate young fellow, that," he remarked.   " Nice face, too.   Can't help thinking that
I've met or seen some one like him lately."

CHAPTER V

Philip Romilly found himself alone at last with
the things which he had craved — darkness, solitude,
the rushing of the salt wind, the sense of open spaces.
On the other, the sheltered side of the steamer, long
lines of passengers were stretched in wicker chairs,
smoking and drinking their coffee, but where he was
no one came save an occasional promenader. Yet
even here was a disappointment. He had come for
peace, for a brief escape from the thrall of memories
which during the last few hours had become charged
with undreamed-of horrors — and there was to be
no peace. In the shadowy darkness which rested
upon the white-churned sea flying past him, he saw
again, with horrible distinctness, the face, the figure
of the man who for those few brief minutes he had
hated with a desperate and passionate hatred. He
saw the broken photograph, the glass splintered into
a thousand pieces. He saw the man himself, choking,
sinking down beneath the black waters; heard the
stifled cry from his palsied lips, saw the slow dawning
agony of death in his distorted features. Some one
was playing a mandolin down in the second class.
He heard the feet of a dancer upon the deck, the little
murmur of applause. Well, after all, this was life.
It was a rebuke of fate to his own illogical and useless
vapourings. Men died every second whilst women

danced, and no one who knew life had any care save
for the measure of their own days.   Some freakish
thought pleaded stridently his own justification.
His mind travelled back down the gloomy avenues of
his past, along those last aching years of grinding
and undeserved poverty.   He remembered his up-
bringing, his widowed mother, a woman used to every
luxury, struggling to make both ends meet in a suburban street, in a hired cottage filled with hired furniture.   He remembered his schooldays, devoid of
pocket money, unable to join in the sports of others,
slaving with melancholy perseverance for a scholar-
ship to lighten his mother's burden.   Always there
was the same ghastly, crushing penuriousness, the
struggle to make a living before his schooldays were
well over, the unbought books he had fingered at the
bookstalls and let drop again, the coarse clothes he
had been compelled to wear, the scanty food he had
eaten, the narrow, driving ways of poverty, culminat-
ing in his mother's death and his own fear — he, at
the age of nineteen years — lest the money for her
funeral should not be forthcoming.   If there were
any hell, surely he had lived in it!   This other,
whose flames mocked him now, could be no worse.
Sin!   Crime!   He remembered the words of the girl
who during these latter years had represented to him
what there might have been of light in life.   He remembered, and it seemed to him that he could meet
that ghostly image which had risen from the black
waters, without shrinking, almost contemptuously.
Fate had mocked him long enough.   It was time, indeed, that he helped himself.

He swung away from the solitude to the other side

of the steamer, paused in a sheltered spot while he lit a cigarette, and paced up and down the more frequented ways. A soft voice from an invisible mass of furs and rugs, called to him.

"Mr. Romilly, please come and talk to me. My rug has slipped — thank you so much. Take this chair next mine for a few minutes, won't you? Mr. Greene has rushed off to the smoking room. I think he has just been told that there is a rival cinema producer on board, and he is trying to run him to ground."

Philip settled himself without hesitation in the vacant place.

"One is forced to envy Mr. Raymond Greene," he sighed. "To have work in life which one loves as he does his is the rarest form of happiness."

"What about your own?" she asked him. "But you are a manufacturer, are you not? Somehow or other, that surprises me."

"And me," he acknowledged frankly. "I mean that I wonder I have persevered at it so long."

"But you are a very young man!"

"Young or old," he answered, "I am one of those who have made a false start in life. I am on my way to new things. Do you think, Miss Dalstan, that your country is a good place for one to visit who seeks new things?"

She turned in her chair a little more towards him. Against the background of empty spaces, the pale softness of her face seemed to gain a new attractiveness.

"Well, that depends," she said reflectively, "upon what these new things might be which you desire.

For an ambitious business man America is a great country."

"But supposing one had finished with business?" he persisted. "Supposing one wanted to develop tastes and a gift for another method of life?"

"Then I should say that New York is the one place in the world," she told him. "You are speaking of yourself?"

"Yes!"

"You have ambitions, I am sure," she continued. "Tell me, are they literary?"

"I would like to call them so," he admitted. "I have written a play and three stories, so bad that no one would produce the play or publish the stories."

"You have brought them with you?"

He shook his head.

"No! They are where I shall never see them again."

"Never see them again?" she repeated, puzzled.

"I mean that I have left them at home. I have left them there, perhaps, to a certain extent deliberately," he went on. "You see, the idea is still with me. I think that I shall rewrite them when I have settled down in America. I fancy that I shall find myself in an atmosphere more conducive to the sort of work I want to do. I would rather not be handicapped by the ghosts of my old failures."

"One's ghosts are hard sometimes to escape from," she whispered.

He clutched nervously at the end of his rug. She looked up and down along the row of chairs. There were one or two slumbering forms, but most were empty. There were no promenaders in sight.

" You know," she asked, her voice still very low,
" why I left the saloon a little abruptly this evening? "

" Why? " he demanded.

" Because," she went on, " I could see the effect
which Mr. Raymond Greene's story had upon you;
because I, also, was in that train, and I have better
eyesight than Mr. Greene.   You were one of the two
men who were walking along the towpath."

" Well? " he muttered.

" You have nothing to tell me? "

" Nothing! "

She waited for a moment.

" At least you have not attempted to persuade me
that you lingered underneath that bridge to escape
from the rain," she remarked.

" If I cannot tell you the truth," he promised, " I
am not going to tell you a lie, but apart from that I
admit nothing.   I do not even admit that it was I
whom you saw."

She laid her hand upon his.   The touch of her
fingers was wonderful, cool and soft and somehow
reassuring.   He felt a sense of relaxation, felt the
strain of living suddenly grow less.

" You know," she said, " all my friends tell me
that I am a restful person.   You are living at high
pressure, are you not?   Try and forget it.   Fate
makes queer uses of all of us sometimes.   She sends
her noblest sons down into the shadows and pitch-
forks her outcasts into the high places of life.   Those
do best who learn to control themselves, to live and
think for the best."

" Go on talking to me," he begged.   " Is it your

voice, I wonder, that is so soothing, or just what you say?"

She smiled reassuringly.

"You are glad because you have found a friend," she told him, "and a friend who, even if she does not understand, does not wish to understand. Do you see?"

"I wish I felt that I deserved it," he groaned.

She laughed almost gaily.

"What a sorting up there would be of our places in life," she declared, "if we all had just what we deserved! . . . Now give me your arm. I want to walk a little. While we walk, if you like, I will try to tell you what I can about New York. It may interest you."

They walked up and down the deck, and by degrees their conversation drifted into a discussion of such recent plays as were familiar to both of them. At the far end of the ship she clung to him once or twice as the wind came booming over the freshening waves. She weighed and measured his criticisms of the plays they spoke of, and in the main approved of them. When at last she stopped outside the companionway and bade him good night, the deck was almost deserted. They were near one of the electric lights, and he saw her face more distinctly than he had seen it at all, realised more adequately its wonderful charm. The large, firm mouth, womanly and tender though it was, was almost the mouth of a protector. She smiled at him as one might smile at a boy.

"You are to sleep well," she said firmly. "Those are my orders. Good night!"

She gave him her hand — a woman's soft and delicate fingers, yet clasping his with an almost virile strength and friendliness. She left him with just that feeling about her — that she was expansive, in her heart, her sympathies, even her brain and peculiar gifts of apprehension. She left him, too, with a curious sense of restfulness, as though suddenly he had become metamorphosed into the woman and had found a sorely-needed guardian. He abandoned without a second thought his intention of going to the smoking-room and sitting up late. The thought of his empty stateroom, a horror to him a few hours ago, seemed suddenly almost alluring, and he made his way there cheerfully. He felt the sleep already upon his eyes.

CHAPTER VI

All the physical exhilaration of his unlived youth seemed to be dancing in Philip Romilly's veins when he awoke the next morning to find an open porthole, the blue sea tossing away to infinity, and his steward's cheerful face at his bedside.

" Bathroom steward says if you are ready, sir, he can arrange for your bath now," the man announced.

Philip sprang out of bed and reached for his Bond Street dressing-gown.

" I'll bring you a cup of tea when you get back, sir," the steward continued. " The bathrooms are exactly opposite."

The sting of the salt water seemed to complete his new-found light-heartedness. Philip dressed and shaved, whistling softly all the time to himself. He even found a queer sort of interest in examining his stock of ties and other garments. The memory of Elizabeth Dalstan's words was still in his brain. They had become the text of his life. This, he told himself, was his birthday. He even accepted without a tremor a letter and telegram which the steward brought him.

" These were in the rack for you, sir," he said. " I meant to bring them down last night but we had a busy start off."

Philip took them up on deck to read. He tore

open the telegram first and permitted himself a little start when he saw the signature. It was sent off from Detton Magna,—

"Why did you not come as promised? What am I to do? BEATRICE."

The envelope of the letter he opened with a little more compunction. It was written on the printed notepaper of the Douglas Romilly Shoe Company, and was of no great length,—

Dear Mr. Romilly,

I understood that you would return to the factory this evening for a few minutes, before taking the train to Liverpool. There were one or two matters upon which I should like some further information, but as time is short I am writing to you at the Waldorf Hotel at New York.

I see that the acceptances due next 4th are unusually heavy, but I think I understood you to say that you had spoken to Mr. Henshaw at the bank concerning these, and in any case I presume there would be no difficulty.

Wishing you every success on the other side, and a safe return,

I am,

Your obedient servant,
J. L. POTTS.

"There is not the slightest doubt," Philip said to himself, as he tore both communications into pieces and watched them flutter away downwards, "that I am on my way to New York. If only one knew what had become of that poor, half-starved art master!"

He went down to breakfast and afterwards strolled

aimlessly about the deck. His sense of enjoyment was so extraordinarily keen that he found it hard to settle down to any of the usual light occupations of idle travellers. He was content to stand by the rail and gaze across the sea, a new wonder to him; or to lie about in his steamer chair and listen, with half-closed eyes, to the hissing of the spray and the faint music of the wind. His mind turned by chance to one of those stories of which he had spoken. A sudden new vigour of thought seemed to rend it inside out almost in those first few seconds. He thought of the garret in which it had been written, the wretched surroundings, the odoriferous food, the thick crockery, the smoke-palled vista of roofs and chimneys. The genius of a Stevenson would have become dwarfed in such surroundings. A phrase, a happy idea, suddenly caught his fancy. He itched for a pencil and paper. Then he looked up to find the one thing wanting. Elizabeth Dalstan, followed by a maid carrying rugs and cushions, had paused, smiling, by his side.

"You have slept and you are better," she said pleasantly. "Now for the next few minutes you must please devote yourself to making me comfortable. Put everything down, Phoebe. Mr. Romilly will look after me."

For a moment he paused before proceeding to his task.

"I want to look at you," he confessed. "Remember I have only seen you under the electric lights of the saloon, or in that queer, violet gloom of last night. Why, you have quite light hair, and I thought it was dark!"

She laughed good-humouredly and turned slowly around.

"Here I am," she announced, "a much bephotographed person. Almost plain, some journalists have dared to call me, but for my expression. On flowing lines, as you see, because I always wear such loose clothes, and yet, believe me, slim. As a matter of fact," she went on pensively, "I am rather proud of my figure. A little journalist who had annoyed me, and to whom I was rude, once called it ample. No one has ever ventured to say more. The critics who love me, and they most of them love me because I am so exceptionally polite to them, and tell them exactly what to say about every new play, allude to my physique as Grecian."

"But your eyes!" he exclaimed. "Last night I thought they were grey. This morning — why, surely they are brown?"

"You see, that is all according to the light," she confided. "If any one does try to write a description of me, they generally evade the point by calling them browny-grey. A young man who was in love with me," she sighed, "but that was long ago, used to say that they reminded him of fallen leaves in a place where the sunlight sometimes is and sometimes isn't. And now, if you please, I want to be made exceedingly comfortable. I want you to find the deck steward and see that I have some beef tea as quickly as possible. I want my box of cigarettes on one side and my vanity case on the other, and I should like to listen to the plot of your play."

He obeyed her behests with scrupulous care, leaned back in his chair and brought into the foreground of his mind the figures of those men and women who had told his story, finding them, to his dismay, unexpectedly crude and unlifelike. And the story itself. Was unhappiness so necessary, after all? They suddenly seemed to crumble away into insignificance, these men and women of his creation. In their place he could almost fancy a race of larger beings, a more extensive canvas, a more splendid, a riper and richer vocabulary.

"Nothing that I have ever done," he sighed, "is worth talking to you about. But if you are going to be my friend —"

"Well?"

"If you are going to be my friend," he went on, with almost inspired conviction, "I shall write something different."

"One can rebuild," she murmured. "One can sometimes use the old pieces. Life and chess are both like that."

"Would you help me, I wonder?" he asked impulsively.

She looked away from him, out across the steamer rail. She seemed to be measuring with her eyes the roll of the ship as it rose and fell in the trough of the sea.

"You are a strange person," she said. "Tell me, are you in the habit of becoming suddenly dependent upon people?"

"Not I," he assured her. "If I were to tell you how my last ten years have been spent, you would not believe me. You couldn't. If I were to speak of a tearing, unutterable loneliness, if I were to speak of poverty — not the poverty you know anything about, but the poverty of bare walls, of coarse food and little enough of it, of everything cheap and miserable and soiled and second-hand — nothing fresh, nothing real —"

He stopped abruptly.

" But I forgot," he muttered. " I can't explain."

" Is one to understand," she asked, a little puzzled, " that you have had difficulties in your business? "

" I have never been in business," he answered quickly. " My name is Romilly, but I am not Romilly the manufacturer. For the last eight years I have lived in a garret in London, teaching false art in a third-rate school some of the time, doing penny-a-line journalistic work when I got the chance ; clerk for a month or two in a brewer's office and sacked for incapacity — those are a few of the real threads in my life."

" At the present moment, then," she observed, " you are an impostor."

" Exactly," he admitted, " and I should probably have been repenting it by now but for your words last night."

She smiled at him and the sun shone once more. It wasn't an ordinary smile at all. It was just as though she were letting him into the light of her understanding, as though some one from the world, entrance into which he had craved, had stooped down to understand and was telling him that all was well. He drew his chair a little closer to hers.

" We are all more or less impostors," she said. " Does any one, I wonder, go about the world telling everybody what they really are, how they really live?

Dear me, how unpleasant and uncomfortable it would be! You are so wise, my new friend. You know the value of impulses. You tell me the truth, and I am your friend. I do not need facts, because facts count for little. I judge by what lies behind, and I understand. Do not weary me with explanations. I like what you have told me. Only, of course, your work must have suffered from surroundings like that. Will it be better for you now?"

"I shall land in New York," he told her, "with at least a thousand pounds. That is about as much as I have spent in ten years. There is the possibility of other money. Concerning that — well, I can't make up my mind. The thousand pounds, of course, is stolen."

"So I gathered," she remarked. "Do you continue, may I ask, to be Douglas Romilly, the manufacturer?"

He shook his head a little vaguely.

"I haven't thought," he confessed. "But of course I don't. I have risked everything for the chance of a new life. I shall start it in a new way and under a new name."

He was suddenly conscious of her pity, of a moistness in her eyes as she looked at him.

"I think," she said, "that you must have been very miserable. Above all things, now, whatever you may have done for your liberty, don't be faint-hearted. If you are in trouble or danger you must come to me. You promise?"

"If I may," he assented fervently.

"Now I must hear the play as it stood in your thoughts when you wrote it," she insisted. "I have a fancy that it will sound a little gloomy. Am I right?"

He laughed.

"Of course you are! How could I write in any other way except through the darkened spectacles? However, there's a way out — of altering it, I mean. I feel flashes of it already. Listen."

The story expanded with relation. He no longer felt confined to its established lines. Every now and then he paused to tell her that this or that was new, and she nodded appreciatively. They walked for a time, watched the seagulls, and bade their farewell to the Irish coast.

"You will have to re-write that play for me," she said, a little abruptly, as she paused before the companionway. "I am going down to my room for a few minutes before lunch now. Afterwards I shall bring up a pencil and paper. We will make some notes together."

Philip walked on to the smoking room. He could scarcely believe that the planks he trod were of solid wood. Raymond Greene met him at the entrance and slapped him on the back:

"Just in time for a cocktail before lunch!" he exclaimed. "I was looking everywhere for a pal. Two Martinis, dry as you like, Jim," he added, turning round to the smoking room steward. "Sure you won't join us, Lawton?"

"Daren't!" was the laconic answer from the man whom he had addressed.

"By-the-bye," Mr. Raymond Greene went on, "let me make you two acquainted. This is Mr. Douglas Romilly, an English boot manufacturer — Mr. Paul

Lawton of Brockton. Mr. Lawton owns one of the largest boot and shoe plants in the States," the introducer went on. " You two ought to find something to talk about."

Philip held out his hand without a single moment's hesitation. He was filled with a new confidence.

" I should be delighted to talk with Mr. Lawton on any subject in the world," he declared, " except our respective businesses."

" I am very glad to meet you, sir," the other replied, shaking hands heartily. " I don't follow that last stipulation of yours, though."

" It simply means that I am taking seven days' holiday," Philip explained gaily, " seven days during which I have passed my word to myself to neither talk business nor think business. Your very good health, Mr. Raymond Greene," he went on, drinking his cocktail with relish. " If we meet on the other side, Mr. Lawton, we'll compare notes as much as you like."

" That's all right, sir," the other agreed. " I don't know as you're not right. We Americans do hang round our businesses, and that's a fact. Still, there's a little matter of lasts I should like to have a word or two with you about some time."

" A little matter of what? " Philip asked vaguely.

" Lasts," the other repeated. " That's where your people and ours look different ways chiefly, that and a little matter of manipulation of our machinery."

" Just so," Philip assented, swallowing the rest of his cocktail. " What about luncheon? There's nothing in the world to give you an appetite like this sea air."

" I'm with you," Mr. Raymond Greene chimed in.
" You two can have your trade talk later on."

He took his young friend's arm, and they descended
the stairs together.

" What the mischief is a last? " he inquired.

" I haven't the least idea," Philip replied carelessly.
" Something to do with boots and shoes, isn't it? "

His questioner stared at him for a moment and
then laughed.

" Say, you're a young man of your word! " he
remarked appreciatively.

CHAPTER VII

Philip Romilly was accosted, late that afternoon, by two young women whose presence on board he had noticed with a certain amount of disapproval. They were obviously of the chorus-girl type, a fact which they seemed to lack the ambition to conceal. After several would-be ingratiating giggles, they finally pulled up in front of him whilst he was promenading the deck.

" You are Mr. Romilly, aren't you? " one of them asked. " Bob Millet told us you were going to be on this steamer. You know Bob, don't you? "

Philip for a moment was taken aback.

" Bob Millet," he repeated thoughtfully.

" Of course! Good old Bob! I don't mind confessing," the young woman went on, " that though we were all out one night together — Trocadero, Empire, and Murray's afterwards — I should never have recognised you. Seems to me you've got thinner and more serious-looking."

" I am afraid my own memory is also at fault," Philip remarked, a little stiffly.

" I am Violet Fox," the young woman who had accosted him continued. " This my friend, Hilda Mason. She's a dear girl but a little shy, aren't you, Hilda? "

" That's just because I told her that we ought to wait until you remembered us," the slighter young

woman, with the very obvious peroxidised hair, protested."

"Didn't seem to be any use waiting for that," her
friend retorted briskly. "Hilda and I are dying for
a cocktail, Mr. Romilly."

He led them with an unwillingness of which they
seemed frankly unaware, towards the lounge. They
drank two cocktails and found themselves unfortunately devoid of cigarettes, a misfortune which it
became his privilege to remedy. They were very
friendly young ladies, if a little slangy, invited him
around to their staterooms, and offered to show him
the runs around New York. Philip escaped after
about an hour and made his way to where Elizabeth
was reclining in her deck chair.

"That fellow Romilly," he declared irritably, "the
other one, I mean, seems to have had the vilest tastes.
If I am to be landed with any more of his ridiculous
indiscretions, I think I shall have to go overboard.
There was an enterprising gentleman named Gayes
in Liverpool, who nearly drove me crazy, then there's
this Mr. Lawton who wants to talk about lasts, and
finally it seems that I dined at the Trocadero and
spent the evening at the Empire and Murray's with
the two very obvious-looking young ladies who
accosted me just now. I am beginning to believe
that Douglas' life was not above suspicion."

She smiled at him tolerantly. An unopened book
lay by her side. She seemed to have been spending
the last quarter of an hour in thought.

"I am rather relieved to hear," she confessed,
"that those two young people are a heritage from
the other Mr. Romilly. No, don't sit down," she

went on. " I want you to do something for me. Go into the library, and on the left-hand side as you enter you will see all the wireless news. Read the bottom item and then come back to me."

He turned slowly away. All his new-found buoyancy of spirits had suddenly left him. He cursed the imagination which lifted his feet from the white decks and dragged his eyes from the sparkling blue sea to the rain-soaked, smut-blackened fields riven by that long thread of bleak, turgid water. The horrors of a murderous passion beat upon his brain. He saw himself hastening, grim and blind, on his devil-sped mission. Then the haze faded from before his eyes. Somehow or other he accomplished his errand. He was in the library, standing in front of those many sheets of typewritten messages, passing them all over, heedless of what their message might be, until he came to the last and most insignificant. Four lines, almost overlapped by another sheet —

STRANGE DISAPPEARANCE OF A LONDON ART TEACHER

Suicide Feared

Acting upon instructions received, the police are investigating a somewhat curious case of disappearance. Philip Romilly, a teacher of art in a London school, visited Detton Magna on Friday afternoon and apparently started for a walk along the canal bank, towards dusk. Nothing has since been heard of him or his movements, and arrangements have been made to drag the canal at a certain point.

The letters seemed to grow larger to him as he stood and read. He remained in front of the message for an inordinately long time. Again his imagination was at work. He saw the whole ghastly business, the police on the canal banks, watching the slow progress of the men with their drags bringing to the surface all the miserable refuse of the turgid waters, the dripping black mud, perhaps at last . . .

He was back again on the deck, walking quite steadily yet seeing little. He made his way to the smoking room, asked almost indifferently for a brandy and soda, and drained it to the last drop. Then he walked up the deck to where Elizabeth was seated, and dropped into a chair by her side.

"So I am missing," he remarked, almost in his ordinary tone. "I really had no idea that I was a person of such importance. Fancy reading of my own disappearance within a few days of its taking place, in the middle of the Atlantic!"

"There was probably some one there who gave information," she suggested.

"There was the young lady whom I went to visit," he assented. "She probably watched me cross the road and turn in at that gate and take the path by the canal side. Yes, she may even have gone to the station to see whether I took the only other train back to London, and found that I did not. She knew, too, that I could only have had a few shillings in my pocket, and that my living depended upon being in London for my school the next morning. Yes, the whole thing was reasonable."

"And they are going to drag the canal," Elizabeth said thoughtfully.

"A difficult business," he assured her. "It is one of the most ghastly, ill-constructed, filthiest strips of water you ever looked upon. It has been the garbage depository of the villages through which it makes its beastly way, for generations. I don't envy the men who have to handle the drags."

"You do not believe, then, that they will find anything — interesting?"

He shrugged his shoulders.

"That type of man," he continued, "must have a morbid mind. There will be dead animals without a doubt, worn-out boots, filthy and decomposed articles of clothing —"

"Don't!" she interrupted. "You know what I mean. Do leave off painting your ghastly pictures. You know quite well what I mean. Philip Romilly is here by my side. What can they hope to find there in his place?"

His evil moments for that afternoon were over. He answered her almost carelessly.

"Not what they are looking for. Have you brought the paper and pencil you spoke of? I have an idea — I am getting fresh ideas every moment now that I picture you as my heroine. It is queer, isn't it, how naturally you fall into the rôle?"

She drew a little nearer to him. He was conscious of a mysterious and unfamiliar perfume, perhaps from the violets half hidden in her furs, or was it something in her hair? It reminded him a little of the world the keys into which he had gripped — the world of joyousness, of light-hearted pleasures, the sunlit world into which he had only looked through other men's eyes.

"Perhaps you knew that I was somewhere across the threshold," she suggested. "Did you drag your

Mona wholly from your brain, or has she her proto-
type somewhere in your world?"

He shook his head.

"Therein lies the weakness of all that I have ever
written," he declared. "There have been so few in
my world from whom I could garner even the glean-
ings of a personality. They are all, my men and
women, artificially made, not born. Twenty-three
shillings a week has kept me well outside the locked
doors."

"Yet, you know, in many ways," she reflected,
"Mona is like me."

"Like you because she was a helper of men," he
assented swiftly, "a woman of large sympathies,
appealing to me, I suppose, because in my solitude,
thoughts of my own weakness taunted me, weakness
because I couldn't break out, I mean. Perhaps for
that reason the thought of a strong woman fascinated
me, a woman large in thoughts and ways, a woman
to whom purposes and tendencies counted most. I
dreamed of a woman sweetly omnipotent, strong
without a shadow of masculinity. That is where my
Mona was to be different from all other created
figures."

"Chance," she declared, "is a wonderful thing.
Chance has pitchforked you here, absolutely to my
side, I, the one woman who could understand what
you mean, who could give your Mona life. Don't
think I am vain," she went on. "I can assure you
that my head isn't the least turned because I have
been successful. I simply know. Listen. I have
few engagements in New York. I should not be
going back at all but to see my mother, who is too

delicate to travel, and who is miserable when I am
away for long. Take this pencil and paper. Let us
leave off dreaming for a little time and give ourselves
up to technicalities. I want to draft a new first act
and a new last one, not so very different from your
version and yet with changes which I want to explain
as we go on. Bring your chair a little nearer — so.
Now take down these notes."

They worked until the first gong for dinner rang.
She sat up in her chair with a happy little laugh.

"Isn't it wonderful!" she exclaimed. "I never
knew time to pass so quickly. There isn't any
pleasure in the world like this," she added, a little impulsively, "the pleasure of letting your thoughts
run out to meet some one else's, some one who understands. Take care of every line we have written, my
friend."

"We might go on after dinner," he suggested
eagerly.

She shook her head.

"I'd rather not," she admitted. "My brain is
too full. I have a hundred fancies dancing about.
I even find myself, as we sit here, rehearsing my ges-
tures, tuning myself to a new outlook. Oh! you
most disturbing person — intellectually of course, I
mean," she added, laughing into his face. "Take
off my rugs and help me up. No, we'll leave them
there. Perhaps, after dinner, we might walk for a
little time."

"But the whole thing is tingling in my brain," he
protested. "Couldn't we go into the library? We
could find a corner by ourselves."

She turned and looked at him, standing up now, the wind blowing her skirts, her eyes glowing, her lips a little parted. Then for the first time he understood her beauty, understood the peculiar qualities of it, the dissensions of the Press as to her appearance, the supreme charm of a woman possessed of a sweet and passionate temperament, turning her face towards the long-wished-for sun. Even the greater things caught hold of him in that moment, and he felt dimly what was coming.

" Do you really wish to work? " she asked.

He looked away from her.

" No! " he answered, a little thickly. " We will talk, if you will."

They neither of them moved. The atmosphere had suddenly become charged with a force indescribable, almost numbing. In the far distance they saw the level line of lights from a passing steamer. Mr. Raymond Greene, with his hands in his ulster pockets, suddenly spotted them and did for them what they seemed to have lost the power to do.

" Hullo! " he exclaimed. " I've been looking for you two everywhere. I don't want to hurt that smoking room steward's feelings. He's not bad at his job. But," he added confidentially, dropping his voice and taking them both by the arm, " I have made a cocktail down in my stateroom — it's there in the shaker waiting for us, something I can't talk about. I've given Lawton one, and he's following me about like a dog. Come right this way, both of you. Steady across the gangway — she's pitching a little. Why, you look kind of scared, Mr. Romilly. Been to sleep, either of you? "

Philip's laugh was almost too long to be natural. Elizabeth, as though by accident, had dropped her veil.   Mr. Raymond Greene, bubbling over with good nature and anticipation, led them towards the stairs.

CHAPTER VIII

Mr. Raymond Greene could scarcely wait until Philip had taken his place at the dinner table that evening, to make known his latest discovery.

" Say, Mr. Romilly," he exclaimed, leaning a little forward, " do you happen to have seen the wireless messages to-day ? — those tissue sheets that are stuck up in the library? "

Philip set down the menu, in which he had been taking an unusual interest.

" Yes, I looked through them this afternoon," he acknowledged.

" There's a little one at the bottom, looks as though it had been shoved in at the last moment. I don't know whether you noticed it. It announced the mysterious disappearance of a young man of the same name as your own — an art teacher from London, I think he was. I wondered whether it might have been any relation? "

" I read the message," Philip admitted. " It certainly looks as though it might have referred to my cousin."

Mr. Raymond Greene became almost impressive in his interested earnestness.

" Talk about coincidences! " he continued. " Do you remember last night talking about subjects for cinema plays? I told you of a little incident I happened to have noticed on the way from London to Liverpool, about the two men somewhere in Derbyshire whom I had seen approaching a tunnel over a canal — they neither of them came out, you know, all the time that the train was standing there."

Philip helped himself a little absently to whisky and soda from the bottle in front of him.

" I remember your professional interest in the situation," he confessed.

" I felt at the time," Mr. Raymond Greene went on eagerly, " that there was something queer about the affair. Listen! I have been putting two and two together, and it seems to me that one of those men might very well have been this missing Mr. Romilly."

Philip shook his head pensively.

" I don't think so," he ventured.

" What's that? You don't think so? " the cinema magnate exclaimed. " Why not, Mr. Romilly? It's exactly the district — at Detton Magna, the message said, in Derbyshire — and it was a canal, too, one of the filthiest I ever saw. Can't you realise the dramatic interest of the situation now that you are confronted with this case of disappearance? I have been asking myself ever since I strolled up into the library before dinner and read this notice — ' *What about the other man?* ' "

Philip had commenced a leisurely consumption of his first course, and answered without undue haste.

" Well," he said, " if this young man Romilly is my cousin, it would be the second or third time already that he has disappeared. He is an ill-balanced, neurotic sort of creature. At times he accepts help — even solicits it — from his more pros-

perous relations, and at times he won't speak to us.
But of one thing I am perfectly convinced, and that
is that there is no man in the world who would be
less likely to make away with himself. He has a
nervous horror of death or pain of any sort, and in
his peculiar way he is much too fond of life ever to
dream of voluntarily shortening it. On the other
hand, he is always doing eccentric things. He probably set out to walk to London — I have known him
do it before — and will turn up there in a fortnight's time."

Mr. Raymond Greene seemed rather to resent
having cold water poured upon his melodramatic
imaginings. He turned to Elizabeth, who had remained silent during the brief colloquy.

"What do you think, Miss Dalstan?" he asked.
"Don't you think that, under the circumstances, I
ought to give information to the British police?"

She laughed at him quite good-naturedly, and yet
in such a way that a less sensitive man than Mr.
Raymond Greene might well have been conscious of
the note of ridicule.

"No wonder you are such a great success in your
profession!" she observed. "You carry the melodramatic instinct with you, day by day. You see
everything through the dramatist's spectacles."

"That's all very well," Mr. Greene protested,
"but you saw the two men yourself, and you've
probably read about the case of mysterious disappearance. Surely you must admit that the coinci-
dence is interesting?"

"Alas!" she went on, shaking her head, "I am
afraid I must throw cold water upon your vivid

imaginings. You see, my eyesight is better than yours and I could see the two men distinctly, whilst you could only see their figures. One of them, the better-dressed, was fair and obviously affluent, and the other was a labourer. Neither of them could in any way have answered the description of the missing man."

Mr. Raymond Greene was a little dashed.

"You didn't say so at the time," he complained.

"I really wasn't sufficiently interested," she told him. "Besides, without knowing anything of Mr. Romilly's cousin, I don't think any person in the world could have had the courage to seek an exit from his troubles by means of that canal."

"But my point," Mr. Raymond Greene persisted, "is that it wasn't suicide at all. I maintain that the situation as I saw it presented all the possibilities of a different sort of crime."

"My cousin hadn't an enemy in the world except himself," Philip intervened.

"And I would give you the filming of my next play for nothing," Elizabeth ventured, "if either of those two men could possibly have been an art teacher. . . . Can I have a little more oil with my salad, please, steward, and I should like some French white wine."

Mr. Raymond Greene took what appeared to be a positive disappointment very good-naturedly.

"Well," he said, "I dare say you are both right, and in any case I shouldn't like to persist in a point of view which might naturally enough become distressing to our young friend here. Tell you what I'll do to show my penitence. I shall order a bottle of wine, and we'll drink to the welfare of the missing

Mr. Philip Romilly, wherever he may be. Pommery,
steward, and bring some ice along."

Philip pushed away his whisky and soda.

" Just in time," he remarked. " I'll drink to poor
Philip's welfare, with pleasure, although he hasn't
been an unmixed blessing to his family."

The subject passed away with the drinking of the
toast, and with the necessity for a guard upon himself gone, Philip found himself eating and drinking
mechanically, watching all the time the woman who
sat opposite to him, who had now engaged Mr. Raymond Greene in an animated conversation on the
subject of the suitability for filming of certain recent
plays. He was trying with a curious intentness to
study her dispassionately, to understand the nature
of the charm on which dramatic critics had wasted
a wealth of adjectives, and of which he himself was
humanly and personally conscious. She wore a high-
necked gown of some soft, black material, with a
little lace at her throat fastened by her only article
of jewellery, a pearl pin. Her hair was arranged
in coils, with a simplicity and a precision which to a
more experienced observer would have indicated the
possession of a maid of no ordinary qualities. Her
mouth became more and more delightful every time
he studied it; her voice, even her method of speech,
were entirely natural and with a peculiarly fascinating inflexion. At times she looked and spoke with
the light-hearted gaiety of a child ; then again there
was the grave and cultured woman apparent in her
well-balanced and thoughtful criticisms. When, at
the end of the meal, she rose to leave the table, he
found himself surprised at her height and the slim

perfection of her figure. His first remark, when he joined her upon the stairs, was an almost abrupt expression of his thoughts.

" Tell me," he exclaimed, " why were all my first impressions of you wrong? To-night you are a revelation to me. You are amazingly different."

She laughed at him.

" I really can't do more than show you myself as I am," she expostulated.

" Ah! but you are so many women," he murmured.

" Of course, if you are going to flatter me! Give me a cigarette from my case, please, and strike a match, and if you don't mind struggling with this wind and the darkness, we will have our walk. There!" she added, as they stood in the companionway. "Now don't you feel as though we were facing an adventure? We shan't be able to see a yard ahead of us, and the wind is singing."

They passed through up the companionway. She took his arm and he suddenly felt the touch of her warm fingers feeling for his other hand. He gripped them tightly, and his last impression of her face, before they plunged into the darkness, was of a queer softness, as though she were giving herself up to some unexpected but welcome emotion. Her eyes were half closed. She had the air of one wrapped in silence. So they walked almost the whole length of the deck. Philip, indeed, had no impulse or desire for speech. All his aching nerves were soothed into repose. The last remnants of his ghostly fears had been swept away. They were on the windward side of the ship, untenanted save now and then by the shadowy forms of other promenaders. The whole ex-

perience, even the regular throbbing of the engines,
the swish of the sea, the rising and falling of a lantern
bound to the top of a fishing smack by which they
were passing, the distant chant of the changing
watch, all the night sights and sounds of the sea-
borne hostel, were unfamiliar and exhilarating. And
inside his hand, even though given him of her great
pity, a woman's fingers lay in his.

She spoke at last a little abruptly.

"There is something I must know about," she
said.

"You have only to ask," he assured her.

"Don't be afraid," she continued. "I wish to ask
you nothing which might give you pain, but I must
know — you see, I am really such a ordinary woman
— I must know about some one whom you went to
visit that day, didn't you, at Detton Magna?"

He answered her almost eagerly.

"I want to talk about Beatrice," he declared.
"I want to tell you everything about her. I know
that you will understand. We were brought up together in the same country place. We were both
thrown upon the world about the same time. That
was one thing, I suppose, which made us kindly
disposed towards one another. We corresponded
always. I commenced my unsuccessful fight in
London. I lived — I can't tell you how — week by
week, month by month. I ate coarse food, I was a
hanger-on to the fringe of everything in life which
appealed to me, fed intellectually on the crumbs of
free libraries and picture galleries. I met no one of
my own station — I was at a public school and my
people were gentlefolk — or tastes. I had no friends

in London before whom I dared present myself, no
money to join a club where I might have mixed with
my fellows, no one to talk to or exchange a single
idea with — and I wasn't always the gloomy sort of
person I have become; in my younger days I loved
companionship.   And the women — my landlady's
daughter, with dyed hair, a loud voice, slatternly in
the morning, a flagrant imitation of her less honest
sisters at night! Who else? Where was I to meet
women when I didn't even know men? I spent my
poor holidays at Detton Magna. Our very loneliness brought Beatrice and me closer together. We
used to walk in those ugly fields around Detton
Magna and exchanged the story of our woes. She
was a teacher at the national school. The children
weren't pleasant, their parents were worse. The
drudgery was horrible, and there wasn't any escape
for her. Sometimes she would sob as we sat side by
side. She, too, wanted something out of life, as I
did, and there seemed nothing but that black wall
always before us. I think that we clung together
because we shared a common misery. We talked
endlessly of a way out. For me what was there?
There was no one to rob — I wasn't clever enough.
There was no way I could earn money, honestly or
dishonestly. And for her, buried in that Derbyshire village amongst the collieries, where there was
scarcely a person who hadn't the taint of the place
upon them — what chance was there for her? There
was nothing she could do, either. I knew in my
heart that we were both ready for evil things, if by
evil things we could make our escape. And we
couldn't. So we tried to lose ourselves in the only

fields left for such as we. We read poetry. We tried to live in that unnatural world where the brains only are nourished and the body languishes. It was a morbid, unhealthy existence, but I plodded along and so did she. Then her weekly letters became different. For the first time she wrote me with reserves. I took a day's vacation and I went down to Detton Magna to see what had happened."

"That was the day," she interrupted softly, "when —"

"That was the day," he assented. "I remember so well getting out of the train and walking up that long, miserable street. School wasn't over, and I went straight to her cottage, as I have often done before. There was a change. Her cheap furniture had gone. It was like one of those little rooms we had dreamed of. There was a soft carpet upon the floor, Chippendale furniture, flowers, hothouse fruit, and on the mantelpiece — the photograph of a man."

He paused, and they took the whole one long turn along the wind-swept, shadowy deck in silence.

"Presently she came," he continued. "The change was there, too. She was dressed simply enough, but even I, in my inexperience, knew the difference. She came in — she, who had spoken of suicide a short time ago — singing softly to herself. She saw me, our eyes met, and the story was told. I knew, and she knew that I knew."

It seemed as though something in his tone might have grated upon her. Gently, but with a certain firmness, she drew her hand away from his.

"You were very angry, I suppose?" she murmured.

Some instinct told him exactly what was passing in her thoughts. In a moment he was on the defensive.

" I think," he said, " that if it had been any other man — but listen. The photograph which I took from the mantelpiece and threw into the fire was the photograph of my own cousin. His father and my father were brought up together. My father chose the Church, his founded the factory in which most of the people in Detton Magna were employed. When my grandfather died, it was found that he was penniless. The whole of his money had gone towards founding the Douglas Romilly Shoe Company. I won't weary with the details. The business prospered, but we remained in poverty. When my mother died I was left with nothing. My uncle made promises and never kept them. He, too, died. My cousin and I quarrelled. He and his father both held that the money advanced by my grandfather had been a gift and not a loan. They offered me a pittance. Well, I refused anything. I spoke plain words, and that was an end of it. And then I came back and I saw his picture, my cousin's picture, upon the mantelpiece. I can see it now and it looks hateful to me. All the old fires burned up in me. I remembered my father's death — a pauper he was. I remembered how near I had been to starvation. I remembered the years I had spent in a garret whilst Douglas had idled time away at Oxford, had left there to trifle with the business his father had founded, had his West End club, hunters, and shooting. It was a vicious, mad, jealous hatred, perhaps, but I claim that it was human. I went out of that little house and it seemed to me that there was a new lust in my heart, a new, craving desire. If I had thrown myself into that canal, they might well have called it temporary insanity. I didn't, but I was mad all the same. Anything else I did — was temporary insanity!"

Her hand suddenly came back again and she leaned towards him through the darkness.

"You poor child," she whispered. "Stop there, please. Don't be afraid to think you've told me this. You see, I am of the world, and I know that we are all only human. Now, twice up and down the deck, and not a word. Then I shall ask you something."

So they passed on, side by side, the touch of her fingers keeping this new courage alive in his heart, his head uplifted even to the stars towards which their rolling mast pointed. It was wonderful, this — to tell the truth, to open the door of his heart!

"Now I am going to ask you something," she said, when they turned for the third time. "You may think it a strange question, but you must please answer it. To me it is rather important. Just what were your feelings for Beatrice?"

"I think I was fond of her," he answered thoughtfully. "I know that I hated her when she came in from the schoolhouse — when I understood. Both of us, in the days of our joint poverty, had scoffed at principles, had spoken boldly enough of sin, but I can only say that when she came, when I looked into her eyes, I seemed to have discovered a new horror in life. I can't analyse it. I am not sure, even now, that I was not more of a beast that I had thought myself.   I am not sure that part of my rage was not because she had escaped and I couldn't."

"But your personal feelings — that is what I want to know about?" she persisted.

He dug down into his consciousness to satisfy her.

"Think of what my life in London had been," he reminded her.   "There wasn't a single woman I knew, with whom I could exchange a word.   All the time I loved beautiful things, and beautiful women, and the thought of them.   I have gone out into the streets at nights sometimes and hung around the entrances to theatres and restaurants just for the pleasure of looking at them with other men.   It didn't do me any good, you know, but the desire was there.   I wanted a companion like those other men had.   Beatrice was the only woman I knew.   I didn't choose her.   It wasn't the selective instinct that made her attractive to me.   It was because she was the only one.   I never felt anything great when I was with her," he went on hoarsely.   "I knew very well that ours were ordinary feelings.   She was in the same position that I was.   There was no one else for her, either.   Do you want me to go on?"

She hesitated.

"Don't be afraid — I am not quite mad," he continued, "only I'll answer for you the part of your question you don't put into words.   Beatrice was nothing to me but an interpretress of her sex.   I never loved her.   If I had, we might in our misery have done the wildest, the most foolish things.   I will tell you why I know so clearly that I never loved her.   I have known it since you have been kind to me, since I have realised what a wonderful thing a woman can be, what a world she can make for the man who cares, whom she cares for."

Her fingers gripped his tightly.

" And now," she said, " I know all that I want to know and all that it is well for us to speak of just now. Dear friend, will you remember that you are sharing your burden with me, and that I, who am accounted something in the world and who know life pretty thoroughly, believe in you and hope for you."

They paused for a moment by the side of the steamer rail. She understood so well his speechlessness. She drew her hand away from his and held it to his lips.

" Please kiss my fingers," she begged. " That is just the seal of our friendship in these days. See how quickly we seem to plough our way through the water. Listen to the throbbing of that engine, always towards a new world for you, my friend. It is to be an undiscovered country. Be brave, keep on being brave, and remember —"

The words seemed to die away upon her lips. A shower of spray came glittering into the dim light, like flakes of snow falling with unexpected violence close to them. He drew her cloak around her and moved back.

" Now," she said, " I think we will smoke, and perhaps, if you made yourself very agreeable to the steward in the smoking room, you could get some coffee."

" One moment," he pleaded. " Remember what? Don't you realise that there is just one word I still need, one little word to crown all that you have said? "

She turned her head towards him. The trouble and brooding melancholy seemed to have fallen from his face. She realised more fully its sensitive lines, its poetic, almost passionate charm. She was carried suddenly away upon a wave of the emotion which she herself had created.

" Oh, but you know!" she faltered. " You see, I trust you even to know when . . . Now your arm, please, until we reach the smoking room, and mind — I must have coffee."

CHAPTER IX

Philip Romilly, on the last day of the voyage, experienced to the full that peculiar sensation of unrest which seems inevitably to prevail when an ocean-going steamer is being slowly towed into port. The winds of the ocean had been left behind. There was a new but pleasant chill in the frosty, sunlit air. The great buildings of New York, at which he had been gazing for hours, were standing, heterogeneous but magnificent, clear-cut against an azure sky. The ferry boats, with their amazing human cargo, seemed to be screeching a welcome as they churned their way across the busy river. Wherever he looked, there was something novel and interesting, yet nothing sufficiently arresting to enable him to forget that he was face to face now with the first crisis of his new life. Since that brief wireless message on the first day out, there had been nothing disquieting in the daily bulletins of news, and he had been able to appreciate to the full the soothing sense of detachment, the friendliness of his fellow voyagers, immeasurably above all the daily association with Elizabeth. He felt like one awaking from a dream as he realised that these things were over. At the first sight of land, it was as though a magician's wand had been waved, a charm broken. His fellow passengers, in unfamiliar costumes, were standing about with their eyes glued upon the distant docks. A queer sense of ostracism possessed him. Perhaps, after all, it had been a dream from which he was now slowly awaking.

He wandered into the lounge to find Elizabeth surrounded by a little group of journalists. She nodded to him pleasantly and waved a great bunch of long-stemmed pink roses which one of them had brought to her. Her greeting saved him from despair. She, at least, was unchanged.

"See how my friends are beginning to spoil me!" she cried out. "Really, I can't tell any of you a thing more," she went on, turning back to them, " only this, and I am sure it ought to be interesting. I have discovered a new dramatist, and I am going to produce a play of his within three months, I hope. I shan't tell you his name and I shan't tell you anything about the play, except that I find more promise in it than anything I have seen or read for months. Mr. Romilly, please wait for me," she called after him. "I want to point out some of the buildings to you."

A dark young man, wearing eyeglasses, with a notebook and pencil in his hand, swung around.

"Is this Mr. Douglas Romilly," he enquired, " of the Romilly Shoe Company? I am from the *New York Star*. Pleased to meet you, Mr. Romilly. You are over here on business, we understand?"

Philip was taken aback and for the moment remained speechless.

"We'd like to know your reason, Mr. Romilly, for paying us a visit," the young man continued, " in your own words. How long a trip do you intend to make, anyway? What might your output be in England per week? Women's shoes and misses', isn't it?"

Elizabeth intervened swiftly, shaking her finger at the journalist.

"Mr. Harris," she said, "Mr. Romilly is my friend, and I am not going to have him spend these few impressive moments, when he ought to be looking about him at the harbour, telling you silly details about his business. You can call upon him at his hotel, if you like — the Waldorf he is going to, I believe — and I am sure he will tell you anything you want to know."

"That's all right, Miss Dalstan," the young man declared soothingly. "See you later, Mr. Romilly," he added. "Maybe you'll let us have a few of your impressions to work in with the other stuff."

Romilly made light of the matter, but there was a slight frown upon his forehead as they passed along the curiously stationary deck.

"I am afraid," he observed, "that this is going to be a terribly hard country to disappear in."

"Don't you believe it," she replied cheerfully. "You arrive here to-day and you are in request everywhere. To-morrow you are forgotten — some one else arrives. That newspaper man scarcely remembers your existence at the present moment. He has discovered Mr. Raymond Greene. . . . Tell me, why do you look so white and unhappy?"

"I am sorry the voyage is over," he confessed.

"So am I, for that matter," she assented. "I have loved every minute of the last few days, but then we knew all the time, didn't we, that it was just an interlude? The things which lie before us are so full of interest."

"It is the next few hours which I fear," he muttered gloomily.

She laughed at him.

"Foolish! If there had been any one on this side who wanted to ask you disagreeable questions, they wouldn't have waited to meet you on the quay. They'd have come down the harbour and held us up. Don't think about that for a moment. Think instead of all the wonderful things we are going to do. You will be occupied every minute of the time until I come back to New York, and I shall be so anxious to see the result. You won't disappoint me, will you?"

"I will not," he promised. "It was only for just a moment that I felt an idiot. It's exciting, you know, this new atmosphere, and the voyage was so wonderful, such a perfect rest. It's like waking up, and the daylight seems a little crude."

She held out her hand.

"You see, the gangways are going down," she pointed out. "I can see many of my friends waiting. Remember, with your new life begins our new alliance. Good luck to you, dear friend!"

Their fingers were locked for a moment together. He looked earnestly into her eyes.

"Whatever the new life may mean for me," he said fervently, "I shall owe to you."

A little rush of people came up the gangway, and Elizabeth was speedily surrounded and carried off. They came across one another several times in the Custom House, and she waved her hand to him gaily.

Philip went through the usual formalities, superintended the hoisting of his trunks upon a clumsy motor truck, and was himself driven without question from the covered shed adjoining the quay. He looked back at the huge side of the steamer, the floor of the Custom House, about which were still dotted little crowds of his fellow passengers. It was the disintegration of a wonderful memory — his farewell. . . .

At the Waldorf he found himself greeted with unexpected cordiality. The young gentleman to whom he applied, after some hesitation, for a room, stretched out his hand and welcomed him to America.

"So you are Mr. Romilly!" he exclaimed. " Well, that's good. We've got your room — Number 602, on the ninth floor."

" Ninth floor!" Philip gasped.

" If you'd like to be higher up we can change you," the young man continued amiably. " Been several people here enquiring for you. A young man from the ' Boot and Shoe Trades Reporter ' was here only half an hour ago, and here's a cable. No mail yet."

He handed the key to a small boy and waved Philip away. The small boy proved fully equal to his mission.

" You just step this way, sir," he invited encouragingly. " Those packages of yours will be all right. You don't need to worry about them."

He led the way down a corridor streaming with human beings, into a lift from which it appeared to

Philip that he was shot on to the ninth floor, along a thickly-carpeted way into a good-sized and comfortable bedroom, with bathroom attached.

" Your things will be up directly, sir," the small boy promised, holding out his hand.   " I'll see after them myself."

Philip expressed his gratitude in a satisfactory manner and stood for a few moments at the window. Although it was practically his first glimpse of New York, the wonders of the panorama over which he looked failed even to excite his curiosity. The clanging of the surface cars, the roar and clatter of the overhead railway, the hooting of streams of automobiles, all apparently being driven at breakneck speed, alien sounds though they were, fell upon deaf ears. He could neither listen nor observe. Every second's delay fretted him. His plans were all made. Everything depended upon their being carried out now without the slightest hitch. He walked a dozen times to the door, waiting for his luggage, and when at last it arrived he was on the point of using the telephone. He feed the linen-coated porters and dismissed them as rapidly as possible. Then he ransacked the trunks until he found, amidst a pile of fashionable clothing, a quiet and inconspicuous suit of dark grey. In the bathroom he hastily changed his clothes, selected an ordinary Homburg hat, and filled a small leather case with various papers. He was on the point of leaving the room when his eyes fell upon the cable. He hesitated for a moment, gazed at the superscription, shrugged his shoulders, and tore it open. He moved to the window and read it slowly, word for word:

Just seen Henshaw. Most disturbing interview. Tells me you have had notice to reduce overdraft by February 1st. Absolutely declines any further advances. Payments coming in insufficient meet wages and current liabilities. No provision for 4th bills, amounting sixteen thousand pounds. Have wired London for accountant. Await your instructions urgently. Suggest you cable back the twenty thousand pounds lying our credit New York. Please reply. Very worried. Potts.

Word by word, Philip read the cable twice over. Then it fluttered from his fingers on to the table. It told its own story beyond any shadow of a mistake. His cousin's great wealth was a fiction. The business to which his own fortune and the whole of his grandfather's money had been devoted, was even now tottering. He remembered the rumours he had heard of Douglas' extravagance, his establishment in London, the burden of his college debts. And then a further light flashed in upon him. Twenty thousand pounds in America! — lying there, too, for Douglas under a false name! He drew out one of the documents which he had packed and glanced at it more carefully. Then he replaced it, a little dazed. Douglas had planned to leave England, then, with this crisis looming over him. Why? Philip for a moment sat down on the arm of an easy-chair. A grim sense of humour suddenly parted his lips. He threw back his head and laughed. Douglas Romilly had actually been coming to America to disappear! It was incredible but it was true.

He left the cable carefully open upon the dressing-table, and, picking up the small leather case, left the room. He reached the lift, happily escaping the observation of the young lady seated at her desk, and descended into the hall. Once amongst the crowd of people who thronged the corridors, he found it perfectly simple to leave the hotel by one of the side entrances. He walked to the corner of the street and drew a little breath. Then he lit a cigarette and strolled along Broadway, curiously light-hearted, his spirits rising at every step. He was free for ever from that other hateful personality. Mr. Douglas Romilly, of the Douglas Romilly Shoe Company, had paid his brief visit to America and passed on.

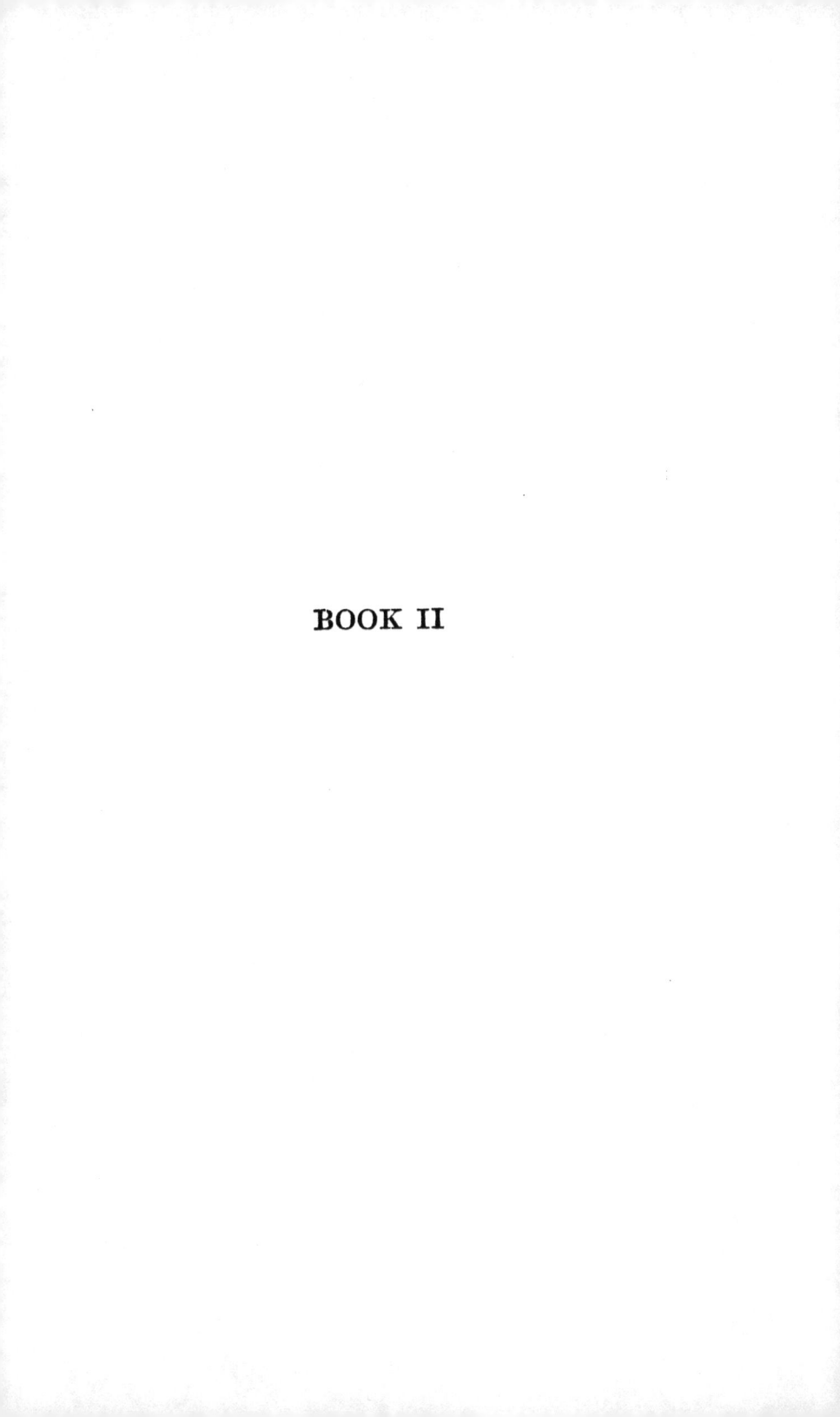

BOOK II

CHAPTER I

After a fortnight of his new life, Philip took stock of himself and his belongings. In the first place, then, he owned a new name, taken bodily from certain documents which he had brought with him from England. Further, as Mr. Merton Ware, he was the monthly tenant of a small but not uncomfortable suite of rooms on the top story of a residential hotel in the purlieus of Broadway. He had also, apparently, been a collector of newspapers of certain dates, all of which contained some such paragraph as this:

DOUGLAS ROMILLY, WEALTHY ENGLISH BOOT MANUFACTURER, DISAPPEARS FROM THE WALDORF ASTORIA HOTEL. WALKS OUT OF HIS ROOM WITHIN AN HOUR OF LANDING AND HAS NOT BEEN HEARD OF SINCE. DOWN TOWN HAUNTS SEARCHED. FOUL PLAY FEARED.

SUPERINTENDENT SHIPMAN DECLARES HIMSELF BAFFLED

Early on Monday morning, the police of the city were invited to investigate a case of curious disappearance. Mr. Douglas Romilly, an English shoe manufacturer, who travelled out from England on board the *Elletania*, arrived at the Waldorf Hotel at four o'clock on Saturday afternoon and was shown to the reservation made for him. Within an hour he was enquired for by several callers, who were shown to his room without result. The apartment was found to be empty and nothing has since been seen or heard of Mr. Romilly. The room assigned to him, which could only have been occupied for a few minutes, has been locked up and the keys handed to the police. A considerable amount of luggage is in their possession, and certain documents of a some-what curious character. From cables received early this afternoon, it would appear that the Douglas Romilly Shoe Company, one of the oldest established firms in England, is in financial difficulties.

Then there was a paragraph in a paper of later date:

NO NEWS OF DOUGLAS ROMILLY

The police have been unable to discover any trace of the missing Englishman. From further cables to hand, it appears that he was in possession of a considerable sum of money, which must have been on his person at the time of disappearance, and it is alleged that there was also a large amount, with which he had intended to make purchases for his business, standing to his credit at a New York bank. Nothing has since been discovered, however, amongst his belongings, of the slightest financial value, nor does any bank in New York admit holding a credit on behalf of the missing man.

"Perhaps it is time," Philip murmured, "that these were destroyed."

He tore the newspapers into pieces and threw them into his waste-basket. On his writing-table were forty or fifty closely written pages of manuscript. In his pocketbook were sixteen hundred dollars, and a document indicating a credit for a very much larger amount at the United Bank of New York, in

favor of Merton Ware and another. The remainder
of his belongings were negligible. He stood at the
window and looked out across the city, the city into
whose labyrinths he was so eager to penetrate — the
undiscovered country. By day and night its voices
were in his ears, the rattle and roar of the overhead
railway, the clanging of the street cars, the heavy
traffic, the fainter but never ceasing foot-fall of the
multitudes. He had sat there before dawn and
watched the queer, pinky-white light steal with ever
widening fingers through the darkness, heard the
yawn of the city as it seemed to shiver and tremble
before the battle of the day. At twilight he had
watched the lights spring up one by one, at first like
pin pricks in the distance, growing and widening until the grotesque shapes of the buildings from which
they sprung had faded into nothingness, and there
was left only a velvet curtain of strangely-lit stars.
At a giddy distance below he could trace the blaze
of Broadway, the blue lights flashing from the electric wires as the cable cars rushed back and forth,
the red and violet glimmer of the sky signs. He
knew it all so well, by morning, by noon and night;
in rainstorm, storms which he had watched come up
from oceanwards in drifting clouds of vapour; and
in sunshine, clear, brilliant sunshine, a little hard
and austere, to his way of thinking, and unseason-
able.

    " A week," he muttered.   " She said a week.   To
night I will go out."

    He looked at himself in the glass. He wore no
longer the well-cut clothes of Mr. Douglas Romilly's
Saville Row tailor, but a ready-made suit of Schmitt

& Mayer's business reach-me-downs, an American felt hat and square-toed shoes.

"She said a week," he repeated. "It's a fortnight to-day. I'll go to the restaurant at the corner. I must find out for myself what all this noise means, what the city has to say."

He turned towards the door and then stopped short. For almost the first time since he had taken up his quarters here, the lift had stopped outside. There was a brief pause, then his bell rang. For a moment Philip hesitated. Then he stepped forward and opened the door, looking out enquiringly at his caller.

"You Mr. Merton Ware?"

He admitted the fact briefly. His visitor was a young woman dressed in a rather shabby black indoor dress, over which she wore an apron. She was without either hat or gloves. Her fingers were stained with purple copying ink, and her dark hair was untidily arranged.

"I live two stories down below," she announced, handing him a little card. "Miss Martha Grimes — that's my name — typewriter and stenographer, you see. The waiter who brings our meals told me he thought you were some way literary, so I just stepped up to show you my prospectus. If you've any typewriting you want doing, I'm on the spot, and I don't know as you'd get it done much cheaper anywhere else — or better."

There was nothing particularly ingratiating about Miss Martha Grimes, but, with the exception of a coloured waiter, she happened to be the first human being with whom Philip had exchanged a word for several days. He felt disinclined to hurry her away.

"Come in," he invited, holding the door open. "So you do typing, eh? What sort of a machine do you use?"

"Remington," she answered. "It's a bit knocked about — a few of the letters, I mean — but I've got some violet ink and I can make a manuscript look all right. Half a dollar a thousand words, and a quarter for carbon copies. Of course, if you'd got a lot of stuff," she went on, her eyes lighting hopefully upon the little collection of manuscript upon his table, "I might quote you a trifle less."

He picked up some of his sheets and glanced at them.

"Sooner or later," he admitted, "I shall have to have this typed. It isn't quite ready yet, though."

He was struck by the curious little light of anticipation which somehow changed her face, and which passed away at his last words. Under pretence of gathering together some of those loose pages, he examined her more closely and realised that he had done her at first scant justice. She was very thin, and the expression of her face was spoilt by the discontented curve of her lips. The shape of her head, however, was good. Her dark hair, notwithstanding its temporary disarrangement, was of beautiful quality, and her eyes, though dull and spiritless-looking, were large and full of subtle promise. He replaced the sheets of manuscript.

"Sit down for a moment," he begged.

"I'd rather stand," she replied.

"Just as you please," he assented, smiling. "I was just wondering what to do about this stuff."

She hesitated for a moment, then a little sulkily she seated herself.

"I suppose you think I'm a pretty forward young person to come up here and beg for work. I don't care if you do," she went on, swinging her foot back and forth. "One has to live."

"I am very pleased that you came," he assured her. "It will be a great convenience to me to have my typing done on the premises, and although I am afraid there won't be much of it, you shall certainly do what there is."

"Story writer?" she enquired.

"I am only a beginner," he told her. "This work I am going to give you is a play."

She looked at him with a shade of commiseration in her face.

"Sickening job, ain't it, writing for the stage unless you've got some sort of pull?"

"This is my first effort," he explained.

"Well, it's none of my business," she said gloomily. "All I want is the typing of it, only you should see some of the truck I've had! I've hated to send in the bill. Waste of good time and paper! I don't suppose yours is like that, but there ain't much written that's any good, anyway."

"You're a hopeful young person, aren't you?" he remarked, taking a cigarette from the mantelpiece and lighting it. "Have one?"

"No, thank *you!*" she replied, rising briskly to her feet. "I'm not that sort that sits about and smokes cigarettes with strange young men. If you'll

let me know when that work's going to be ready, I'll
send the janitor up for it."

He smiled deprecatingly.

"You're not afraid of me, by any chance, are
you?" he asked.

Her eyes glowed with contempt as she looked him
up and down.

"Afraid of you, sir!" she repeated.   "I should
say not! I've met all sorts of men and I know something about them."

"Then sit down again, please," he begged.

She hesitated for a moment, then subsided once
more unwillingly into the chair.

"Don't know as I want to stay up here gossiping,"
she remarked.   "You'd much better be getting on
with your work. Give me one of those cigarettes,
anyway," she added abruptly.

"Do you live in the building?" he enquired, as he
obeyed her behest.

"Two flats below with pop," she replied.   "He's
a bad actor, very seldom in work, and he drinks.
There are just the two of us. Now you know as
much as is good for you. You're English, ain't
you?"

"I am," Philip admitted.

"Just out, too, by the way you talk."

"I have been living in Jamaica," he told her, "for
many years — clerk in an office there."

"Better have stayed where you were, I should
think, if you've come here hoping to make a living
by that sort of stuff."

"Perhaps you're right," he agreed, "but you see
I am here — been here a week or two, in fact."

" Done much visiting around? " she enquired.

" I've scarcely been out," he confessed. " You see, I don't know the city except from my windows. It's wonderful from here after twilight."

" Think so," she replied dully. " It's a hard, hammering, brazen sort of place when you're living in it from hand to mouth. Not but what we don't get along all right," she added, a little defiantly. " I'm not grumbling."

" I am sure you're not," he assented soothingly. " Tell me — to-night I am a little tired of work. I thought of going out. Be a Good Samaritan and tell me where to find a restaurant in Broadway, somewhere where crowds of people go but not what they call a fashionable place. I want to get some dinner — I haven't had anything decent to eat for I don't know how long — and I want to breathe the same atmosphere as other people."

She looked at him a little enviously.

" How much do you want to spend? " she asked bluntly.

" I don't know that that really matters very much. I have some money. Things are more expensive over here, aren't they? "

" I should go to the New Martin House," she advised him, " right at the corner of this block. It's real swell, and they say the food's wonderful."

" I could go as I am, I suppose? " he asked, glancing down at his clothes.

She stared at him wonderingly.

" Say, where did you come from? " she exclaimed. " You ain't supposed to dress yourself out in glad clothes for a Broadway restaurant, not even the best of them."

" Have you been to this place yourself? " he enquired.

" Nope! "

" Come with me," he invited suddenly.

She arose at once to her feet and threw the remains of her cigarette into the grate.

" Say, Mr. Ware," she pronounced, " I ain't that sort, and the sooner you know it the better, especially if I'm going to do your work. I'll be going."

" Look here," he remonstrated earnestly, " you don't seem to understand me altogether. What do you mean by saying you're not that sort? "

" You know well enough," she answered defiantly. " I guess you're not proposing to give me a supper out of charity, are you? "

" I am asking you to accompany me," he declared, " because I haven't spoken to a human being for a week, because I don't know a soul in New York, because I've got enough money to pay for two dinners, and because I am fiendishly lonely."

She looked at him and it was obvious that she was more than half convinced. Her brightening expression transformed her face. She was still hesitating, but her inclinations were apparent.

" Say, you mean that straight? " she asked. " You won't turn around afterwards and expect a lot of soft sawder because you've bought me a meal? "

" Don't be a silly little fool," he answered goodhumouredly. " All I want from you is to sit by my side and talk, and tell me what to order."

Her face suddenly fell.

"No good," she sighed. "Haven't got any clothes."

"If I am going like this," he expostulated, "why can't you go as you are? Take your apron off. You'll be all right."

"There's my black hat with the ribbon," she reminded herself. "It's no style, and Stella said yesterday she wouldn't be seen in a dime show in it."

"Never you mind about Stella," he insisted confidently. "You clap it on your head and come along."

She swung towards the door.

"Meet you in the hall in ten minutes," she promised. "Can't be any quicker. This is your trouble, you know. I didn't invite myself."

Philip opened the door, a civility which seemed to somewhat embarrass her.

"I shall be waiting for you," he declared cheerfully.

CHAPTER II

Philip stepped into his own little bedroom and made scanty preparations for this, his first excursion. Then he made his way down into the shabby hall and was seated there on the worn settee when his guest descended. She was wearing a hat which, so far as he could judge, was almost becoming. Her gloves, notwithstanding their many signs of mending, were neat, her shoes carefully polished, and although her dress was undeniably shabby, there was something in her carriage which pleased him. Her eyes were fixed upon his from the moment she stepped from the lift. She was watching for his expression half defiantly, half anxiously.

"Well, you see what I look like," she remarked brusquely. "You can back out of it, if you want to."

"Don't be silly," he replied. "You look quite all right. I'm not much of a beau myself, you know. I bought this suit over the counter the other day, without being measured for it or anything."

"Guess you ain't used to ready-made clothes," she observed, as they stepped outside.

"You see, in England — and the Colonies," he added hastily, "things aren't so expensive as here. What a wonderful city this is of yours, Martha!"

"Miss Grimes, please," she corrected him.

"I beg your pardon," he apologised.

"That's just what I was afraid of," she went on querulously. "You're beginning already. You think because you're giving me a meal, you can take all sorts of liberties. Calling me by my Christian name, indeed!"

"It was entirely a slip," he assured her. "Tell me what theatre that is across the way?"

She answered his question and volunteered other pieces of information. Philip gazed about him, as they walked along Broadway, with the eager curiosity of a provincial sightseer. She laughed at him a little scornfully.

"You'll get used to all the life and bustle presently," she told him. "It won't seem so wonderful to you when you walk along here without a dollar to bless yourself with, and your silly plays come tumbling back. Now this is the Martin House. My! Looks good inside, don't it?"

They crossed the threshold, Philip handed his hat to the attendant and they stood, a little undecided, at the top of the brilliantly-lit room. A condescending maître d'hôtel showed them to a retired table in a distant corner, and another waiter handed them a menu.

"You know, half of this is unintelligible to me," Philip confessed. "You'll have to do the ordering — that was our bargain, you know."

"You must tell me how much you want to spend, then?" she insisted.

"I will not," he answered firmly. "What I want is a good dinner, and for this once in my life I don't care what it costs. I've a few hundred dollars in

my pocket, so you needn't be afraid I shan't be able
to pay the bill. You just order the things you like,
and a bottle of claret or anything else you prefer."

She turned to the waiter, and, carefully studying
the prices, she gave him an order.

" One portion for two, remember, of the fish and
the salad," she enjoined. " Two portions of the
chicken, if you think one won't be enough."

She leaned back in her place.

" It's going to cost you, when you've paid for the
claret, a matter of four dollars and fifty cents, this
dinner," she said, " and I guess you'll have to give
the waiter a quarter. Are you scared? "

He laughed at her once more.

" Not a bit! "

She looked at his long, delicate fingers — studied
him for a moment. Nothwithstanding his clothes,
there was an air of breeding about him, unconceal-
able, a thing apart, even, from his good looks.

" Clerk, were you? " she remarked. " Seems to
me you're used to spending two dollars on a meal all
right. I'm not! "

" Neither am I," he assured her. " One doesn't
have much opportunity of spending money in —
Jamaica."

" You seem kind of used to it, somehow," she persisted. " Have you come into money, then? "

" I've saved a little," he explained, with a rather
grim smile, " and I've — well, shall we say come into
some? "

" Stolen it, maybe," she observed indifferently.

" Should you be horrified if I told that I had? "

" I don't know," she answered. " I'm one of those

who's lived honest, and I sometimes wonder whether it pays."

"It's a great problem," he sighed.

"It is that," she admitted gloomily. "I've got a friend — she used to live in our place, just below me — Stella Kimbell, her name is. She and I learnt our typewriting together and started in the same office. We stood it, somehow, for three years, sometimes office work, sometimes at home. We didn't have much luck. It was always better for me than for Stella, because she was good-looking, and I'm not."

"I shouldn't say that," he remonstrated. "You've got beautiful eyes, you know."

"You stop it!" she warned him firmly. "My eyes are my own, and I'll trouble you not to make remarks about them."

"Sorry," Philip murmured, duly crushed.

"The men were after her all the time," the girl continued, reminiscently. "Last place we were at, a drygoods store not far from here, the heads of the departments used to make her life fairly miserable. She held out, though, but what with fines, and one thing or another, they forced her to leave. So I did the same. We drifted apart then for a while. She got a job at an automobile place, and I was working at home. I remember the night she came to me — I was all alone. Pop had got a three-line part somewhere and was bragging about it at all the bars in Broadway. Stella came in quite suddenly and almost out of breath.

"'Kid,' she said, 'I'm through with it.'

"'What do you mean?' I asked her.

"Then she threw herself down on the sofa and she

sobbed — I never heard a girl cry like that in all my life. She shrieked, she was pretty nearly in hysterics, and I couldn't get a word out of her. When she was through at last, she was all limp and white. She wouldn't tell me anything. She simply sat and looked at the stove. Presently she got up to go. I put my hands on her shoulders and I forced her back in the chair.

"'You've got to tell me all about it, Stella,' I insisted.

"And then of course I heard the whole story. She'd got fired again. These men are devils!"

"Don't tell me more about it unless you like," he begged sympathetically. "Where is she now?"

"In the chorus of ' Three Frivolous Maids.' She comes in here regularly."

"Sorry for herself?"

"Not she! Last time I saw her she told me she wouldn't go back into an office, or take on typewriting again, for anything in the world. She was looking prettier than ever, too. There's a swell chap almost crazy about her. Shouldn't wonder if she hasn't got an automobile."

"Well, she answers our question one way, then," he remarked thoughtfully. "Tell me, Miss Grimes, is everything to eat in America as good as this fish?"

"Some cooking here," she observed, looking rather regretfully at her empty plate. "I told you things were all right. There's grilled chicken — Maryland chicken — coming, and green corn."

"Have I got to eat the corn like that man opposite?" he asked anxiously.

"You can eat it how you like," she answered.

"Watch me, if you want to. I don't care. I ain't tasted green corn since I can remember, and I'm going to enjoy it."

"You don't like your claret, I'm afraid," he remarked.

She sipped it and set down the glass a little disparagingly.

"If you want to know what I would like," she said, "it's just a Martini cocktail. We don't drink wines over here as much as you folk, I guess."

He ordered the cocktails at once. Every now and then he watched her. She ate delicately but with a healthy and unashamed appetite. A little colour came into her cheeks as the room grew warmer, her lower lip became less uncompromising. Suddenly she laid down her knife and fork. Her eyes were agleam with interest. She pulled at his sleeve.

"Say, that's Stella!" she exclaimed excitedly. "Look, she's coming this way! Don't she look stunning!"

A girl, undeniably pretty, with dark, red-gold hair, wearing a long ermine coat and followed by a fashionably dressed young man, was making her way up the room. She suddenly recognised Philip's companion and came towards her with outstretched hand.

"If it isn't Martha!" she cried. "Isn't this great! Felix, this is Miss Grimes — Martha Grimes, you know," she added, calling to the young man who was accompanying her. "You must remember — why, what's the matter with you, Felix?"

She broke off in her speech. Her companion was

staring at Philip, who was returning his scrutiny with an air of mild interrogation.

"Say," the young man enquired, "didn't I meet you on the *Elletania?* Aren't you Mr. Douglas Romilly?"

Philip shook his head.

"My name is Ware," he pronounced, "Merton Ware. I have certainly never been on the *Elletania* and I don't remember having met you before."

The young man whose name was Felix appeared almost stupefied.

"Gee whiz!" he muttered. "Excuse me, sir, but I never saw such a likeness before — never!"

"Well, shake hands with Miss Grimes quickly and come along," Stella enjoined. "Remember I only have half an hour for dinner now. You coming to see the show, Martha?"

"Not to-night," that young woman declared firmly.

The two passed on after a few more moments of amiable but, on the part of the young man, somewhat dazed conversation. Philip had resumed the consumption of his chicken. He raised an over-filled glass to his lips steadily and drank it without spilling a drop.

"Mistook me for some one," he remarked coolly.

She nodded.

"Man who disappeared from the Waldorf Astoria. They made quite a fuss about him in the newspapers. I shouldn't have said you were the least like him — to judge by his pictures, anyway."

Philip shrugged his shoulders. He seemed very little interested.

" I don't often read the newspapers. . . . So that is Stella."

" That is Stella," she assented, a little defiantly. " And if I were she — I mean if I were as good-looking as she is — I'd be in her place."

" I wonder whether you would? " he observed thoughtfully.

" Oh! don't bother me with your problems," she replied. " Does it run to coffee? "

" Of course it does," he agreed, " and a liqueur, if you like."

" If you mean a cordial, I'll have some of that green stuff," she decided. " Don't know when I shall get another dinner like this again."

" Well, that rests with you," he assured her. " I am very lonely just now. Later on it will be different. We'll come again next week, if you like."

" Better see how you feel about it when the time comes," she answered practically. " Besides, I'm not sure they'd let me in here again. Did you see Stella's coat? Fancy feeling fur like that up against your chin! Fancy —"

She broke off and sipped her coffee broodingly.

" Those things are immaterial in themselves," he reminded her. " It's just a question how much happiness they have brought her, whether the thing pays or not."

" Of course it pays! " she declared, almost passionately. " You've never seen my rooms or my drunken father. I can tell you what they're like, though. They're ugly, they're tawdry, they're untidy, when I've any work to do, they're scarcely clean. Our meals are thrown at us — we're always

behind with the rent. There isn't anything to look
at or listen to that isn't ugly. You haven't known
what it is to feel the grim pang of a constant hideous-
ness crawling into your senses, stupefying you
almost with a sort of misery — oh, I can't describe
it!"

"I have felt all those things," he said quietly.

"What did you do?" she demanded. "No, perhaps you had luck. Perhaps it's not fair to ask you
that. It wouldn't apply. What should you do if
you were me, if you had the chance to get out of it
all the way that she has?"

"I am not a woman," he reminded her simply.
"If I answer you as an outsider, a passer-by —
mind, though, one who thinks about men and women
— I should say try one of her lesser sins, one of the
sins that leaves you clean. Steal, for instance."

"And go to prison!" she protested angrily.
"How much better off would you be there, I wonder,
and what about when you came out? Pooh! Pay
your bill and let's get out of this."

He obeyed, and they made their way into the
crowded street. He paused for a moment on the
pavement. The pleasure swirl was creeping a little
into his veins.

"Would you like to go to a theatre?" he asked.

She shook her head.

"You do as you like. I'm going home. You
needn't bother about coming with me, either."

"Don't be foolish," he protested. "I only mentioned a theatre for your sake. Come along."

They walked down Broadway and turned into
their own street. They entered the tenement build-

ing together and stepped into the lift. She held out her hand a little abruptly.

" Good night! "

" Good night! " he answered. " You get out first, don't you? I'll polish that stuff up to-night, the first part of it, so that you can get on with the typing."

Some half-developed fear which had been troubling her during the walk home, seemed to have passed. Her face cleared.

" Don't think I am ungrateful," she begged, as the lift stopped. " I haven't had a good time like this for many months. Thank you, Mr. Ware, and good night! "

She stepped through the iron gates on to her own floor, and Philip swung up to his rooms. Somehow, he entered almost light-heartedly. The roar of the city below was no longer provocative. He felt as though he had stretched out a hand towards it, as though he were in the way of becoming one of its children.

CHAPTER III

A few nights later Philip awoke suddenly to find himself in a cold sweat, face to face with all the horrors of an excited imagination. Once more he felt his hand greedy for the soft flesh of the man he hated, tearing its way through the stiff collar, felt the demoniacal strength shooting down his arm, the fever at his finger tips. He saw the terrified face of his victim, a strong man but impotent in his grasp; heard the splash of the turgid waters; saw himself, his lust for vengeance unsatisfied, peering downwards through the dim and murky gloom. It was not only a physical nightmare which seized him. His brain, too, was his accuser. He saw with a hideous clarity that even the excuse of motive was denied him. It was a sense of personal loss which had driven him out on to that canal path, a murderer at heart. It was something of which he had been robbed, an acute and burning desire for vengeance, personal, entirely egotistical. It was not the wrong to the woman which he resented, had there been any wrong. It was the agony of his own personal misery. He rose from his bed and stamped up and down his little chamber in a fear which was almost hysterical. He threw wide open the windows, heedless of a driving snowstorm. The subdued murmur of the city, with its paling lights, brought him no relief. He longed frantically for some one who knew the truth, for Elizabeth before any one, with her soft, cool touch, her gentle, protective sympathy. He was a fool to think he could live alone like this, with such a burden to bear! Perhaps it would not be for long. The risks were many. At any moment he might hear the lift stop, steps across the corridor, the ring at his bell, the plainly-clad, businesslike man outside, with his formal questions, his grim civility. He fumbled about in his little dressing-case until he came to a small box containing several white pills. He gripped them in his hand and looked around, listening. No, it was fancy! There was still no sound in the building. When at last he went back to bed, however, the little box was tightly clenched in his hands.

In the morning he went through his usual programme. He arose soon after eight, lighted his little spirit lamp, made his coffee, cut some bread and butter, and breakfasted. Then he lit a cigarette and sat down at his desk. His imagination, however, seemed to have burnt itself out in the night. Ideas and phrases were denied to him. He was thankful, about eleven o'clock, to hear a ring at the bell and find Martha Grimes outside with a little parcel under her arm. She was wearing the same shabby black dress and her fingers were stained with copying ink. Her almost too luxuriant hair was ill-arranged and untidy. Even her eyes seemed to have lost their lustre.

" I've finished," she announced, handing him the parcel. " Better look and see whether it's all right. I can't do it up properly till I've had the whole."

He cut the string and looked at a few of the sheets. The typing was perfect. He began to express his approval but she interrupted him.

"It's better stuff than I expected," she declared grudgingly. "I thought you were only one of these miserable amateurs. Where did you learn to write like that?"

Somehow, her praise was like a tonic.

"Do you like it?" he asked eagerly.

"Oh! my likes or dislikes don't matter," she replied. "It's good stuff. You'll find the account in there. If you'd like to pay me, I'd like to have the money."

He glanced at the neat little bill and took out his pocketbook.

"Sit down for a minute," he begged. "I'm stuck this morning — can't write a line. Take my easy-chair and smoke a cigarette — I have nothing else to offer you."

For a moment she seemed about to refuse. Then she flung herself into his easy-chair, took a cigarette, and, holding it between her lips, almost scarlet against the pallor of her cheeks, stretched upwards towards the match which he was holding.

"Stella and her boy were over to see me last night," she announced, a little abruptly.

"The young lady with the ermines," he murmured.

"And her boy, Felix Martin. It was through him they came — I could see that all right. He was trying all the time to pump me about you."

"About me?"

"Oh! you needn't trouble to look surprised," she

remarked. " I guess you remember the bee he had in his bonnet that night."

" Mistook me for some one, didn't he? " Philip murmured.

She nodded.

" Kind of queer you don't read our newspapers! It was a guy named Romilly — Douglas Romilly — who disappeared from the Waldorf Hotel. Strange thing about it," she went on, " is that I saw photographs of him in the newspapers, and I can't recognise even a likeness."

" This Mr. Felix Martin doesn't agree with you, apparently," Philip observed.

" He don't go by the photographs," Martha Grimes explained. " He believes that he crossed from Liverpool with this Mr. Douglas Romilly, and that you," she continued, crossing her legs and smoothing down her skirt to hide her shabby shoes, " are so much like him that he came down last night to see if there was anything else he could find out from me before he paid a visit to police headquarters."

There was a moment's silence. Philip was apparently groping for a match, and the girl was keeping her head studiously turned away from him.

" What business is it of his? "

" There was a reward offered. Don't know as that would make much difference to Felix Martin, though. According to Stella's account, he is pretty well a millionaire already."

" It would be more useful to you, wouldn't it? " Philip remarked.

" Five hundred dollars ! " Martha sighed. " Don't
seem to me just now that there's much in the world
you couldn't buy with five hundred dollars."

" Well, what did you tell Mr. Felix Martin ? "

" Oh, I lied, sure! He'd found out ' he date you
came into your rooms here — the day this man
Romilly disappeared — but I told him that I'd known
you and done work for you before then — long
enough before the *Elletania* ever reached New York.
That kind of stumped him."

" Why did you do that ? " Philip demanded.

" Dunno," the girl replied, with a shrug of the
shoulders. " Just a fancy. I guessed you wouldn't
want him poking around."

" But supposing I had been Douglas Romilly, you
might at least have divided the reward," he reminded
her.

" There's money and money," Martha declared.
" We spoke of that the other day. Stella's got
money — now. Well, she's welcome. My time will
come, I suppose, but if I can't have clean money, I
haven't made up my mind yet whether I wouldn't
rather try the Hudson on a foggy morning."

" Well, I am not Douglas Romilly, anyway,"
Philip announced.

She looked up at him almost for the first time
since her entrance.

" I kind of thought you were," she admitted. " I
might have saved my lies, then."

He shook his head.

" You have probably saved me from more than
you know of," he replied. " I am not Douglas
Romilly, but —"

"You're not Merton Ware, either," she interrupted.

"Quite right," he agreed. "I started life as Philip Merton Ware the day I took these rooms, and if the time should come," he went on, "that any one seriously set about the task of finding out exactly who I was before I was Merton Ware, you and I might as well take that little journey — was it to the Hudson, you said, on a foggy morning? — together."

They sat in complete silence for several moments, Then she threw the end of her cigarette into the fire.

"Well, I'm glad I didn't lie for nothing," she declared. "I didn't quite tumble to the Douglas Romilly stunt, though. They say he has left his business bankrupt in England and brought a fortune out here. You don't look as though you were overdone with it."

"I certainly haven't the fortune that Douglas Romilly is supposed to have got away with," he said quietly. "I have enough money for my present needs, though — enough, by-the-by, to pay you for this typing," he added, counting out the money upon the table.

"Any more stuff ready?"

"With luck there'll be some this afternoon," he promised her. "I had a bad night last night, but I think I'll be able to work later in the day."

She looked at him curiously, at his face, absolutely devoid of colour, his eyes, restless and overbright, his long, twitching fingers.

"Bad conscience or drugs?" she asked.

"Bad conscience," he acknowledged. "I've been

where you have been — Miss Grimes. I looked over the edge and I jumped. I'd stay where you are, if I were you."

"Maybe I shall, maybe I shan't," she replied doggedly. "Stella wants to bring a boy around to see me. 'You bring him,' I said. 'I'll talk to him.' Then she got a little confused. Stella's kind, in her way. She came back after Mr. Martin had gone down the passage. 'See here, kid,' she said, 'you know as well as I do I can't bring any one round to see you while you are sitting around in those rags. Let me lend you —' Well, I stopped her short at that. 'My own plumes or none at all,' I told her, 'and I'd just as soon he didn't come, anyway.'"

"You're a queer girl," Philip exclaimed. "Where's your father to-day?"

"Usual place," she answered,—"in bed. He never gets up till five."

"Let me order lunch up here for both of us, from the restaurant," he suggested.

She shook her head.

"No, thanks!"

"Why not?" he persisted.

"I'm going round to the office to see if I can get any extra work."

"But you've got to lunch some time," he persisted.

She laughed a little hardly.

"Have I? We girls haven't got to eat like you men. I'll call up towards the evening and see if you've anything ready for me."

She was gone before he could stop her. He turned back to his desk and seated himself. The sight of his last finished sentence presented itself suddenly in a new light. There was a suggestiveness about it which was almost poignant. He took up his pen and began to write rapidly.

CHAPTER IV

It was a few minutes after six that evening when Philip was conscious of a knock at his door. He swung around in his chair, blinking a little.

"Come in!"

Martha Grimes entered. She was in outdoor apparel, that is to say she wore her hat and a long mackintosh. She remained standing upon the threshold.

"Just looked up to see if you've got any more work ready," she explained.

He sprang to his feet and stood there, for a moment, unsteadily.

"Come in and shut the door," he ordered. "Look! Look!" he added, pointing to his table. "Thirty-three sheets! I've been working all the time. I've been living, I tell you, living God knows where! — not in this accursed little world. Here, let's pick up the sheets. There's enough work for you."

She looked at him curiously.

"Have you been in that chair ever since?" she asked.

"Ever since," he assented enthusiastically.

"Any lunch?"

"Not a scrap. Never thought about it."

"You'll make yourself sick, that's what you'll

do," she declared. " Go out and get something at once."

" Never even thought about lunch," he repeated, half to himself. " Where have you been? "

" Some luck," she replied. " First place I dropped in at. Found there was a girl gone home for the day, fainted. Lots of work to do, so they just stuck me down in her chair. Three dollars they gave me. The girl's coming back to-morrow, though, worse luck."

" When did you have your lunch? "

" Haven't had any. I'm going to make myself a cup of tea now."

He reached for his hat.

" Not on your life! " he exclaimed. " Come along, Miss Martha Grimes. I have written lines — you just wait till you type them! I tell you it's what I have had at the back of my head for months. It's there now on paper — living, flaring words. Come along."

" Where to? "

" We are going to eat," he insisted. " I am faint, and so are you. We are going to that same place, and we'll have lunch and dinner in one."

" Nothing doing," she snapped. " You'll see some more people who recognise you."

He waved his hand contemptuously.

" Who cares! If you don't come along with me, I'll go up town to the Waldorf or the Ritz Carlton. I'll waste my money and advertise myself. Come along — that same little quiet corner. I don't suppose your friends will be there again."

" Stella won't," she admitted doubtfully. " She's

going to Sherry's. I'd just as soon be out," she went on ruminatingly. " Shouldn't be surprised if she didn't bring that guy in, after all."

He had already rung the bell of the lift.

" Look at me!" she exclaimed ironically. " Nice sort of an object I am to take out! Got a raincoat on — though it's dry enough — because my coat's gone at the seams."

" If you don't stop talking like that," he declared, " I'll march into one of those great stores and order everything a woman wants to wear. Look at me. Did you ever see such clothes!"

"A man's different," she protested. " Besides, you've got a way with you of looking as though you could wear better clothes if you wanted to — something superior. I don't like it. I should like you better if you were common."

" You're going to like me better," he assured her, " because we are going to have a cocktail together within the next three minutes. Look at you — pale as you can stick. I bet you haven't had a mouthful of food all day. Neither have I, except a slice of bread and butter with my tea this morning. We're a nice sort of couple to talk about clothes. What we want is food."

She swayed for a moment and pretended that she tripped. He caught her arm and steadied her. She jerked it from him.

" Have your own way," she yielded.

They reached the corner of the street, plunged into the surging crowds of Broadway, passed into the huge restaurant, were once more pounced upon by a businesslike but slightly patronizing maître

d'hôtel, and escorted to a remote table in a sort
of annex of the room. Philip pushed the menu
away.

"Two cocktails — the quickest you ever mixed
in your life," he ordered. "Quicker than that,
mind."

The man was back again almost at once with two
frosted glasses upon a tray. They laughed together almost like children as they set them down
empty.

"I know what I want, and you, too, by the look
of you," he continued —" a beefsteak, with some
more of that green corn you gave me the other day,
and fried potatoes, and Burgundy. We'll have some
oysters first while we wait."

She sighed.

"I don't mean to come here with you again," she
said, a little impatiently. "I don't know why I
give in to you. You're not strong, you know. You
are a weak man. Women will always look after
you; they'll always help you in trouble — I suppose they'll always care for you. Can't think why I
do what you want me to. Guess I was near starving."

He laughed.

"You don't know much about me yet," he reminded her.

"You don't know much about yourself," she retorted glibly. "Why, according to your own con-
fession, you only started life a few weeks ago. I
fancy what went before didn't count for much.
You've been fretted and tied up somewhere. You
haven't had the chance of getting big like so many

of our American men. What are you going to do
with this play of yours? "

" Miss Elizabeth Dalstan has promised to produce
it," he told her.

She looked at him in some surprise.

" Elizabeth Dalstan? " she repeated. " Why,
she's one of our best actresses."

" I understood so," he replied. " She has heard
the story — in fact I wrote out one of the scenes
with her. She is going to produce it as soon as it's
finished."

" Well, all you poor idiots who write things have
some fine tale to tell their typewriter," she remarked.
" You seem as though you mean it, though. Where
did you meet Elizabeth Dalstan? "

" I came over with her on the *Elletania*," he answered thoughtlessly.

She gave a little start. Then she turned upon
him almost in anger.

" Well, of all the simpletons! " she exclaimed.
" So that's the way you give yourself away, is it?
Just here from Jamaica, eh! Nothing to do with
Douglas Romilly! Never heard of the *Elletania*,
did you! I'd like to see you on the grid at police
headquarters for five minutes, with one of our men
asking you a few friendly questions! You'd look
well, you would! You ought to go about with a
nurse! "

Philip had all the appearance of a guilty child.

" You see," he explained penitently, " I am new
to this sort of thing. However, you know now."

" Still ready to swear that you're not Douglas
Romilly, I suppose? "

"On my honour I am not," he replied.

"Kind of funny that you should have been on the steamer, after all," she jeered.

"Perhaps so, but I am not Douglas Romilly," he persisted.

She was silent for a moment, then she shrugged her shoulders.

"What do I care who you are?" she said. "Here, help me off with this raincoat, please. It's warm in here, thank goodness!"

He looked at her as she sat by his side in her plain black dress, and was impressed for the first time with a certain unsuspected grace of outline, which made him for the moment oblivious of the shabbiness of her gown.

"You have rather a nice figure," he told her with a sudden impulse of ingenuousness.

She turned upon him almost furiously. Something in his expression, however, seemed to disarm her. She closed her lips again.

"You are nothing but a child!" she declared. "You don't mean anything. I'd be a fool to be angry with you."

The waiter brought their steak. Philip was conscious of something in his companion's eyes which almost horrified him. It was just that gleam of hungry desire which has starvation for its background.

"Don't let's talk," he pleaded. "There isn't any conversation in the world as good as this."

The waiter served them and withdrew, casting a curious glance behind. They were, from his point of view, a strange couple, for, cosmopolitan though the restaurant was, money was plentiful in the neighbourhood, and clients as shabby as these two seldom presented themselves. He pointed them out to a maître d'hôtel, who in his turn whispered a few words concerning them to a dark, lantern-jawed man, with keen eyes and a hard mouth, who was dining by himself. The latter glanced at them and nodded.

" Thank you, Charles," he said, " I've had my eye on them. The girl's a pauper, daughter of that old fool Grimes, the actor. Does a little typewriting — precious little, I should think, from the look of her. The man's interesting. Don't talk about them. Understand? "

The maître d'hôtel bowed.

" I understand, Inspector. Not much any one can tell you, sir."

" Pays his bill in American money, I suppose? " the diner asked.

" I'll ascertain for you, Mr. Dane," Charles replied. " I believe he is an Englishman."

" Name of Merton Ware," the inspector agreed, nodding, " just arrived from Jamaica. Writes some sort of stuff which the girl with him typewrites. That's his story. He's probably as harmless as a baby."

Charles bowed and moved away. His smile was inscrutable.

CHAPTER V

New York became a changed city to Philip. Its roar and its turmoil, its babel of tongues speaking to him always in some alien language, were suddenly hushed! He was no longer conscious of the hard unconcern of a million faces, of the crude buildings in the streets, the cutting winds, the curious, depressing sense of being on a desert island, the hermit clutching at the sleeves of imaginary multitudes. A few minutes' journey in a cable car which seemed to crawl, a few minutes' swift walking along the broad thoroughfare of Fifth Avenue, where his feet seemed to fall upon the air and the passersby seemed to smile upon him like real human beings, and he was in her room. It was only an hotel sitting room, after all, but eloquent of her, a sitting room filled with great bowls of roses, with comfortable easy-chairs, furniture of rose-coloured satin, white walls, and an English fire upon the grate. Elizabeth was in New York, and the world moved differently.

She came out to him from an inner room almost at once. His eyes swept over her feverishly. He almost held his breath. Then he gave a great sigh of satisfaction. She came with her hands outstretched, a welcoming smile upon her lips. She

was just as he had expected to find her.   There was
nothing in her manner to indicate that they had not
parted yesterday.

"Welcome to New York, my dramatist!" she exclaimed. "I am here, you see, to the day, almost to
the hour."

He stood there, holding her hands.   His eyes
seemed to be devouring her.

"Go on talking to me," he begged. "Let me
hear you speak.   You can't think — you can't imagine how often in the middle of the night, I have
waked up and thought of you, and the cold shivers
have come because, after all, I fancied that you
must be a dream, that you didn't really exist,
that that voyage had never existed. Go on talking."

"You foolish person!" she laughed, patting his
hands affectionately. "But then, of course, you
are a little overwrought.   I am very real, I can assure you.   I have been in Chicago, playing, but
there hasn't been a night when I haven't thought of
the times when we used to talk together in the darkness, when you let me into your life, and I made
up my mind to try and help you.   Foolish person!
Sit down in that great easy-chair and draw it up to
the fire."

He sank into it with a little sigh of content.   She
threw herself on to the couch opposite to him.   Her
hands drooped down a little wearily on either side,
her head was thrown back.   Against the background
of rose-silk cushions, her cheeks seemed unexpectedly
pale.

"I am tired with travelling," she murmured, " and

I hate Chicago, and I have worried about you. Day by day I have read the papers. Everything has gone well?"

"So far as I know," he answered. "I did exactly as we planned — or rather as you planned. The papers have been full of the disappearance of Douglas Romilly. You read how wonderfully it has all turned out? Fate has provided him with a real reason for disappearing. It seems that the business was bankrupt."

"You mustn't forget, though," she reminded him, "that that also supplies a considerable motive for tracking him down. He is supposed to have at least twenty thousand pounds with him."

"I have all the papers," he went on. "They prove that he knew the state the business was in. They prove that he really intended to disappear in New York. The money stands to the credit of Merton Ware — and another at a bank with which his firm apparently had had no connections, a small bank in Wall Street."

"So that," she remarked, "is where you get your pseudonym from?"

"It makes the identification so easy," he pointed out, "and no one knew of it except he. I could easily get a witness presently to prove that I am Merton Ware."

"You haven't drawn the money yet, then?"

"I haven't been near the bank," he replied. "I still have over a thousand dollars — money he had with him. Sometimes I think that if I could I'd like to leave that twenty thousand pounds where it is. I should like some day, if I could do so without

suspicion, to let the creditors of the firm have it
back again. What do you think? "

She nodded.

" I would rather you didn't touch it yourself,"
she agreed. " I think you'll find, too, that you'll
be able to earn quite enough without wanting it.
Nothing disturbing has happened to you at all,
then? "

" Once I had a fright," he told her. " I was in
a restaurant close to my hotel. I was there with
a young woman who is typing the play for me."

She looked towards him incredulously.

" You were there with a typewriter? " she exclaimed.

" I suppose it seems queer," he admitted. " It
didn't to me. She is a plain, shabby, half starved
little thing, fighting her own battle bravely. She
came to me for work — she lives in the flat below —
and it seemed to me that she was just as hungry
for a kind word as I was lonely, and I took her out
with me. Twice I have taken her. Her name is
Miss Grimes."

" I am not in the least sure that I approve," she
said, " but go on."

" A friend of hers came into the restaurant, a girl
in the chorus of a musical comedy here, and she had
with her a young man. I recognised him at once.
We didn't come across one another much, but he was
on the steamer."

Elizabeth's face was full of concern.

" Go on."

" He asked me twice if I wasn't Mr. Romilly. I
assured him that he was mistaken. I don't think I

gave myself away. The next day he went to see the girl I was with, Martha Grimes."

"Well, what did she tell him?"

"She told him that she had been typing my work for over a month, that I had come from Jamaica, and that my name was Merton Ware."

Elizabeth gazed into the fire for several moments, and Philip watched her. It was a woman's face, grave and thoughtful, a little perturbed just then, as though by some unwelcome thought. Presently she looked back at him, looked into his eyes long and earnestly.

"My friend," she said, "you are like no one else on earth. Perhaps you are one of those horrible people who have what they call an unholy influence over my sex. You have known this girl for a matter of a few days, and she lies for you. And there's five hundred dollars reward. I suppose she knew about that?"

"Yes, she knew," he admitted. "She simply isn't that sort. I suppose I realised that, or I shouldn't have been kind to her."

"It's a puzzle," she went on. "I think there must be something in you of the weakling, you know, something that appeals to the mothering instinct in women. I know that my first feeling for you was that I wanted to help you. Tell me what you think of yourself, Mr. Philip Merton Ware? Are you a faithful person? Are you conscientious? Have you a heart, I wonder? How much of the man is there underneath that strong frame of yours? Are you going to take just the things that are given you in life, and make no return? For the moment, you see, I am forgetting that you are my friend and that I like you. I am thinking of you from the point of view of an actress — as a psychical problem. Philip, you idiot!" she broke off, suddenly stamping her foot, " don't sit there looking at me with your great eyes. Tell me you are glad I've come back. Tell me you feel something, for goodness' sake!"

He was on his knees before she could check him, his arms, his lips praying for her. She thrust him back.

"It was my fault," she declared, " but don't, please. Yes, of course you have feelings. I don't know why you tempted me to that little outburst."

"You'll tempt me to more than that," he cried passionately. "Do you think it's for your help that I've thought of you? Do you think it's because you're an angel to me, because you've comforted me in my darkest, most miserable hours that I've dreamed of you and craved for you? There's more than that in my thoughts, dear. It's because you are you, yourself, that I've longed for you through the aching hours of the night, that I've sat and written like a man beside himself just for the joy of thinking that the words I wrote would be spoken by you. Oh! if you want me to tell you what I feel —"

She suddenly leaned forward, took his head between her hands and kissed his forehead.

"Now get back, please, to your chair," she begged. "You've stilled the horrible, miserable little doubt that was tearing at my heartstrings. I just had it before, once or twice, and then — isn't it

foolish! — your telling me about this little typewriter girl! I must go and see her. We must be
kind to her."

He resumed his seat with a little sigh.

"She thought a great deal more of me and my
work when I told her that you were probably going
to act in my play."

Her expression changed. She was more serious,
at the same time more eager.

"Ah! The play!" she exclaimed. "I can see
that you have brought some of it."

He drew the roll of manuscript from his pocket.

"Shall I read it?" he suggested.

She almost snatched it away. "No! I can't
wait for that. Give it to me, quickly."

She leaned forward so that the firelight fell upon
the pages. Little strands of soft brown hair
drooped over her face. In studying her, Philip almost forgot his own anxiety. He had known so few
women, yet he had watched so many from afar off,
endowed them with their natural qualities, built up
their lives and tastes for them, and found them all
so sadly wanting. To him, Elizabeth represented
everything that was desirable in her sex, from the
flowing lines of her beautiful body to the sympathy
which seemed to be always shining out of her eyes.
Notwithstanding her strength, she was so exquisitely
and entirely feminine, a creature of silk and laces,
free from any effort of provocativeness, yet subtly,
almost clamorously human. He forgot, in those few
moments, that she had become the arbitress of his
material fate — that he was a humble author, watching the effect of his first attempts upon a mistress

in her profession. He remembered only that she was
the woman who was filling his life, stealing into every
corner of it, permeating him with love, pointing him
onwards towards a life indescribable, unrealisable. . . .

She swung suddenly towards him. There was a
certain amount of enthusiasm in her face but even
more marked was her relief.

"Oh! I am so glad," she cried. "You know, I
have had qualms. When you told me the story in
your own words, picking your language so carefully,
and building it all up before me, well, you know what
I said. I gave you more than hope — I promised
you success. And then, when I got away into the
hard, stagey world of Chicago, and my manager
talked business to me, and my last playwright
preached of technique, I began to wonder whether,
after all, you could bring your ideas together like
this, whether you would have a sense of perspective
— you know what I mean, don't you? And you have
it, and the play is going to be wonderful, and I shall
produce it. Why don't you look pleased, Mr.
Author? You are going to be famous."

He smiled.

"I don't care about fame," he said. "And for
the rest, I think I knew."

"Conceited!" she exclaimed.

"It wasn't that," he protested. "It was simply
when I sat down in that little room, high up over
the roofs and buildings of a strange city, shut myself in and told myself that it was for you — well,
the thoughts came too easily. They tumbled over
one another. And when I looked away from my

work, I saw the people moving around me, and I knew that I had made my dreams real, and that's the great thing, isn't it? . . . Elizabeth!"

"Well?"

"I am lonely in that little room."

"You lonely, taking out typewriters to dine!" she mocked tenderly.

"It is lonely," he repeated, "and I am afraid of you here in all this luxury. I am so far away. I come from my attic to this, and I am afraid. Do you know why?"

She sat quite still for a moment. Dimly she felt the presage of a coming change in their relations. Up to now she had been the mistress, she had held him so easily in check with her practised skill, with an unfinished sentence, a look, a touch. And now the man was rising up in him, and she felt her powers weaken.

"Shall I change my abode?" she murmured.

"Ah! but you would be just as wonderful and as far away even if we changed places — if you sat in my attic and I took your place here. That isn't why I torture myself, why I am always asking myself if you are real, if the things we talk about are real, if the things we feel belong to ourselves, well up from our own hearts for one another or are just the secondary emotions of other people we catch up without knowing why. This is foolish, but you understand — you do understand. It is because you keep me so far away from yourself, when my fingers are burning for yours, when even to touch your face, to feel your cheek against mine, would banish every fear I have ever had. Elizabeth, you do understand!

I have never kissed you, I have never held you for one moment in my arms — and I love you!"

He was leaning over her chair and she held him tightly by the shoulders. There was nothing left of that hidden fear in his dark eyes. They shone now with another light, and she began to tremble.

"I wanted to wait a little, Philip, but if you feel like that — well, I can't."

He took her silently into his arms. With the half closing of her eyes, the first touch of her responsive lips, himself dimly conscious of the change, he passed into the world where stronger men live.

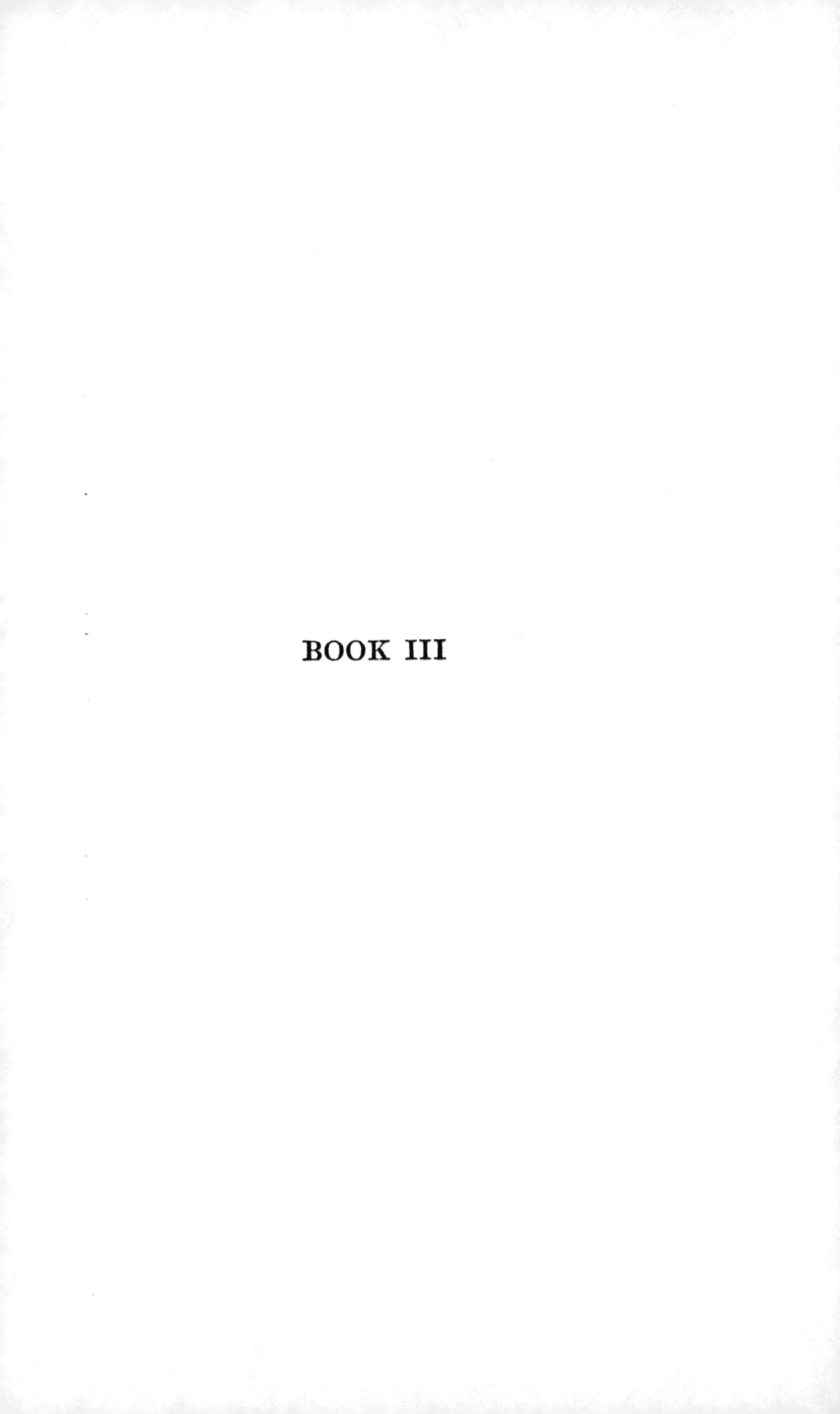

BOOK III

CHAPTER I

Three months later, a very different Philip stood in the smaller of a handsome suite of reception rooms in a fashionable Fifth Avenue hotel. He was wearing evening clothes of the most approved cut and carried himself with a dignity and assurance entirely transforming. The distinction of birth and breeding, little apparent in those half-starved, passionate days of his misery, had come easily to the surface. His shoulders, too, seemed to have broadened, and his face had lost its cadaverous pallor.

The apartment in which he stood was plainly but handsomely furnished as a small withdrawing room. On the oak chiffonier stood a silver tray on which were half a dozen frosted cocktails. Through the curtains was apparent a room beyond, in which a round table, smothered with flowers, was arranged for supper; in the distance, from the public restaurant, came the sound of softly played music. Philip glanced at the clock. The whole of the anxieties of this momentous evening had passed. Telephone messages had reached him every quarter of an hour. The play was a great success. Elizabeth was coming to him with her producer and a few theatrical friends, flushed with triumph. They were all to meet for the first time that night the man who for the last three months had lived as a hermit —

Merton Ware, the author of " The House of Shams," the new-found dramatist.

A maître d'hôtel appeared in the space between the two rooms, and bowed.

" Everything is quite ready, Mr. Ware," he said, in the friendly yet deferential manner of an American head-waiter. " Won't you take a cocktail, sir, while you are waiting? "

" Very thoughtful of you, Louis. I think I will," Philip assented, taking a little case from his pocket and lighting a cigarette.

The man passed him a glass upon a small salver.

" You'll pardon the liberty, I am sure, sir," he continued, dropping his voice a little. " I've just heard that ' The House of Shams ' seems to be a huge success, sir. If I might take the liberty of offering my congratulations! "

Philip smiled genially.

" You are the first, Louis," he said. " Thank you very much indeed."

" I think you will find the supper everything that could be desired, Mr. Ware," the man went on. " Our head chef, Monsieur Raconnot, has given it his personal attention. The wine will be slightly iced, as you desired. I shall be outside in the corridor to announce the guests."

" Capital, Louis! " Ware replied, sipping his cocktail. " It will be another quarter of an hour yet before we see anything of them, I am afraid."

The man disappeared and left Philip once more alone. He looked through the walls of the room as though, indeed, he could see into the packed theatre

and could hear the cries for " Author!" which even
then were echoing through the house. From the
moment when Elizabeth, abandoning her reserve, had
given him the love he craved, a new strength seemed
to have shone out of the man. Step by step he had
thought out subtly and with infinite care every small
detail of his life. It was he who had elected to live
those three months in absolute seclusion. It was
he, indirectly, who had arranged that many more
photographs of Douglas Romilly, the English shoe
manufacturer, should appear in the newspapers.
One moment's horror he had certainly had. He
could see the little paragraph now, almost lost in
the shoals of more important news:

GHASTLY DISCOVERY IN A DERBYSHIRE CANAL

Yesterday the police recovered the body of a man who
had apparently been dead for some weeks, from a canal
close to Detton Magna. The body was unrecognisable
but it is believed that the remains are those of Mr. Philip
Romilly, the missing art teacher from London, who is
alleged to have committed suicide in January last.

The thought of that gruesome find scarcely
blanched his cheeks. His nerves now were stronger
and tenser things. He crushed back those memories
with all the strength of his will. Whatever might
lie behind, he had struck for the future which he
meant to live and enjoy. They were only weaklings
who brooded over an unalterable past. It was for
the present and the near future that he lived, and
both, in that moment, were more alluring than ever
before. Even his intellectual powers seemed to have

developed in his new-found happiness. The play which he had written, every line of which appeared to gain in vital and literary force towards its conclusion, was only the first of his children. Already other images and ideas were flowing into his brain. The power of creation was triumphantly throwing out its tendrils. He was filled with an amazing and almost inspired confidence. He was ready to start upon fresh work that hour, to-morrow, or when he chose. And before him now was the prospect of stimulating companionship. Elizabeth and he had decided that the time had come for him to take his fate into his hands. He was to be introduced to the magnates of the dramatic profession, to become a clubman in the world's most hospitable city, to mix freely in the circles where he would find himself in constant association with the keenest brains and most brilliant men of letters in the world. He was safe. They had both decided it.

He walked to the mirror and looked at himself. The nervous, highly-strung, half-starved, neurotic stripling had become the perfectly assured, well-mannered, and well-dressed man of the world. He had studied various details with a peculiar care, suffered a barber to take summary measures with his overlong black hair, had accustomed himself to the use of an eyeglass, which hung around his neck by a thin, black ribbon. Men might talk of likenesses, men who were close students of their fellows, yet there was no living person who could point to him and say —" You are, beyond a shadow of doubt, a man with whom I travelled on the *Elletania*." The thing was impossible.

Louis once more made a noiseless appearance. There was the slightest of frowns upon his face.

"A gentleman wishes a word with you before the arrival of your guests, Mr. Ware," he announced.

"A journalist?" Philip enquired carelessly.

"I do not think so, sir."

Even as he spoke the door was opened and closed again. The man who had entered bowed slightly to Philip. He was tall and clean-shaven, self-assured, and with manner almost significantly reserved. He held a bowler hat in his hand and glanced towards Louis. He had the air of being somewhat out of place in so fashionable a rendezvous.

"Good evening, Mr. Ware!" he began. "Could I have just a word with you?"

Philip nodded to Louis, who at once left the room. The newcomer drew a little nearer.

"My name, sir," he said, "is Dane — Edward Dane."

Philip bowed politely. He was just a little annoyed at the intrusion, an annoyance which he failed altogether to conceal.

"What do you want with me?" he asked. "I am expecting some friends to supper in about ten minutes."

"Ten minutes will perhaps be sufficient for what I have to say," the other promised. "You don't know me, then, Mr. Ware?"

"Never saw you before, to the best of my knowledge," Philip replied nonchalantly. "Are you a journalist?"

The man laid his hat upon a corner of the table.

"I am a detective," he said, "attached to the

Cherry Street headquarters. Your last rooms, **Mr. Ware**, were in my beat."

Philip nodded with some slight indication of interest. He faced his ordeal with the courage of a man of steel.

"That so?" he remarked indifferently. "Well, Mr. Dane, I have heard a good deal about you American detectives. Pleased to meet you. What can I do for you?"

The detective eyed Philip steadfastly. There was just the shadow of something that looked like admiration in his hard, grey eyes.

"Well, Mr. Ware," he said, "nothing that need disturb your supper party, I am sure. Over in this country we sometimes do things in an unusual way. That's why I am paying you this visit. I have been watching you for exactly three months and fourteen days."

"Watching me?" Philip repeated.

"Precisely! No idea why, I suppose?"

"Not the slightest."

The detective glanced towards the clock. Barely two minutes had passed.

"Well," he explained, "I got on your tracks quick enough when you skipped from the Waldorf and blossomed out in a second-rate tenement house as Merton Ware."

"So I was at the Waldorf, was I?" Philip murmured.

"You crossed from Liverpool on the *Elletania*," the man continued, "registered at the Waldorf as Mr. Douglas Romilly of the Douglas Romilly Shoe Company, went to your room, changed your clothes, and disappeared. Of course, a disappearance of that sort," he went on tolerantly, " might be possible in London. In New York, to even attempt it is farcical."

" Dear me," remarked Philip, " this is very interesting. Let me ask you this question, though. If you were so sure of your facts, why didn't you arrest me at once instead of just watching me? "

The man's eyes were like gimlets. He seemed as though he were trying, with curious and professional intensity, to read the thoughts in Philip's brain.

" There is no criminal charge against Douglas Romilly that I know of," he said.

" There's a considerable reward offered for his discovery," Philip reminded him.

" I can claim that at any moment," the man replied. " I have had my reasons for waiting. It's partly those reasons that have brought me here. For one thing, Mr. Douglas Romilly was supposed to be able to put his hand on a matter of a hundred thousand dollars somewhere in New York. You haven't shown many signs up till now, Mr. Ware, of having any such sum in your possession."

" I see," Philip assented. " You wanted the money as well."

" The creditors of the Douglas Romilly Shoe Company are wanting it pretty badly," the man proceeded, " but that wasn't all. I wanted to find out what your game was. That I don't know, even now. That is why I have come to you. Have I the pleasure of speaking to Mr. Douglas Romilly? "

" I really don't see," Philip protested thoughtfully, " why I should go into partnership with you in this affair. You see, in the long run, our interests might not be altogether identical."

Mr. Dane smiled grimly.

"That's a fairly shrewd calculation, Mr. Ware," he admitted. "You ain't bound to answer any question you don't want to. This is just a friendly chat and no more."

"Besides," Philip continued, lighting another cigarette, "I think I understood you to say that you had already arrived at the conclusion that I was Douglas Romilly?"

"Not precisely that," the detective replied. "All that I discovered was that you were the man who registered at the Waldorf Hotel as Mr. Douglas Romilly."

"Well, the only name I choose to acknowledge at present is the name of Merton Ware," Philip declared. "If you think there is any mystery about me, any connection with the gentleman whom I believe you call Mr. Douglas Romilly, well, the matter is one for your investigation. You will forgive me if I remind you that my guests will be here in a matter of a few minutes, and permit me to ask you one more question. Why do you come here to me in this very unofficial manner? If I am really an impostor, you are giving me every opportunity of clearing out."

Mr. Edward Dane shook his head. He was fingering the brim of his hat.

"Oh, no, Mr. Ware!" he declared smoothly. "Our detective system may have some faults, but when a man's name is put on the list where yours figures, he has not one chance in a million of leaving the country or of gaining any place of hiding. I shall know where you lunch to-morrow and with whom you dine, and with whom you spend your time. The law, sir, will keep its eye upon you."

"Really, that seems very friendly," Philip said coolly. "Shall I have the privilege of your personal surveillance?"

"I think not, Mr. Ware. To tell you the truth, this is rather a p. p. c. visit. I've booked my passage on the *Elletania*, sailing to-morrow from New York. I am taking a trip over to England to make a few enquiries round about the spot where this Mr. Douglas Romilly hails from — Detton Magna, isn't it?"

Philip made no reply, yet even his silence might well have been the silence of indifference.

"At the last moment," the detective concluded, "it flashed in upon me that there might be some ridiculous explanation of the few little points about your case which, I must confess, have puzzled me. For that reason, I decided to seek an interview with you before I left. You have, however, I gather, nothing to say to me?"

"Nothing at all, Mr. Dane, except to wish you a pleasant voyage," Philip declared. "I won't detain you a moment longer. I hear my guests in the corridor. Good night, sir!" he added, opening the door. "I appreciate your call very much. Come and see me again when you return from England."

Mr. Dane lingered for a moment upon the threshold, hat in hand, a somewhat ominous figure. There was no attempt at a handshake between the two men. The detective was imperturbable. Philip, listening to Elizabeth's voice, had shown his first sign of impatience.

"I shall surely do that, Mr. Ware!" the other promised, as he passed out.

The door closed. Philip stood for a moment in the empty room, listening to the man's retreating footsteps. Then he turned slowly around. His cheeks were blanched, his eyes were glazed with reminiscent horror. He looked through the wall of the room — a long way back.

"We shall find Mr. Ware in here, I expect." He could hear the voices of his approaching guests.

He ground his heel into the carpet and swung around. He anticipated Louis, threw open the curtain, and stood there waiting to welcome his guests, a smile upon his lips, his hands outstretched towards Elizabeth.

CHAPTER II

Elizabeth's face was glowing with joy. For the first time Philip realised that she, too, had had her anxieties.

"You dear, dear man!" she exclaimed. "To think what you have missed! It would have been the evening of your life. It's a success, do you hear? — a great success! It was wonderful!"

He seemed, almost to himself, to be playing a part, he was so calm yet so gracefully happy.

"I am glad for both our sakes," he said.

She indicated the others with a little wave of the hand.

"I don't think you know a soul, do you?" she asked. "They none of them quite believe in your existence down at the theatre. This is my leading man, Noel Bridges. You should have seen how splendid he was as Carriston."

Mr. Noel Bridges, with a deprecating smile towards Elizabeth, held out his hand. He was tall and of rather a rugged type for the New York stage. Like the rest of the little party, his eyes were full of curiosity as he shook hands with Philip.

"So you are something human, after all," he remarked. "We began to think you lived underground and only put your head up every now and then for a little air. I am glad to meet you, Mr. Ware. I enjoy acting in your play very much indeed, and I hope it's only the first of many."

"You are very kind," Philip murmured cordially.

Elizabeth glanced around the little group.

"Dear me, I am forgetting my manners," she declared. "I ought to have presented you to Sara Denison first. Sara is really the star of your play, Mr. Ware, although I have the most work to do. She loves her part and has asked about you nearly every day."

Miss Denison, a young lady of the smaller Gibson type, with large eyes and a very constant smile, greeted Philip warmly.

"Do you know," she told him, "that this is the first time I have ever been in a play in which the author hasn't been round setting us to rights most of the time? I can't imagine how you kept away, Mr. Ware."

"Perhaps," observed Philip, "my absence has contributed to your success. I am sure I shouldn't have known what to tell you. You see, I am so absolutely ignorant of the technique."

"I've got to shake hands with you, Mr. Ware," a stout, middle-aged, clean-shaven man, with narrow black eyes and pale cheeks, declared, stepping forward. "These other folk don't count for much by the side of me. I am the manager of the theatre, and I'm thundering glad that your first play has been produced at the 'New York,' sir. There's good stuff in it, and if I am any judge, and I'm supposed to be, there's plenty of better stuff behind. Shake hands, if you please, sir. You know me by name —

Paul Fink. I hope you'll see my signature at the bottom of a good many fat cheques before you've finished writing plays."

"That's very nice of you, Mr. Fink," Philip declared. "Now I am sure you all want your supper."

At a sign from Philip, the maître d'hôtel handed round the tray of cocktails. Mr. Fink raised his glass.

"Here's success to the play," he exclaimed, "and good luck to all of us!"

He tossed off the contents of the glass and they all followed his example. Then they took their places at the little round table and the service of supper began. The conversation somewhat naturally centered around Philip. The three strangers were all interested in his personality and the fact that he had no previous work to his credit. It was unusual, almost dramatic, and for a time both Elizabeth and he himself found themselves hard put to it to escape the constant wave of good-natured but very pertinent questions.

"You'll have a dose of our newspapermen to-morrow, sir," Mr. Fink promised him. "They'll be buzzing around you all day long. They'll want to know everything, from where you get your clothes and what cigarettes you smoke, to how you like best to do your work and what complexioned typist you prefer. They're some boys, I can tell you."

Philip's eyes met Elizabeth's across the table. The same instinct of disquietude kept them both, for a moment, silent.

"I am afraid," Elizabeth sighed, "that Mr. Ware

will find it rather hard to appreciate some of our journalistic friends."

" They're good fellows," Mr. Fink declared heartily, " white men, all of them. So long as you don't try to put 'em off on a false stunt, or anything of that sort, they'll sling the ink about some. Ed Harris was in my room just after the second act, and he showed me some of his stuff. I tell you he means to boost us."

Elizabeth laid her hand upon her manager's arm.

" They're delightful, every one of them," she agreed, " but, Mr. Fink, you have such influence with them, I wonder if I dare give you just a hint? Mr. Ware has passed through some very painful times lately. He is so anxious to forget, and I really don't wonder at it myself. I am sure he will be delighted to talk with all of them as to the future and his future plans, but do you think you could just drop them a hint to go quietly as regards the past? "

Mr. Fink was a little perplexed but inclined to be sympathetic. He glanced towards Philip, who was deep in conversation with Sara Denison.

" Why, I'll do my best, Miss Dalstan," he promised. " You know what the boys are, though. They do love a story."

" I am not going to have Mr. Ware's story published in every newspaper in New York," Elizabeth said firmly, " and the newspaper man who worms the history of Mr. Ware's misfortunes out of him, and then makes use of it, will be no friend of mine. Ask them to be sports, Mr. Fink, there's a dear."

"I'll do what I can," he promised. "Mr. Ware isn't the first man in the world who has funked the limelight, and from what I can see of him it probably wasn't his fault if things did go a little crooked in the past. I'll do my best, Miss Dalstan, I promise you that. I'll look in at the club to-night and drop a few hints around."

Elizabeth patted his hand and smiled at him very sweetly. The conversation flowed back once more into its former channels, became a medley of confused chaff, disjointed streams of congratulation, of toast-drinking and pleasant speeches. Then Mr. Fink suddenly rose to his feet.

"Say," he exclaimed, "we've all drunk one another's healths. There's just one other friend I think we ought to take a glass of wine with. Gee, he'd give something to be with us to-night! You'll agree with me, Miss Dalstan, I know. Let's empty a full glass to Sylvanus Power!"

There was a curious silence for a second or two, then a clamour of assenting voices. For a single moment Philip felt a sharp pang at his heart. Elizabeth was gazing steadily out of the room, a queer tremble at her lips, a look in her eyes which puzzled him, a look almost of fear, of some sort of apprehension. The moment passed, but her enthusiasm, as she raised her glass, was a little overdone, her gaiety too easily assumed.

"Why, of course!" she declared. "Fancy not thinking of Sylvanus!"

They drank his health noisily. Philip set down his glass empty. A curious instinct kept his lips sealed. He crushed down and stifled the memory of that sudden stab. He did not even ask the one natural question.

" Say, where is Sylvanus Power these days? " Mr. Fink enquired.

" In Honolulu, when last I heard," Elizabeth replied lightly, " but then one never knows really where he is."

Philip became naturally the central figure of the little gathering. Mr. Fink was anxious to arrange a little dinner, to introduce him to some fellow workers. Noel Bridges insisted upon a card for the Lambs Club and a luncheon there. Philip accepted gratefully everything that was offered to him. It was no good doing things by halves, he told himself. The days of his solitude were over. Even when, after the departure of his guests, he glanced for a moment into the anteroom beyond and remembered those few throbbing moments of suspense, they came back to him with a curious sense of unreality — they belonged, surely, to some other man, living in some other world!

" You are happy? " Elizabeth murmured, as she took his arm and they waited in the portico below for her automobile.

He had no longer any idea of telling her of that disquieting visit. The touch of her hair blown against his cheek, as he had helped her on with her cloak, something in her voice, some slight diffidence, a queer, half expostulating look in the eyes that fell with a curious uneasiness before his, drove every thought of future danger out of his mind. He had at least the present! He answered without a moment's hesitation.

" For the first time in my life ! "

She gave the chauffeur a whispered order as she stepped into the car.

" I have told him to go home by Riverside Drive," she said, as they glided off. " It is a little farther, and I love the air at this time of night."

He clasped her fingers — suddenly felt, with the leaning of her body, her heart beating against his. With that wave of passion there was an instant and portentous change in their attitudes. The soft protectiveness which had sometimes seemed to shine out of her face, to envelop him in its warmth, had disappeared. She was no longer the stronger. She looked at him almost with fear, and he was electrically conscious of all the vigour and strength of his stunted manhood, was master at last of his fate, accepting battle, willing to fight whatever might come for the sake of the joy of these moments. She crept into his arms almost humbly.

CHAPTER III

The success of "The House of Shams" was as immediate and complete as was the social success of its author. After a few faint-hearted attempts, Philip and Elizabeth both agreed that the wisest course was to play the bold game — to submit himself to the photographer, the interviewer, and, to some judicious extent, to the wave of hospitality which flowed in upon him from all sides. He threw aside, completely and utterly, every idea of leading a more or less sheltered life. His photograph was in the Sunday newspapers and the magazines. It was quite easy, in satisfying the appetite of journalists for copious personal details, especially after the hints dropped by Mr. Fink, to keep them carefully off the subject of his immediate past. There had been many others in the world who, on attaining fame, had preferred to gloss over their earlier history. It seemed to be tacitly understood amongst this wonderful freemasonry of newspaper men that Mr. Merton Ware was to be humoured in this way. He was a man of the present. Character sketches of him were to be all foreground. But, nevertheless, Philip had his trials.

"Want to introduce you to one of our chief 'movie' men," Noel Bridges said to him one day in the smoking room of "The Lambs." "He is much interested in the play, too. Mr. Raymond Greene, shake hands with Mr. Merton Ware."

Mr. Raymond Greene, smiling and urbane, turned around with outstretched hand, which Philip, courteous, and with all that charm of manner which was making him speedily one of the most popular young men in New York, grasped cordially.

"I am very happy to meet you, Mr. Greene," he said. "You represent an amazing development. I am told that we shall all have to work for you presently or find our occupation gone."

With a cool calculation which had come to Philip in these days of his greater strength, he had purposely extended his sentence, conscious, although apparently he ignored the fact, that all the time Mr. Raymond Greene was staring in his face with a bewilderment which was not without its humorous side. He was too much a man of the world, this great picture producer, to be at a loss for words, to receive an introduction with any degree of clumsiness.

"But surely," he almost stammered, "we have met before?"

Philip shook his head doubtfully.

"I don't think so," he said. "As a matter of fact, I am sure we haven't, because you are one of the men whom I hoped some day to come across over here. I couldn't possibly have forgotten a meeting with you."

Mr. Raymond Greene's blue eyes looked as though they saw visions.

"But surely," he expostulated, "the *Elletania* — my table on the *Elletania*, when Miss Dalstan crossed —"

Philip laughed easily.

"Why," he exclaimed, "are you going to be like the others and take me for — wasn't it Mr. Romilly? — the man who disappeared from the Waldorf? Why, I've been tracked all round New York because of my likeness to that man."

"Likeness!" Mr. Raymond Greene muttered. "Likeness!"

There was a moment's silence. Then Mr. Greene knew that the time had arrived for him to pull himself together. He had carried his bewilderment to the very limits of good breeding.

"Well, well!" he continued. "Fortunately, it's six o'clock, and I can offer you gentlemen a cocktail, for upon my word I need it! Come to look at you, Mr. Ware, there's a trifle more what I might term *savoir faire,* about you. That chap on the boat was a little crude in places, but believe me, sir," he went on, thrusting his arm through Ware's and leading him towards the bar, "you don't want to be annoyed at those people who have mistaken you for Romilly, for in the whole course of my life, and I've travelled round the world a pretty good deal, I never came across a likeness so entirely extraordinary."

"I have heard other people mention it," Noel Bridges intervened, "although not quite with the same conviction as you, Mr. Greene. Curiously enough, however, the photograph of Romilly which they sent out from England, and which was in all the Sunday papers, didn't strike me as being particularly like Mr. Ware."

"It was a damned bad photograph, that," Mr. Raymond Greene pronounced. " I saw it — couldn't

make head nor tail of it, myself. Well, the world
is full of queer surprises, but this is the queerest I
ever ran up against. Believe me, Mr. Ware, if this
man Romilly who disappeared had been a millionaire,
you could have walked into his family circle and been
made welcome at the present moment. Why, I don't
believe his own wife or sister, if he had such ap-
pendages, would have been able to tell that you
weren't the man."

"Unfortunately," Bridges remarked, as he sipped
the cocktail which the cinema man had ordered, "this
chap Romilly was broke, wasn't he? — did a scoot
to avoid the smash-up? They say that he had a
few hundred thousand dollars over here, ostensibly
for buying material, and that he has taken the lot
out West."

"Well, I must say he didn't seem that sort on
the steamer," Mr. Raymond Greene declared, "but
you never can tell. Looked to me more like a school-
teacher. Some day, Mr. Ware, I want you to come
along to my office — it's just round the corner in
Broadway there — and have a chat about the play."

"You don't want to film us before we've finished
its first run, surely?" Philip protested, laughing.
"Give us a chance!"

"Well, we'll talk about that," the cinema magnate
promised.

They were joined by other acquaintances, and
Philip presently made his escape. One of the moments which he had dreaded more than any other had
come and passed. Even if Mr. Raymond Greene had
still some slight misgivings, he was, to all effects and
purposes, convinced. Philip walked down the street,

feeling that one more obstacle in the path of his absolute freedom had been torn away. He glanced at
his watch and boarded a down-town car, descended
in the heart of the city region of Broadway, and
threaded his way through several streets until he
came to the back entrance of a dry goods store.
Here he glanced once more at his watch and commenced slowly to walk up and down. The time-
keeper, who was standing in the doorway with his
hands in his pockets, watched him with interest.
When Philip approached for the third time, he addressed him in friendly fashion.

" Waiting for one of our gals, eh? "

Philip stifled his quick annoyance and answered in
as matter-of-fact a tone as possible.

" Yes! How long will it be before they are out
from the typewriting department? "

" Typewriting department? " the man repeated.
" Well, that depends some upon the work. They'll
be out, most likely, in ten minutes or so. I guessed
you were after one of our showroom young ladies.
We get some real swells down here sometimes — motor cars of their own. The typists ain't much, as a
rule. It's a skinny job, theirs."

" The young ladies from here appear to be prosperous," Ware remarked. " I watched them last
night coming out. My friend happened to be late,
and I had to leave without seeing her."

" That's nothing to go by, their clothes ain't,"
the man replied. " They spend all their money on
their backs instead of putting it inside. If it's Miss
Grimes you're waiting for, you're in luck, for here
she is, first out."

Philip drew a little into the background. The girl came down the stone passage, passed the time-keeper without appearing to notice his familiar " Good-evening! " and stepped out into the murky street. Philip, who saw her face as she emerged from the gloom, gave a little start. She seemed paler than ever, and she walked with her eyes fixed upon vacancy, as though almost unconscious of her whereabouts. She crossed the sidewalk without noticing the curbstone, and stumbled at the unexpected depth of it. Philip stepped hastily forward.

" Miss Grimes! " he exclaimed. " Martha! . . . Why do you look at me as though I were a ghost? "

She started violently. It was certain that she saw him then for the first time.

" You! Mr. Ware! Sorry, I didn't see you."

He insisted upon shaking hands. There was a little streak of colour in her cheeks now.

" I came to meet you," he explained. " I came yesterday and missed you. I have been to your rooms four times and only found out with difficulty where you were working. The last time I called, I rang the bell six times, but the door was locked."

" I was in bed," she said shortly. " I can't have gentlemen callers there at all now. Father's gone off on tour. Thank you for coming to meet me, but I don't think you'd better stop."

" Why not? " he asked gently.

" Because I don't want to be seen about with you," she declared, " because I don't want you to look at me, because I want you to leave me alone," she added, with a little passionate choke in her voice.

He turned and walked by her side.

"Martha," he said, "you were very kind to me when I needed it, you were a companion to me when I was more miserable than I ever thought any human being could be. I was in a quandary then — in a very difficult position. I took a plunge. In a way I have been successful."

"Oh, we all know that!" she replied bitterly. "Pictures everywhere, notices in the paper all the time — you and your fine play! I've seen it. Didn't think much of it myself, but I suppose I'm not a judge."

"Tell me why you came out there looking as though you'd seen a ghost?" he asked.

"Discharged," she answered promptly.

"Why?"

"Fainted yesterday," she went on, "and was a bit wobbly to-day. The head clerk said he wanted some one stronger."

"Brute!" Philip muttered. "Well, that's all right, Martha. I have some work for you."

"Don't want to do your work."

"Little fool!" he exclaimed. "Martha, do you know you're the most obstinate, pig-headed, prejudiced, ill-tempered little beast I ever knew?"

"Then go along and leave me," she insisted, stopping short, "if I'm all that."

"You're also a dear!"

She drew a little breath and looked at him fiercely.

"Now don't be silly," he begged. "I'm starving. I had no lunch so that I could dine early. Here we are at Durrad's."

"I'm not going inside there with you," she declared.

"Look here," he expostulated, "are we going to do a wrestling act on the sidewalk? It will be in all the papers, you know."

"Spoil your clothes some, wouldn't it?" she remarked, looking at them disparagingly.

"It would indeed, also my temper," he assured her. "We are going to have a cocktail, you and I, within two minutes, young lady, and a steak afterwards. If you want to go in there with my hand on your neck, you can, but I think it would look better —"

She set her feet squarely upon the ground and faced him.

"Mr. Ware," she said, "I am in rags — any one can see that. Listen. I will not go into a restaurant and sit by your side to have people wonder what woman from the streets you have brought in to give a meal to out of charity. Do you hear that? I can live or I can die, just by myself. If I can't keep myself, I'll die, but I won't. Nothing doing. You hear?"

She had been so strong and then something in his eyes, that pitying, half anxious expression with which he listened, suddenly seemed to sap her determination. She swayed a little upon her feet — she was indeed very tired and very weak. Philip took instant advantage of her condition. Without a moment's hesitation he passed his arm firmly through hers, and before she could protest she was inside the place, being led to a table, seated there with her back to the wall, with a confused tangle of

words still in her throat, unuttered. Then two great
tears found their way into her eyes. She said nothing because she could not. Philip was busy talking
to the waiter. Soon there was a cocktail by her
side, and he was drinking, smiling at her, perfectly
good-natured, obviously accepting her momentary
weakness and his triumph as a joke.

"Got you in, didn't I?" he observed pleasantly.
"Now, remember you told me the way to drink
American cocktails — one look, one swallow, and
down they go."

She obeyed him instinctively. Then she took out
a miserable little piece of a handkerchief and wiped
her eyes.

"What's gone wrong?" he asked briskly. "Tell
me all about it."

"Father went off on tour," she explained. "He
left the rent owing for a month, and he's been writing for money all the time. The agent who comes
round doesn't listen to excuses. You pay, or out
you go into the street. I've paid somehow and
nearly starved over it. Then I got this job after
worrying about it Lord knows how long, and this
evening I'm discharged."

"How much a week was it?" he enquired, with
sympathy.

"Ten dollars," she replied. "Little enough, but
I can't live without it."

He changed his attitude, suddenly realising the
volcanic sensitiveness of her attitude towards him
and life in general. Instinctively he felt that at a
single ill-considered word she would even then, in
her moment of weakness, have left him, have pushed

him on one side, and walked out to whatever she
might have to face.

"What a fool you are!" he exclaimed, a little
brusquely.

"Am I!" she replied belligerently.

"Of course you are! You call yourself a daughter of New York, a city whose motto seems to be
pretty well every one for himself. You know you
did my typing all right, you know my play was a
success, you know that I shall have to write another. What made you take it for granted that I
shouldn't want to employ you, and go and hide
yourself? Lock the door when I came to see you,
because it was past eight o'clock, and not answer my
letters?"

"Can't have men callers now dad's away," she
told him, a little brusquely. "It's not allowed."

"Oh, rubbish!" he answered irritably. "That
isn't the point. You've kept away from me. You've
deliberately avoided me. You knew that I was just
as lonely as you were."

Then she blazed out. The sallowness of her
cheeks, the little dip under her cheekbones — she had
grown thinner during the last week or so — made her
eyes seem larger and more brilliant than ever.

"You lonely! Rubbish! Why, they're all running after you everywhere. Quite a social success,
according to the papers! I say, ain't you afraid?"

"Horribly," he admitted, "and about the one person I could have talked to about it chucks me."

"I don't know anything about you, or what you've
done," she said. "I only know that the tecs —"

He laid his hand upon her fingers. She snatched

them away but accepted his warning. They **were** served then with their meal, and their **conversation** drifted into other channels.

"Well," he continued presently, in a perfectly matter-of-fact tone, " I've found you now, and you've got to be sensible. It's true I've had a stroke of luck, but that might fall away at any moment. I've typing waiting for you, or I can get you a post at the New York Theatre. You'd better first do my typing. I'll have it in your rooms to-morrow morn- ing by nine o'clock. And would you like something in advance?"

"No!" she replied grudgingly. "I'll have what I've earned, when I've earned it."

He sipped his claret and studied her meditatively.

"You're not much of a pal, are you?"

She scoffed at him, looked him up and down, at his well-fitting clothes, his general air of prosperity.

"Pal!" she jeered. "Look at you — Merton Ware, the great dramatist, and me — a shabby, ugly, bad-tempered, indifferent typewriter. Bad-tem- pered," she repeated. "Yes, I am that. I didn't start out to be. I just haven't had any luck."

"It will all come some day," he assured her cheer- fully.

"I think if you'd stayed different," she went on thoughtfully, "if you hadn't slipped away into the clouds . . . shows what a selfish little beast I am! Can't imagine why you bother about me."

"Shall I tell you why, really?" he asked. "Be- cause you saved me — I don't know what from. The night we went out I was suffering from a lone- liness which was the worst torture I have ever felt.

It was there in my throat and dragging down my heart, and I just felt as though any way of ending it all would be a joy. All these millions of hard-faced people, intent on their own prosperity or their own petty troubles, goaded me, I think, into a sort of silent fury. Just that one night I craved like a madman for a single human being to talk to — well, I shall never forget it, Martha —"

" Miss Grimes!" she interrupted under her breath. He laughed.

" That doesn't really matter, does it? " he asked. " You've never been afraid that I should want to make love to you, have you? "

She glanced round into the mirror by their side, looked at her wan face, the shabby little hat, the none too tidily arranged hair which drooped over her ears; down at her shapeless jacket, her patched skirt, the shoes which were in open rebellion. Then she laughed, curiously enough without any note of bitterness.

" Seems queer, doesn't it, even to think of such a thing! I've been up against it pretty hard, though. A man who gives a meal to a girl, even if she is as plain as I am, generally seems to think he's bought her, in this city. Even the men who are earning money don't give much for nothing. But you are different," she admitted. " I'll be fair about it — you're different."

" You'll be waiting for the work at nine o'clock to-morrow morning? " he asked, as indifferently as possible.

" I will," she promised.

He leaned back and told her little anecdotes about

the play, things that had happened to him during the last few weeks, speaking often of Elizabeth Dalstan. By degrees the nervous unrest seemed to pass away from her. When they had finished their meal and drunk their coffee, she was almost normal. She smoked a cigarette and even accepted the box which he thrust into her hand. When he had paid the bill, she rose a little abruptly.

"Well," she said, "you've had your way, and a kind, nice way it was. Now I'll have mine. I don't want any politeness. When we leave this place I am going to walk home, and I am going to walk home alone."

"That's lucky," he replied, "because I have to be at the theatre in ten minutes to meet a cinema man. Button up your coat and have a good night's sleep."

They left the place together. She turned away with a farewell nod and walked rapidly eastwards. He watched her cross the road. A poor little waif, she seemed, except that something had gone from her face which had almost terrified him. She carried herself, he fancied, with more buoyancy, with infinitely more confidence, and he drew a sigh of relief as he called for a taxi.

CHAPTER IV

Elizabeth paused for breath at the top of the third flight of stairs. She leaned against the iron balustrade.

"You poor dear!" she exclaimed. "How many times a day did you have to do this?"

"I didn't go out very often," he reminded her, "and it wasn't every day that the lift was out of order. It's only one more flight."

She looked up the stairs, sighed, and raised her smart, grey, tailor-made skirt a little higher over her shoes.

"Well," she announced heroically, "lead on. If they would sometimes dust these steps — but, after all, it doesn't matter to you now, does it? Fancy that poor girl, though."

He smiled a little grimly.

"A few flights of stairs aren't the worst things she has had to face, I'm afraid," he said.

"I am rather terrified of her," Elizabeth confided, supporting herself by her companion's shoulder. "I think I know that ultra-independent type. Kick me if I put my foot in it. Is this the door?"

Philip nodded and knocked softly. There was a sharp "Come in!"

"Put the key down, please," the figure at the typewriter said, as they entered.

The words had scarcely left Martha's lips before she turned around, conscious of some other influence in the room. Philip stepped forward.

" Miss Grimes," he said, " I have brought Miss Dalstan in to see you. She wants —"

He paused. Something in the stony expression of the girl who had risen to her feet and stood now facing them, her ashen paleness unrelieved by any note of colour, her hands hanging in front of her patched and shabby frock, seemed to check the words upon his lips. Her voice was low but not soft. It seemed to create at once an atmosphere of anger and resentment.

" What do you want? " she demanded.

" I hope you don't mind — I am so anxious that you should do some work for me," Elizabeth explained. " When Mr. Ware first brought me in his play, I noticed how nicely it was typewritten. You must have been glad to find it turn out such a success."

" I take no interest in my work when once it is typed," Martha Grimes declared, " and I am very sorry but I do not like to receive visitors. I am very busy. Mr. Ware knows quite well that I like to be left alone."

Elizabeth smiled at her delightfully.

" But it isn't always good for us, is it," she reminded her, " to live exactly as we would like, or to have our own way in all things? "

There was a moment's rather queer silence. Martha Grimes seemed to be intent upon studying the appearance of her visitor, the very beautiful woman familiar to nearly every one in New York, perhaps at that moment America's most popular actress. Her eyes seemed to dwell upon the little strands of fair hair that escaped from beneath her smart but simple hat, to take in the slightly deprecating lift of the eyebrows, the very attractive, half appealing smile, the smart grey tailormade gown with the bunch of violets in her waistband. Elizabeth was as quietly dressed as it was possible for her to be, but her appearance nevertheless brought a note of some other world into the shabby little apartment.

" It's the only thing I ask of life," Martha said, " the only thing I get. I want to be left alone, and I will be left alone. If there is any more work, I will do it. If there isn't, I can find some somewhere else. But visitors I don't want and won't have."

Elizabeth was adorably patient. She surreptitiously drew towards her a cane chair, a doubtful-looking article of furniture upon which she seated herself slowly and with great care.

" Well," she continued, with unabated pleasantness, " that is reasonable as far as it goes, only we didn't quite understand, and it is such a climb up here, isn't it? I came to talk about some work, but I must get my breath first."

" Miss Dalstan thought, perhaps," Philip intervened diffidently, " that you might consider accepting a post at the theatre. They always keep two stenographers there, and one of them fills up her time by private work, generally work for some one connected with the theatre. In your case you could, of course, go on with mine, only when I hadn't enough for you, and of course I can't compose as fast as you can type, there would be something else, and the salary would be regular."

"I should like a regular post," the girl admitted sullenly. "So would any one who's out of work, of course."

"The salary," Elizabeth explained, "is twenty-five dollars a week. The hours are nine to six. You have quite a comfortable room there, but when you have private work connected with the theatre you can bring it home if you wish. Mr. Ware tells me that you work very quickly. You will finish all that you have for him to-day, won't you?"

"I shall have it finished in half an hour."

"Then will you be at the New York Theatre to-morrow morning at nine o'clock," Elizabeth suggested. "There are some parts to be copied. It will be very nice indeed if you like the work, and I think you will."

The girl stood there, irresolute. It was obvious that she was trying to bring herself to utter some form of thanks. Then there was a loud knock at the door, which was opened without waiting for any reply. The janitor stood there with a small key in his hand, which he threw down upon a table.

"Key of number two hundred, miss," he said. "Let me have it back again to-night."

He closed the door and departed.

"Two hundred?" Philip exclaimed. "Why, that's my old room, the one up above."

"I must see it," Elizabeth insisted. "Do please let us go up there. I meant to ask you to show it me."

"You are not thinking of moving, are you, Miss Grimes?" Philip enquired.

She snatched at the key, but he had just possessed himself of it and was swinging it from his forefinger.

"I don't know," she snapped. "I was going up there, anyway. You can't have the key to-day."

"Why not?" Philip asked in surprise.

"Never mind. There are some things of mine up there. I—"

She broke off. They both looked at her, perplexed. Philip shook his head good-naturedly.

"Miss Grimes," he said, "you forget that the rooms are mine till next quarter day. I promise you we will respect any of your belongings we may find there. Come along, Elizabeth."

"We'll see you as we come down," the latter promised, nodding pleasantly.

"I don't know as you will," the girl retorted fiercely. "I may not be here."

They climbed the last two flights of stairs together.

"What an extraordinary young woman!" Elizabeth exclaimed. "Is there any reason for her being quite so rude to me?"

"None that I can conceive," he answered. "She is always like that."

"And yet you took an interest in her!"

"Why not? She is human, soured by misfortune, if you like, with an immense stock of bravery and honesty underneath it all. She has had a drunken father practically upon her hands, and life's been pretty sordid for her. Here we are."

He fitted the key into the lock and swung the door open. The clear afternoon light shone in upon the little shabby room and its worn furniture. There were one or two insignificant belongings of Philip's still lying about the place, and on the writing-table, exactly opposite the spot where he used to sit, a little blue vase, in which was a bunch of violets. Somehow or other it was the one arresting object in the room. They both of them looked at it in equal amazement.

"Is any one living here?" Elizabeth enquired.

"Not to my knowledge," he replied. "No one could take it on without my signing a release."

They moved over to the desk. Elizabeth stooped down and smelt the violets, lifted them up and looked at the cut stalks.

"Is this where you used to sit and write?" she asked.

He nodded.

"But I never had any flowers here," he observed, gazing at them in a puzzled manner.

Elizabeth looked at the vase and set it down. Then she turned towards her companion and shook her head.

"Oh, my dear Philip," she sighed, "you really don't know what makes that girl so uncouth?"

"You mean Martha? Of course I don't. You think that she . . . Rubbish!"

He stopped short in sudden confusion. Elizabeth passed her arm through his. She replaced the vase very carefully, looked once more around the room, and led him to the door.

"Never mind," she said. "It isn't anything

serious, of course, but it's wonderful, Philip, what memories a really lonely woman will live on, what she will do to keep that little natural vein of sentiment alive in her, and how fiercely she will fight to conceal it. You can go on down and wait for me in the hall. I am going in to say good-by to Miss Martha Grimes. I think that this time I shall get on better with her."

CHAPTER V

Philip waited nearly a quarter of an hour for Elizabeth. When at last she returned, she was unusually silent. They drove off together in her automobile. She held his fingers under the rug.

"Philip dear," she said, "I think it is time that you and I were married."

He turned and looked at her in amazement. There was a smile upon her lips, but rather a plaintive one. He had a fancy, somehow, that there had been tears in her eyes lately.

"Elizabeth!"

"If we are ever going to be," she went on softly, "why shouldn't we be married quietly, as people are sometimes, and then tell every one afterwards?"

He held the joy away from him, struggling hard for composure.

"But a little time ago," he reminded her, "you wanted to wait."

"Yes," she confessed, "I, too, had my — my what shall I call it — fear? — my ghost in the background?"

"Ah! but not like mine," he faltered, his voice unsteady with a surging flood of passion. "Elizabeth, if you really mean it, if you are going to take the risk of finding yourself the wife of the villain in a *cause célèbre*, why — why — you know very well that even the thought of it can draw me up into heaven. But, dear — my sweetheart — remember! We've played a bold game, or rather I have with your encouragement, but we're not safe yet."

" Do you know anything that I don't? " she asked feverishly.

" Well, I suppose I do," he admitted. " It isn't necessarily serious," he went on quickly, as he saw the colour fade from her cheeks, " but on the very night that our play was produced, whilst I was waiting about for you all at the restaurant, a man came to see me. He is one of the keenest detectives in New York — Edward Dane his name is. He knew perfectly well that I was the man who had disappeared from the Waldorf. He told me so to my face."

" Then why didn't he — why didn't he do something? "

" Because he was clever enough to suspect that there was something else behind it all," Philip said grimly. " You see, he'd discovered that I hadn't used any of the money. He couldn't fit in any of my doings with the reports they'd had about Douglas. Somehow or other — I can't tell how — another suspicion seems to have crept into the man's brain. All the time he talked to me I could see him trying to read in my face whether there wasn't something else! He'd stumbled across a puzzle of which the pieces didn't fit. He has gone to England — gone to Detton Magna — gone to see whether there are any missing pieces to be found. He may be back any day now."

" But what could he discover? " she faltered.

"God knows!" Philip groaned. "There's the whole ghastly truth there, if fortune helped him, and he were clever enough, if by any devilish chance the threads came into his hand. I don't think — I don't think there was ever any fear from the other side. I had all the luck. But, Elizabeth, sometimes I am terrified of this man Dane. I didn't mean to tell you this, but it's too late now. Do you know that I am watched, day by day? I pretend not to notice it — I am even able, now and then, to shut it out from my own thoughts — but wherever I go there's some one shadowing me, some one walking in my footsteps. I'm perfectly certain that if you were to go to police headquarters here, you could find out where I have spent almost every hour since I took that room in Monmouth House."

She gripped his fingers fiercely.

"Philip! Philip!"

He leaned forward, gazing with peculiar, almost passionate intentness, into the faces of the people as they swept along Broadway.

"Look at them, Elizabeth!" he muttered. "Look at that mob of men and women sweeping along the pavements there, every kind and shape of man, every nationality, every age! They are like the little flecks on the top of a wave. I watched them when I first came and I felt almost reckless. You'd think a man could plunge in there and be lost, wouldn't you? He can't! I tried it. Is there anywhere else in the world, I wonder? Is there anywhere in the living world where one can throw off everything of the past, where one can take up a new life, and memory doesn't come?"

She shook her head. She was more composed now. The moment of feverish excitement had passed. Her shrewd and level common sense had begun to reassert itself.

" There isn't any such place, Philip," she told him, " and if there were it wouldn't be worth while your trying to find it. We are both a little hysterical this evening. We've lost our sense of proportion. You've played for your stake. You mustn't quail; if the worst should come, you must brave it out. I believe, even then, you would be safe. But it won't come — it shan't ! "

He gripped her hands. They were slowing up now, caught in a maze of heavy traffic a few blocks from the theatre. His voice was firm. He had regained his self-control.

" What an idiot I have been ! " he exclaimed scornfully. " Never mind, that's past. There is just one more serious word, though, dear."

She responded immediately to the change in his manner, and smiled into his face.

" Well? "

" My only real problem," he went on earnestly, " is this. Dare I hold you to your word, Elizabeth? Dare I, for instance, say ' yes ' to the wonderful suggestion of yours? — make you my wife and risk having people look at you in years to come, point at you with pity and say that you married a murderer who died a shameful death ! Fancy how the tragedy of that would lie across your life — you who are so wonderful and so courted and so clever ! "

" Isn't that my affair, Philip? " she asked calmly.

" No," he answered, " it's mine ! "

She turned and laughed at him. For a moment
she was her old self again.

" You refuse me? "

His eyes glowed.

" We'll wait," he said hoarsely, " till Dane comes
back from England! "

The car had stopped outside the theatre. Hat in
hand, and with his face wreathed in smiles, the com-
missionaire had thrown open the door. The people
on the pavement were nudging one another —
a famous woman was about to descend. She turned
back to Philip.

" Come in with me," she begged. " Somehow, I
feel cold and lonely to-night. It hasn't anything
to do with what we were talking about, but I feel as
though something were going to happen, that something were coming out of the shadows, something
that threatens either you or me. I'm silly, but
come."

She clung to him as they crossed the pavement.
For once she forgot to smile at the little curious
crowd. She was absorbed in herself and her feelings.

" Life is so hard sometimes! " she exclaimed, as
they lingered for a moment near the box office.
" There's that poor girl, Philip, friendless and lonely.
What she must suffer! God help her — God help
us all! I am sick with loneliness myself, Philip.
Don't leave me alone. Come with me to my room.
I only want to see if there are any letters. We'll
go somewhere near and dine first, before I change.
Philip, what is the matter with me? I don't want
to go a step alone. I don't want to be alone for a
moment."

He laughed reassuringly and drew her closer to
him. She led the way down the passage towards
her own suite of apartments. They passed one or
two of the officials of the theatre, whom she greeted
with something less than her usual charm of manner. As they reached the manager's office there
was the sound of loud voices, and the door was
thrown open. Mr. Fink appeared, and with him a
somewhat remarkable figure — a tall, immensely
broad, ill-dressed man, with a strong, rugged face
and a mass of grey hair; a huge man, who seemed,
somehow or other, to proclaim himself of a bigger
and stronger type than those others amongst whom
he moved. He had black eyes, and the heavy jaw of
an Irishman. His face was curiously unwrinkled.
He stood there, blocking the way, his great hands
suddenly thrust forward.

" Betty, by the Lord that loves us! " he exclaimed.
" Here's luck! I was on my way out to search for
you. Got here on the Chicago Limited at four
o'clock. Give me your hands and say that you are
glad to see me."

If Elizabeth were glad, she showed no sign of it.
She seemed to have become rooted to the spot, suddenly dumb. Philip, by her side, heard the quick
indrawing of her breath.

" Sylvanus! " she murmured. " You! Why, I
thought you were in China."

" There's no place on God's earth can hold me for
long," was the boisterous reply. " I did my business there in three days and caught a Japanese
boat back. Such a voyage and such food! But
New York will make up for that. You've got a

great play, they tell me. I must hear all about it.
Shake my hands first, though, girl, as though you
were glad to see me. You seem to have shrunken
since I saw you last — to have grown smaller.
Didn't London agree with you? "

The moment of shock had passed. Elizabeth had
recovered herself. She gave the newcomer her hands
quite frankly. She even seemed, in a measure, glad
to see him.

" These unannounced comings and goings of yours
from the ends of the earth are so upsetting to your
friends," she declared.

" And this gentleman? Who is he? "

Elizabeth laughed softly.

" I needn't tell you, Mr. Ware," she said, turning
to Philip, " that this dear man here is an eccentric.
I dare say you've heard of him. It is Mr. Sylvanus
Power, and Sylvanus, this is Mr. Merton Ware, the
author of our play —' The House of Shams.' "

Philip felt his hand held in a grasp which, firm
though it was, seemed to owe its vigour rather to
the long, powerful fingers than to any real cordiality.
Mr. Sylvanus Power was studying him from behind his bushy eyebrows.

" So you're Merton Ware," he observed. " I
haven't seen your play yet — hope to to-night. An
Englishman, eh? "

" Yes, I am English," Philip assented coolly.
" You come from the West, don't you? "

There was a moment's silence. Elizabeth laughed
softly.

" Oh, there's no mistake about Mr. Power! " she
declared. " He brings the breezy West with him, to

Wall Street or Broadway, Paris or London. You
can't shake it off or blow it away."

"And I don't know as I am particularly anxious
to, either," Mr. Power pronounced. "Are you going to your rooms here, Betty? If so, I'll come
along. I guess Mr. Ware will excuse you."

Philip was instantly conscious of the antagonism
in the other's manner. As yet, however, he felt little
more than amusement. He glanced towards Elizabeth, and the look in her face startled him. The
colour had once more left her cheeks and her eyes
were full of appeal.

"If you wouldn't mind?" she begged. "Mr.
Power is a very old friend and we haven't met for so
long."

"You needn't expect to see anything more of
Miss Dalstan to-night, either of you," the newcomer
declared, drawing her hand through his arm, "except on the stage, that is. I am going to take her
out and give her a little dinner directly. Au revoir,
Fink! I'll see you to-night here. Good-day to you,
Mr. Ware."

Philip stood for a moment motionless. The voice
of Mr. Sylvanus Power was no small thing, and he
was conscious that several of the officials of the
place, and the man in the box office, had heard every
word that had passed. He felt, somehow, curiously
ignored. He watched the huge figure of the West-
erner, with Elizabeth by his side, disappear down
the corridor. Mr. Fink, who had also been looking
after them, turned towards him.

"Say, that's some man, Sylvanus Power!" he exclaimed admiringly. "He is one of our multi-mil-

lionaires, Mr. Ware. What do you think of him?"

"So far as one can judge from a few seconds' conversation," Philip remarked, "he seems to possess all the qualities essential to the production of a multi-millionaire in this country."

Mr. Fink grinned.

"Sounds a trifle sarcastic, but I guess he's a new type to you," he observed tolerantly.

"Absolutely," Philip acknowledged, as he turned and made his way slowly out of the theatre.

CHAPTER VI

Philip's disposition had been so curiously affected by the emotions of the last few months that he was not in the least surprised to find himself, that evening, torn by a very curious and unfamiliar spasm of jealousy. After an hour or so of indecision he made his way, as usual, to the theatre, but instead of going at once to Elizabeth's room, he slipped in at the back of the stalls. The house was crowded, and, seated in the stage box, alone and gloomy, his somewhat austere demeanour intensified by the severity of his evening clothes, sat Sylvanus Power with the air of a conqueror. Philip, unaccountably restless, left his seat in a very few minutes, and, making his way to the box office, scribbled a line to Elizabeth. The official to whom he handed it looked at him in surprise.

"Won't you go round yourself, Mr. Ware?" he suggested. "Miss Dalstan has another ten minutes before she is on."

Philip shook his head.

"I'm looking for a man I know," he replied evasively. "I'll be somewhere about here in five minutes."

The answer came in less than that time. It was just a scrawled line in pencil:

Forgive me, dear. I will explain everything in the morning, if you will come to my rooms at eleven o'clock. This evening I have a hateful duty to perform and I cannot see you.

Philip, impatient of the atmosphere of the theatre, wandered out into the streets with the note in his pocket. Broadway was thronged with people, a heterogeneous, slowly-moving throng, the hardest crowd to apprehend, to understand, of any in the world. He looked absently into the varying stream of faces, stared at the whirling sky-signs, the lights flashing from the tall buildings, heard snatches of the music from the open doors of the cafés and restaurants. Men, and even women, elbowed him, unresenting, out of the way, without the semblance of an apology. It seemed to him that his presence there, part of the drifting pandemonium of the pavement, was in a sense typical of his own existence in New York. He had given so much of his life into another's hands and now the anchor was dragging. He was suddenly confronted with the possibility of a rift in his relations with Elizabeth; with a sudden surging doubt, not of Elizabeth herself but simply a feeling of insecurity with regard to their future. He only realised in those moments how much he had leaned upon her, how completely she seemed to have extended over him and his troubled life some sort of sheltering influence, to which he had succumbed with an effortless, an almost fatalistic impulse, finding there, at any rate, a refuge from the horrors of his empty days. It was all abstract and impersonal at first, this jealousy which had come so suddenly to disturb the serenity of an almost too per-

fect day, but as the hours passed it seemed to him
that his thoughts dwelt more often upon the direct
cause of his brief separation from Elizabeth. He
turned in at one of the clubs of which he had been
made a member, and threw himself gloomily into an
easy-chair. His thoughts had turned towards the
grim, masterful personality of the man who seemed
to have obtruded himself upon their lives. What did
it mean when Elizabeth told him she was engaged for
to-night? She was supping with him somewhere —
probably at that moment seated opposite to him at
a small, rose-shaded table in one of the many restaurants of the city which they had visited together.
He, Sylvanus Power, his supplanter, was occupying
the place that belonged to him, ordering her supper,
humouring her little preferences, perhaps sharing
with her that little glow of relief which comes with the
hour of rest, after the strain of the day's work. The
suggestion was intolerable. To-morrow he would
have an explanation! Elizabeth belonged to him.
The sooner the world knew it, the better, and this
man first of all. He read her few lines again, hastily
pencilled, and evidently written standing up. There
was a certain ignominy in being sent about his business, just because this colossus from the West had
appeared and claimed — what? Not his right! —
he could have no right! What then? . . .

Philip ordered a drink, tore open an evening paper,
and tried to read. The letters danced before his
eyes, the whisky and soda stood neglected at his elbow. Afterwards he found himself looking into
space. There was something cynical, challenging almost, in the manner in which that man had taken

Elizabeth away from him, had acknowledged his introduction, even had treated the author of a play, a writer, as some sort of a mountebank, making his living by catering for the amusements of the world. How did that man regard such gifts as his, he wondered? — Sylvanus Power, of whom he had seen it written that he was one of the conquerors of nature, a hard but splendid utilitarian, the builder of railways in China and bridges for the transit of his metals amid the clouds of the mountain tops. In the man's absence, his harshness, almost uncouthness, seemed modified. He was a rival, without a doubt, and to-night a favoured one. How well had he known Elizabeth? For how long? Was it true, that rumour he had once heard — that the first step in her fortunes had been due to the caprice of a millionaire? He found the room stifling, but the thought of the streets outside unnerved him. He looked about for some distraction.

The room was beginning to fill — actors, musicians, a few journalists, a great many men of note in the world of Bohemia kept streaming in. One or two of them nodded to him, several paused to speak.

"Hullo, Ware!" Noel Bridges exclaimed. "Not often you give us a look in. What are you doing with yourself here all alone?"

Philip turned to answer him, and suddenly felt the fire blaze up again. He saw his questioner's frown, saw him even bite his lip as though conscious of having said a tactless thing. The actor probably understood the whole situation well enough.

"I generally go into the Lotus," Philip lied. "To-night I had a fancy to come here."

"The Lotus is too far up town for us fellows," Bridges remarked. "We need a drink, a little supper, and to see our pals quickly when the night's work is over. I hear great things of the new play, Mr. Ware, but I don't know when you'll get a chance to produce it. Were you in the house to-night?"

"Only for a moment."

"Going stronger than ever," Bridges continued impressively. "Yes, thanks, I'll take a Scotch high-ball," he added, in response to Philip's mute invitation, "plenty of ice, Mick. There wasn't a seat to be had in the house, and I wouldn't like to say what old Fink had to go through before he could get his box for the great Sylvanus."

"His box?" Philip queried.

"The theatre belongs to Sylvanus Power, you know," Bridges explained. "He built it five years ago."

"For a speculation?"

The actor fidgeted for a moment with his tumbler.

"No, for Miss Dalstan," he replied.

Philip set his teeth hard. The temptation to pursue the conversation was almost overpowering. The young man himself, though a trifle embarrassed, seemed perfectly willing to talk. At least it was better to know the truth! Then another impulse suddenly asserted itself. Whatever he was to know he must learn from her lips and from hers only.

"Well, I should think it's turned out all right," he remarked.

Noel Bridges shrugged his shoulders.

"The rent, if it were figured out at a fair interest on the capital, would be something fabulous," he declared. "You see, the place was extravagantly built — without any regard to cost. The dressing rooms, as you may have noticed, are wonderful, and all the appointments are unique. I don't fancy the old man's ever had a quarter's rent yet that's paid him one per cent. on the money. See you later, perhaps, Mr. Ware," the young man concluded, setting down his tumbler. "I'm going in to have a grill. Why don't you come along?"

Philip hesitated for a second and then, somewhat to the other's surprise, assented. He was conscious that he had been, perhaps, just a little unresponsive to the many courtesies which had been offered him here and at the other kindred clubs. They had been ready to receive him with open arms, this little fraternity of brain-workers, and his response had been, perhaps, a little doubtful, not from any lack of appreciation but partly from that curious diffidence, so hard to understand but so fundamentally English, and partly because of that queer sense of being an impostor which sometimes swept over him, a sense that he was, after all, only the ghost of another man, living a subjective life; that, reason it out however he might, there was something of the fraud in any personality he might adopt. And yet, deep down in his heart he was conscious of so earnest a desire to be really one of them, this good-natured, good-hearted, gay-spirited little throng, with their delightful intimacies, their keen interest in each other's welfare, their potent, almost mysterious geniality, which seemed to draw the stranger of kindred tastes so closely under its influence. Philip, as he sat at the long table with a dozen or so other men, did his best that night to break through the fetters, tried hard to remember that his place amongst them, after all, was honest enough. They were writers and actors and journalists. Well, he too was a writer. He had written a play which they had welcomed with open arms, as they had done him. In this world of Bohemia, if anywhere, he surely had a right to lift up his head and breathe — and he would do it. He sat with them, smoking and talking, until the little company began to thin out, establishing all the time a new reputation, doing a great deal to dissipate that little sense of disappointment which his former non-responsiveness had created.

"He's a damned good fellow, after all," one of them declared, as at last he left the room. "He is losing his Britishness every day he stays here."

"Been through rough times, they say," another remarked.

"He is one of those," an elder member pronounced, taking his pipe for a moment from his mouth, "who was never made for happiness. You can always read those men. You can see it behind their eyes."

Nevertheless, Philip walked home a saner and a better man. He felt somehow warmed by those few hours of companionship. The senseless part of his jealousy was gone, his trust in Elizabeth reëstablished. He looked at the note once more as he undressed. At eleven o'clock on the following morning in her rooms!

CHAPTER VII

Something of his overnight's optimism remained
with Philip when at eleven o'clock on the following
morning he was ushered into Elizabeth's rooms. It
was a frame of mind, however, which did not long sur-
vive his reception. From the moment of his arrival,
he seemed to detect a different atmosphere in his
surroundings,— the demeanour of Phoebe, his
staunch ally, who admitted him without her usual
welcoming smile; the unanalysable sense of something
wanting in the dainty little room, overfilled with
strong-smelling, hothouse flowers in the entrance and
welcome of Elizabeth herself. His eyes had ached for
the sight of her. He was so sure that he would know
everything the moment she spoke. Yet her coming
brought only confusion to his senses. She was different — unexpectedly, bewilderingly different. She
had lost that delicate serenity of manner, that
almost protective affection which he had grown to
lean upon and expect. She entered dressed for the
street, smoking a cigarette, which was in itself
unusual, with dark rings under her eyes, which
seemed to be looking all around the room on some
pretext or other, but never at him.

" Am I late? " she asked, a little breathlessly. " I
am so sorry. Tell me, have you anything particular
to do? "

"Nothing," he answered.

"I want to go out of the city — into the country, at once," she told him feverishly. "The car is waiting. I ordered it for a quarter to eleven. Let us start."

"Of course, if you wish it," he assented.

He opened the door but before she passed through he leaned towards her. She shook her head. His heart sank. What could there be more ominous than this!

"I am not well," she muttered. "Don't take any notice of anything I say or do for a little time. I am like this sometimes — temperamental, I suppose. All great actresses are temperamental. I suppose I am a great actress. Do you think I am, Philip?"

He was following her down-stairs now. He found it hard, however, to imitate the flippancy of her tone.

"The critics insist upon it," he observed drily. "Evidently your audience last night shared their opinion."

She nodded.

"I love them to applaud like that, and yet — audiences don't really know, do they? Perhaps —"

She relapsed into silence, and they took their places in the car. She settled herself down with a little sigh of content and drew the rug over her.

"As far as you can go, John," she told the man, "but you must get back at six o'clock. The country, mind — not the shore."

They started off.

"So you were there last night?" she murmured, leaning back amongst the cushions with an air of relief.

" I was there for a few moments. I wrote my note to you in the box office."

She shook the memory away.

" And afterwards? "

" I went to one of the clubs down-town."

" What did you do there? " she enquired. " Gossip? "

" Some of the men were very kind to me," he said. " I had supper with Noel Bridges, amongst others."

" Well? " she asked, almost defiantly.

" I don't understand."

She looked intently at him for a moment.

" I forgot," she went on. " You are very chivalrous, aren't you? You wouldn't ask questions. . . . See, I am going to close my eyes. It is too horrible here, and all through Brooklyn. When we are in the lanes I can talk. This is just one of those days I wish that we were in England. All our country is either suburban or too wild and restless. Can you be content with silence for a little time? "

" Of course," he assured her. " Besides, you forget that I am in a strange country. Everything is worth watching."

They passed over Brooklyn Bridge, and for an hour or more they made slow progress through the wide-flung environs of the city. At last, however, the endless succession of factories and small tenement dwellings lay behind them. They passed houses with real gardens, through stretches of wood whose leaves were opening, whose branches were filled with the sweet-smelling sap of springtime. Elizabeth seemed to wake almost automatically from a kind of stupor. She pushed back her veil, and Philip,

stealing eager glances towards her, was almost
startled by some indefinable change. Her face
seemed more delicate, almost the face of an invalid,
and she lay back there with half-closed eyes. The
strength of her mouth seemed to have dissolved, and
its sweetness had become almost pathetic. There
were signs of a great weariness about her. The
fingers which reached out for the little speaking-tube
seemed to have become thinner.

" Take the turn to the left, John," she instructed,
" the one to Bay Shore. Go slowly by the lake and
stop where I tell you."

They left the main road and travelled for some
distance along a lane which, with its bramble-grown
fences and meadows beyond, was curiously reminiscent of England. They passed a country house,
built of the wood which was still a little unfamiliar
to Philip, but wonderfully homelike with its cluster
of outbuildings, its trim lawns, and the turret clock
over the stable entrance. Then, through the leaves
of an avenue of elms, they caught occasional glimpses
of the blue waters of the lake, which they presently
skirted. Elizabeth's eyes travelled over its placid
surface idly, yet with a sense of passive satisfaction.
In a few minutes they passed into the heart of a
little wood, and she leaned forward.

" Stop here, close to the side of the road, John.
Stop your engine, please, and go and sit by the lake."

The man obeyed at once with the unquestioning
readiness of one used to his mistress' whims. For
several minutes she remained silent. She had the
air of one drinking in with almost passionate eagerness the sedative effect of the stillness, the soft spring

air, the musical country sounds, the ripple of the breeze in the trees, the humming of insects, the soft splash of the lake against the stony shore. Philip himself was awakened into a peculiar sense of pleasure by this, almost his first glimpse of the country since his arrival in New York. A host of half forgotten sensations warmed his heart. He felt suddenly intensely sympathetic, perhaps more genuinely tender than he had ever felt before towards the woman by his side, whose hour of suffering it was. His hand slipped under the rug and held her fingers, which clutched his in instantaneous response. Her lips seemed unlocked by his slight action.

" I came here alone two years ago," she told him, " and since then often, sometimes to study a difficult part, sometimes only to think. One moment."

She released her fingers from his, drew out the hatpins from her hat, unwound the veil and threw them both on to the opposite seat. Then she laid her hands upon her forehead as though to cool it. The little breeze from the lake rippled through her hair, bringing them every now and then faint whiffs of perfume from the bordering gardens.

" There! " she exclaimed, with a little murmur of content. " That's a man's action, isn't it? Now I think I am getting brave. I have something to say to you, Philip."

He felt her fingers seeking his again and held them tightly. It was curious how in that moment of crisis his thoughts seemed to wander away. He was watching the little flecks of gold in her hair, wondering if he had ever properly appreciated the beautiful curve of her neck. Even her voice seemed somehow attuned to the melody of their surroundings, the confused song of the birds, the sighing of the lake, the passing of the west wind through the trees and shrubs around.

"Philip," she began, clinging closely to him, "I have brought you here to tell you a story which perhaps you will think, when you have heard it, might better have been told in my dressing-room. Well, I couldn't. Besides, I wanted to get away. It is about Sylvanus Power."

He sat a little more upright. His nerves were tingling now with eagerness.

"Yes?"

"I met him," she continued, "eight years ago out West, when I was in a travelling show. I accepted his attentions at first carelessly enough. I did not realise the sort of man he was. He was a great personage even in those days, and I suppose my head was a little turned. Then he began to follow us everywhere. There was a scandal, of course. In the end I left the company and came to New York. He went to China, where he has always had large interests. When I heard that he had sailed — I remember reading it in the paper — I could have sobbed with joy."

Philip moved a little uneasily in his place. Some instinct told him, however, how greatly she desired his silence — that she wanted to tell her story her own way.

"Then followed three miserable years, during which I saw little of him. I knew that I had talent, I was always sure of making a living, but I got no further. It didn't seem possible to get any further.

Nothing that I could do or say seemed able to procure for me an engagement in New York. Think of me for a moment now, Philip, as a woman absolutely and entirely devoted to her work. I loved it. It absorbed all my thoughts. It was just the one thing in life I cared anything about. I simply ached to get at New York, and I couldn't. All the time I had to play on tour, and you won't quite understand this, dear, but there is nothing so wearing in life as for any one with my cravings for recognition there to be always playing on the road."

She paused for a few minutes. There was a loud twittering of birds. A rabbit who had stolen carefully through the undergrowth scurried away. A car had come through the wood and swept past them, bringing with it some vague sense of disturbance. It was some little time before she settled down again to her story.

" At the end of those three years," she went on, " Sylvanus Power had become richer, stronger, more masterful than ever. I was beginning to lose heart. He was clever. He studied my every weakness. He knew quite well that with me there was only one way, and he laid his schemes with regard to me just in the same fashion as he schemed to be a conqueror of men, to build up those millions. We were playing near New York and one day he asked me to motor in there and lunch with him. I accepted. It was in the springtime, almost on such a day as this. We motored up in one of his wonderful cars. We lunched — I remember how shabby I felt — at the best restaurant in New York, where I was waited upon like a queen. Somehow or other, the man had always

the knack of making himself felt wherever he went.
He strode the very streets of New York like one of
its masters and the people seemed to recognise it.
Afterwards he took me into Broadway, and he ordered
the car to stop outside the theatre where I am now
playing. I looked at it, and I remember I gave
a little cry of interest.

"'This is the new theatre that every one is talking
about, isn't it?' I asked him eagerly.

"'It is,' he answered. 'Would you like to see
inside?'

" Of course, I was half crazy with curiosity. The
doors flew open before him, and he took me everywhere. You know yourself what a magnificent place
it is — that marvellous stage, the auditorium all in
dark green satin, the seats like armchairs, the dressing rooms like boudoirs — the wonderful spacious-
ness of it! It took my breath away. I had never
imagined such splendour. When we had finished
looking over the whole building, I clutched his arm.

"'I can't believe that it isn't some sort of fairy
palace!' I exclaimed. 'And to think that no one
knows who owns the place or when it is going to
be opened!'

"'I'll tell you all about that,' he answered. 'I
built it, I own it, and it will be opened just when
you accept my offer and play in it.'

" It all seemed too amazing. For a time I couldn't
speak coherently. Then I remember thinking that
whatever happened, whatever price I had to pay,
I must stand upon the stage of that theatre and win.
My lips were quite dry. His great voice seemed to
have faded into a whisper.

"'Your offer?' I repeated.

"'Yourself,' he answered gruffly."...

There was a silence which seemed to Philip interminable. All the magic of the place had passed away, its music seemed no longer to be singing happiness into his heart. Then at last he realised that she was waiting for him to speak.

"He wanted — to marry you?" he faltered.

"He had a wife already."

Splash! John was throwing stones into the lake, a pastime of which he was getting a little tired. A huge thrush was thinking about commencing to build his nest, and in the meantime sat upon a fallen log across the way and sang about it. A little tree-climbing bird ran round and round the trunk of the nearest elm, staring at them, every time he appeared, with his tiny black eyes. A squirrel, almost overhead, who had long since come to the conclusion that they were harmless, decided now that they had the queerest manners of any two young people he had ever watched from his leafy throne, and finally abandoned his position. Elizabeth had been staring down the road ever since the last words had passed her lips. She turned at last and looked at her companion. He was once more the refugee, the half-starved man flying from horrors greater even than he had known. She began to tremble.

"Philip!" she cried. "Say anything, but speak to me!"

Like a flash he seemed to pass from his own, almost the hermit's way of looking out upon life from the old-fashioned standpoint of his inherent puritanism, into a closer sympathy with those others,

the men and women of the world into which he had
so lately entered, the men and women who had welcomed him so warm-heartedly, human beings all of
them, who lived and loved with glad hearts and much
kindliness. The contrast was absurd, the story itself
suddenly so reasonable. No other woman on tour
would have kept Sylvanus Power waiting for three
years. Only Elizabeth could have done that. It
was such a human little problem. People didn't
live in the clouds. He wasn't fit for the clouds himself. Nevertheless, when he tried to speak his throat
was hard and dry, and at the second attempt he
began instead to laugh. She gripped his arm.

" Philip! " she exclaimed. " Be reasonable! Say
what you like, but look and behave like a human
being. Don't make that noise! " she almost shrieked.

He stopped at once.

" Forgive me," he begged humbly. " I can't help
it. I seem to be playing hide and seek with myself.
You haven't finished the story yet — if there is anything more to tell me."

She drew herself up. She spoke absolutely without faltering.

" I accepted Sylvanus Power's terms," she went
on. " He placed large sums of money in Fink's
hands to run the theatre. There was a wonderful
opening. You were not interested then or you might
have heard of it. I produced a new play of Clyde
Fitch's. It was a great triumph. The house was
packed. Sylvanus Power sat in his box. It was
to be his night. Through it all I fought like a
woman in a nightmare. I didn't know what it meant.
I knew hundreds of women who had done in a small

way what I was prepared to do magnificently. In all my acquaintance I think that I scarcely knew one who would have refused to do what I was doing. And all the time I was in a state of fierce revolt. I had moments when my life's ambitions, when New York itself, the Mecca of my dreams, and that marvellous theatre, with its marble and silk, seemed suddenly to dwindle to a miserable, contemptible little doll's house. And then again I played, and I felt my soul as I played, and the old dreams swept over me, and I said that it wasn't anything to do with personal vanity that made me crave for the big gifts of success; that it was my art, and that I must find myself in my art or die."

The blood was flowing in his veins again. She was coming back to him. He was ashamed — he with his giant load of sin! His voice trembled with tenderness.

"Go on," he begged.

"I think that the reason I played that night as though I were inspired was because of the great passionate craving at my heart for forgetfulness, to shut out the memory of that man who sat almost gloomily alone in his box, waiting. And then, after it was all over, the wonder and the glory of it, he appeared suddenly in my dressing-room, elbowing his way through excited journalists, kicking bouquets of flowers from his path. We stood for a moment face to face. He came nearer. I shrank away. I was terrified! He looked at me in cold surprise.

"'Three minutes,' he exclaimed, 'to say good-by. I'm off to China. Stick at it. You've done well for a start, but remember a New York audience wants holding. Choose your plays carefully. Trust Fink.'

"'You're going away?' I almost shrieked.

He glanced at his watch, leaned over, and kissed me on the forehead.

"'I'll barely make that boat,' he muttered, and rushed out." . . .

Philip was breathless. The strange, untold passion of the whole thing was coming to him in waves of wonderful suggestion.

"Finish!" he cried impatiently. "Finish!"

"That is the end," she said. "I played for two years and a half, with scarcely a pause. Then I came to Europe for a rest and travelled back with you on the *Elletania*. Last night I saw Sylvanus Power again for the first time. Don't speak. My story is in two halves. That is the first. The second is just one question. That will come before we reach home. . . . John!" she called.

The man approached promptly — he was quite weary of throwing stones.

"Take us somewhere to lunch," his mistress directed, "and get back to New York at six o'clock."

CHAPTER VIII

It was not until they were crossing Brooklyn Bridge, on their way into the city, that she asked him that question. They crawled along, one of an interminable, tangled line of vehicles of all sorts and conditions, the trains rattling overhead, and endless streams of earnest people passing along the footway. Below them, the evening sunlight flashed upon the murky waters, glittered from the windows of the tall buildings, and shone a little mercilessly upon the unlovely purlieus of the great human hive. The wind had turned cool, and Elizabeth, with a little shiver, had drawn her furs around her neck. All through the day, during the luncheon in an unpretentious little inn, and the leisurely homeward drive, she had been once more entirely herself, pleasant and sympathetic, ignoring absolutely the intangible barrier which had grown up between them, soon to be thrown down for ever or to remain for all time.

" We left our heroine," she said, " at an interesting crisis in her career. I am waiting to hear from you — what would you have done in her place? "

He answered her at once, and he spoke from the lesser heights. He was fiercely jealous.

" It is not a reasonable question," he declared. " I am not a woman. I am just a man who has led an unusually narrow and cramped life until these last few months."

" That is scarcely fair," she objected. " You
profess to have loved — to love still, I hope. That
in itself makes a man of any one. Then you, too,
have sinned. You, too, are one of those who have
yielded to passion of a sort. Therefore, your judg-
ment ought to be the better worth having."

He winced as though he had been struck, and
looked at her with eyes momentarily wild. He felt
that the deliberate cruelty of her words was of
intent, an instinct of her brain, defying for the
moment her heart.

" I don't know," he faltered. " I won't answer
your question. I can't. You see, the love you speak
of is my love for you. You ask me to ignore that
— I, who am clinging on to life by ne rope."

" You are like all men," she sig ed. " We do
not blame you for it — perhaps v love you the
more — but when a great crisis cmes you think
only of yourselves. You disappoint me a little,
Philip. I fancied that you might have thought a
little of me, something of Sylvanus Power."

" I haven't your sympathy for other people," he
declared hoarsely.

" No," she assented, " sympathy is the one thing
a man lacks. It isn't your fault, Philip. You are
to be pitied for it. And, after all, it is a woman's
gift, isn't it? "

There followed then a silence which seemed interminable. It was not until they were nearing the
theatre that he suddenly spoke with a passion which
startled her.

" Tell me," he insisted, " last night? I can't help
asking. I was in hell!"

He told himself afterwards that there couldn't be any possible way of reconciling cruelty so cold-blooded with all that he knew of Elizabeth. She behaved as though his question had fallen upon deaf ears. The car had stopped before the entrance to the theatre. She stepped out even before he could assist her, hurried across the pavement and looked back at him for one moment only before she plunged into the dark passage. She nodded, and there was an utterly meaningless smile upon her lips.

"Good-by!" she said. "Do you mind telling John he needn't wait for me?"

Then she disappeared. He stood motionless upon the pavement, a little dazed. Two or three people jostled against him. A policeman glanced at him curiously. A lady with very yellow hair winked in his face. Philip pulled himself together and simultaneously felt a touch upon his elbow. He glanced into the . ce of the girl who had accosted him, and for a moment he scarcely recognised her.

"Wish you'd remember you're in New York and not one of your own sleepy old towns," Miss Grimes remarked brusquely. "You'll have a policeman say you're drunk, in a minute, if you stand there letting people shove you around."

He fell into step by her side, and they walked slowly along. Martha was plainly dressed, but she was wearing new clothes, new shoes, and a new hat.

"Don't stare at me as though you never saw me out of a garret before," she went on, a little sharply. "Your friend Miss Dalstan is a lady who understands things. When I arrived at the theatre this morning I found that it was to be a permanent job all right, and there was a little advance for me waiting in an envelope. That fat old Mr. Fink began to cough and look at my clothes, so I got one in first. ' This is for me to make myself look smart enough for your theatre, I suppose?' I said. ' Give me an hour off, and I'll do it.' So he grinned, and here I am. Done a good day's work, too, copying the parts of your play for a road company, and answering letters. What's wrong with you? "

The very sound of her voice was a tonic. He almost smiled as he answered her.

" Just a sort of hankering for the moon and a sudden fear lest I mightn't get it."

" You're spoilt, that's what's the matter with you," she declared brusquely.

" It never occurred to me," he said gloomily, " that life had been over-kind."

" Oh, cut it out! " she answered. " Here you are, not only set on your feet but absolutely held up there; all the papers full of Merton Ware's brilliant play, and Merton Ware, the new dramatist, with his social gifts — such an acquisition to New York Society! Why, it isn't so very long ago, after all, that you hadn't a soul in New York to speak to. I saw something in your face that night. I thought you were hungry. So you were, only it wasn't for food. It cheered you up even to talk with me. And look at you to-day! Clubs and parties and fine friends, and there you were, half dazed in Broadway! Be careful, man. You don't know what it is to be down and out. You haven't been as near it as I have, anyway, or you'd lift your head up and be thankful."

204 THE CINEMA MURDER

"Martha," he began earnestly —

"Miss Grimes!" she interrupted firmly. "Don't let there be any mistake about that. I hate familiarity."

"Miss Grimes, then," he went on. "You talk about my friends. Quite right. I should think I have been introduced to nearly a thousand people since the night my play was produced. I have dined at a score of houses and many scores of restaurants. The people are pleasant enough, too, but all the time it's Merton Ware the dramatist they are patting on the back. They don't know anything about Merton Ware the man. Perhaps there are some of them would be glad to, but you see it's too soon, and they seem to live too quickly here to make friends. I am almost as lonely as I was, so far as regards ordinary companionship. Last night I felt the first little glow of real friendliness — just the men down at the club."

"You've put all your eggs into one basket, that's what you've done," she declared.

"That's true enough," he groaned.

"And like all men — selfish brutes!" she proceeded deliberately — "you expect everything. Fancy expecting everything from a woman like Miss Dalstan! Why, you aren't worthy of it, you know."

"Perhaps not," he admitted, "but you see, Miss Grimes, there is something in life which seems to have passed you by up till now."

"Has it indeed!" she objected. "You think I've never had a young man, eh? Perhaps you're right. Haven't found much time for that sort of rubbish. Anyway, this is where I hop on a trolley car."

" Wait a moment," he begged. " Don't leave me yet. You've nothing to do, have you? "

" Nothing particular," she confessed, " except go home and cook my dinner."

" Look here," he went on eagerly, " I feel like work. I've got the second act of my new play in my mind. Come round with me and let me try dictating it. I'll give you something to eat in my rooms. It's for the theatre, mind. I never tried dictating. I believe I could do it to you."

" In your rooms," she repeated, a little doubtfully.

" They won't talk scandal about us, Miss Grimes," he assured her. " To tell you the truth, I want to be near the telephone."

" In case she rings you up, eh? "

" That's so. I said something I ought not to have done. I ought to have waited for her, but it was something that had been tearing at me ever since last night, and I couldn't bear it."

" Some blunderers, you men," Miss Grimes sighed. " Well, I'm with you."

He led her almost apologetically to the lift of the handsome building in which his new rooms were situated. They were very pleasant bachelor rooms, with black oak walls and green hangings, prints upon the wall, a serviceable writing-table, and a deep green carpet. She looked around her and at the servant who had come forward at their entrance, with a little sniff.

" Shall you be changing to-night, sir? " he asked.

" Not to-night," Philip answered quickly. " Tell the waiter to send up a simple dinner for two — I can't bother to order.   And two cocktails," he added, as an afterthought.

Martha stared after the disappearing manservant disparagingly.

" Some style," she muttered.   " A manservant, eh? Don't know as I ever saw one before off the stage."

" Don't be silly," he remonstrated.   " He has four other flats to look after besides mine.   It's the way one lives, nowadays, cheaper than ordinary hotels or rooms.   Take off your coat."

She obeyed him, depositing it carefully in a safe place.   Then she strolled around the room, finding pictures little to her taste, and finally threw herself into an easy-chair.

" Are we going to work before we eat? " she asked.

" No, afterwards," he told her.   " Have a cigarette? "

She held it between her fingers but declined a match.

" I'll wait for the cocktails," she decided.   " Now listen here, Mr. Ware, there's a word or two I'd like to say to you."

" Go ahead," he invited listlessly.

" You men," she continued, looking him squarely in the face, " think a lot too much of yourselves. You think so much of yourselves that as often as not you've no time to think of other folk.   A month or so ago who were you?   You were hiding in a cheap tenement house, scared out of your wits, dressed pretty near as shabbily as I was, with a detective on your track, and with no idea of what you were going to do for a living.   And now look at you.   Who's done it all? "

" Of course, my play being successful," he began —
She broke in at once.

" You and your play! Who took your play?
Who produced it at the New York Theatre and
acted in it so that people couldn't listen without a
sob in their throats and a tingling all over? Yours
isn't the only play in the world! I bet Miss Dalstan
has a box full of them. She probably chose yours
because she knew that you were feeling pretty miserable, because she'd got sorry for you coming over
on the steamer, because she has a great big heart,
and is always trying to do something for others.
She's made a man of you. Oh! I know a bit about
plays. I know that with the royalties you're drawing you can well afford rooms like these and anything else you want. But that isn't all she's done.
She's introduced you to her friends, she's taken
more notice of you than any man around. She
takes you out automobile driving, she lets you spend
all your spare time in her rooms. She don't mind
what people say. You dine with her and take her
home after the play. You have more of her than
any other person alive. Say, what I want to ask
is — do you think you're properly grateful? "

" I couldn't ever repay Miss Dalstan," he acknowledged, a little sadly, " but —"

" Look here, no ' buts '! " she interrupted. " You
think I don't know anything. Perhaps I don't, and
perhaps I do. I was standing in the door of the
office when you two came in from your automobile
drive this afternoon. I saw her come away without
wishing you good-by, then I saw her turn and nod,
looking just as usual, and I saw her face after-

wards. If I had had you, my man, as close to me then as you are now, I'd have boxed your ears."

He moved uneasily in his chair. There was no doubt about the girl's earnestness. She was leaning a little forward, and her brown eyes were filled with a hard, accusing light. There was a little spot of colour, even, in her sallow cheeks. She was unmistakably angry.

"I'd like to know who you are and what you think yourself to make a woman look like that?" she wound up.

The waiter entered with the cocktails and began to lay the cloth for dinner. Philip paced the room uneasily until he had gone.

"Look here, my little friend," he said, when at last the door was closed, "there's a great deal of sound common sense in what you say. I may be an egoist — I dare say I am. I've been through the proper training for it, and I've started life again on a pretty one-sided basis, perhaps. But — have you ever been jealous?"

"Me jealous!" she repeated scornfully. "What of, I wonder?"

There was a suspicious glitter in her eyes, a queer little tremble in her tone. His question, however, was merely perfunctory. She represented little more to him, at that moment, than the incarnation of his own conscience.

"Very likely you haven't," he went on. "You are too independent ever to care much for any one. Well, I've been half mad with jealousy since last night. That is the truth of it. There's another man wants her, the man who built the theatre for her. She told me about him yesterday while we were out together."

" Don't you want her to be happy? " the girl asked bluntly.

" Of course I do."

" Then leave her alone to choose. Don't go about looking as though you had a knife in your heart, if you find her turn for a moment to some one else. You don't want her to choose you, do you, just because you are a weakling, because her great kind heart can't bear the thought of making you miserable? Stand on your feet like a man and take your luck. . . . Can I take off my hat? I can't eat in this."

The waiter had entered with the dinner. Merton opened the door of his room and paced up and down, for a few moments, thoughtfully. When she reappeared she took the seat opposite Philip and suddenly smiled at him, an exceedingly rare but most becoming performance. Her mouth seemed at once to soften, and even her eyes laughed at him.

" Here you ask me to dine," she said, " because you are lonely, and I do nothing but scold you! Never mind. I was typewriting something of yours this morning — I've forgotten the words, but it was something about the discipline of affection. You can take my scolding that way. If I didn't adore Miss Dalstan, and if you hadn't been kind to me, I should never take the trouble to make myself disagreeable."

He smiled back at her, readily falling in with her altered mood. She seemed to have talked the ill-humour out of her blood, and during the service of the meal she told him of the comfort of her work, the charm of the other girl in the room, with whom she was already discussing a plan to share an apartment. When she came to speak, however remotely, of Miss Dalstan, her voice seemed instinctively to soften. Philip found himself wondering what had passed between the two women in those few moments when Elizabeth had left him and gone back to Martha's room. By some strange miracle, the strong, sweet, understanding woman had simply taken possession of the friendless child. The thought of her sat now in Martha's heart, an obsession, almost a worship. Perhaps that was why the sense of companionship between the two, notwithstanding certain obvious disparities, seemed to grow stronger every moment.

They drank their coffee and smoked cigarettes afterwards in lazy fashion. Suddenly Martha sprang up.

" Say, I came here to work! " she exclaimed.

" And I brought you under false pretences," he confessed. " My brain's not working. I can't dictate. We'll try another evening. You don't mind? "

" Of course not," she answered, glancing at the clock. " I'll be going."

" Wait a little time longer," he begged.

She resumed her seat. There was only one heavily shaded lamp burning on the table, and through the little cloud of tobacco smoke she watched him. His eyes were sometimes upon the timepiece, sometimes on the telephone. He seemed always, although his attitude was one of repose, to be listening, waiting. It was half-past nine — the middle of the second act. They knew quite well that for a quarter of an hour Elizabeth would be in her dressing room. She could ring up if she wished. The seconds ticked monotonously away. Martha found herself, too, sharing that curiously intense desire to hear the ring of the telephone. Nothing happened. A quarter to ten came and passed. She rose to her feet.

"I am going home right now," she announced.

He reached for his hat.

"I'll come with you," he suggested, a little half-heartedly.

"You'll do nothing of the sort," she objected, "or if you do, I'll never come inside your rooms again. Understand that. I don't want any of these Society tricks. See me home, indeed! I'd have you know that I'm better able to take care of myself in the streets of New York than you are. So thank you for your dinner, and just you sit down and listen for that telephone. It will ring right presently, and if it doesn't, go to bed and say to yourself that whatever she decides is best. She knows which way her happiness lies. You don't. And it's she who counts much more than you. Leave off thinking of yourself quite so much and shake hands with me, please, Mr. Ware."

He gripped her hand, opened the door, and watched her sail down towards the lift, whistling to herself, her hands in her coat pockets. Then he turned back into the room and locked himself in.

CHAPTER IX

The slow fever of inaction, fretting in Philip's veins, culminated soon after Martha's departure in a passionate desire for a movement of some sort. The very silence of the room maddened him, the unresponsive-looking telephone, the fire which had burned itself out, the dropping even of the wind, which at intervals during the evening had flung a rainstorm against the windowpane. At midnight he could bear it no longer and sallied out into the streets. Again that curious desire for companionship was upon him, a strange heritage for one who throughout the earlier stages of his life had been content with and had even sought a grim and unending solitude. He boarded a surface car for the sake of sitting wedged in amongst a little crowd of people, and he entered his club, noting the number of hats and coats in the cloakroom with a queer sense of satisfaction. He no sooner made his appearance in the main room than he was greeted vociferously from half a dozen quarters. He accepted every hospitality that was offered to him, drinking cheerfully with new as well as old acquaintances. Presently Noel Bridges came up and gripped his shoulder.

" Come and have a grill with us, Ware," he begged. " There's Seymour and Richmond here, from the Savage Club, and a whole crowd of us. Hullo, Freddy!" he went on, greeting the man with whom

Philip had been talking. " Why don't you come and
join us, too?   We'll have a rubber of bridge afterwards."

" That's great," the other declared.   " Come on,
Ware.   We'll rag old Honeybrook into telling us
some of his stories."

The little party gathered together at the end of
the common table.   Philip had already drunk much
more than he was accustomed to, but the only result
appeared to be some slight slackening of the tension
in which he had been living.   His eyes flashed, and
his tongue became more nimble.   He insisted upon
ordering wine.   He had had no opportunity yet of
repaying many courtesies.   They drank his health,
forced him into the place of honour by the side of
Honeybrook, veteran of the club, and ate their meal
to the accompaniment of ceaseless bursts of laughter,
chaff, the popping of corks, mock speeches, badinage
of every sort.   Philip felt, somehow, that his brain
had never been clearer.   He not only held his own,
but he earned a reputation for a sense of humour
previously denied to him.   And in the midst of it
all the door opened and closed, and a huge man,
dressed in plain dinner clothes, still wearing his theatre hat, with a coat upon his arm and a stick in his
hand, passed through the door and stood for a
moment gazing around him.

" Say, that's Sylvanus Power!" one of the young
men at the table exclaimed.   " Looks a trifle grim,
doesn't he? "

" It's the old man, right enough," Noel Bridges
murmured.   " Wonder what he wants down here?   It
isn't in his beat? "

Honeybrook, the great New York raconteur, father of the club, touched Philip upon the shoulder.

" Hey, presto! " he whispered. " We who think so much of ourselves have become pigmies upon the face of the earth. There towers the representative of modern omnipotence. Those are the hands — grim, strong-looking hands, aren't they? — that grip the levers of modern American life. Rodin ought to do a statue of him as he stands there — art and letters growing smaller as he grows larger. We exist for him. He builds theatres for our plays, museums for our pictures, libraries for our books."

" Seems to me he is looking for one of us," Noel Bridges remarked.

" Some pose, isn't it! " a younger member of the party exclaimed reverently, as he lifted his tankard.

All these things were a matter of seconds, during which Sylvanus Power did indeed stand without moving, looking closely about the room. Then his eye at last lit upon the end of the table where Philip and his friends were seated. He approached them without a word. Noel Bridges ventured upon a greeting.

" Coming to join us, Mr. Power? " he asked.

Sylvanus Power, if he heard the question, ignored it. His eyes had rested upon Philip. He stood over the table now, looming before them, massive, in his way awe-inspiring.

" Ware," he said, " I've been looking for you."

Instinctively Philip rose to his feet. Tall though he was, he had to look up at the other man, and his slender body seemed in comparison like a willow

wand. Nevertheless, the light in his eyes was illumi-
native. There was no shrinking away. He stood
there with the air of one prepared to welcome, to
incite and provoke storm whatever might be brewing.

"I have been to your rooms," Sylvanus Power
went on. "They knew nothing about you there."

"They wouldn't," Philip replied. "I go where
I choose and when I choose. What do you want
with me?"

Conversation in the room was almost suspended.
Those in the immediate locality, well acquainted with
the gossip of the city, held the key to the situation.
Every one for a moment, however, was spellbound.
They felt the coming storm, but they were powerless.

"I sought you out, Ware," Sylvanus Power continued, his harsh voice ringing through the room,
"to tell you what probably every other man here
knows except you. If you know it you're a fool,
and I'm here to tell you so."

"Have you been drinking?" Philip asked calmly.

"Maybe I have," Sylvanus Power answered, "but
whisky can't cloud my brain or stop my tongue.
You're looking at my little toy here," he went on,
twirling in his right hand a heavy malacca cane
with a leaden top. "I killed a man with that once."

"The weapon seems sufficient for the purpose,"
Philip answered indifferently.

"Any other man," Sylvanus Power went on,
"would have sat in the chair for that. Not I! You
don't know as much of me as you need to, Merton
Ware. I'm no whippersnapper of a pen-slinger,
earning a few paltry dollars by writing doggerel
for women and mountebanks to act. I've hewn my

way with my right arm and my brain, from the streets to the palace. They say that money talks. By God! if it does I ought to shout, for I've more million dollars than there are men in this room."

"Nevertheless," Philip said, growing calmer as he recognised the man's condition, "you are a very insufferable fellow."

There had been a little murmur throughout the room at the end of Sylvanus Power's last blatant speech, but at Philip's retort there was a hushed, almost an awed silence. Mr. Honeybrook rose to his feet.

"Sir," he said, turning to Power, "to the best of my belief you are not a member of this club."

"I am a member of any club in America I choose to enter," the intruder declared. "As for you writing and acting popinjays, I could break the lot of you if I chose. I came to see you, Ware. Come out from your friends and talk to me."

Philip pushed back his chair, made his way deliberately round the head of the table, brushing aside several arms outstretched to prevent his going. Sylvanus Power stood in an open space between the tables, swinging his cane, with its ugly top, in the middle of his hand. He watched Philip's approach and lowered his head a little, like a bull about to charge.

"If you have anything to say to me," Philip observed coolly, "I am here, but I warn you that there is one subject which is never discussed within these walls. If you transgress our unwritten rule, I shall neither listen to what you have to say nor will you be allowed to remain here."

"And what is that subject?" Sylvanus Power thundered.

"No woman's name is mentioned here," Philip told him calmly.

Several of the men had sprung to their feet. It seemed from Power's attitude as though murder might be done. Philip, however, stood his ground almost contemptuously, his frame tense and poised, his fists clenched. Suddenly the strain passed. The man whose face for a moment had been almost black with passion, lowered his cane, swayed a little upon his feet, and recovered himself.

"So you know what I've come here to talk about, young man?" he demanded.

"One can surmise," Philip replied. "If you think it worth while, I will accompany you to my rooms or to yours."

Philip in those few seconds made a reputation for himself which he never lost. The little company of men looked at one another in mute acknowledgment of a courage which not one of them failed to appreciate.

"I'll take you at your word," Sylvanus Power decided grimly. "Here, boys," he went on, moving towards the table where Philip had been seated, "give me a drink — some rye whisky. I'm dry."

Not a soul stirred. Even Noel Bridges remained motionless. Heselton, the junior manager of the theatre, met the millionaire's eye and never flinched. Mr. Honeybrook knocked the ash from his cigar and accepted the rôle of spokesman.

"Mr. Power," he said, "we are a hospitable company here, and we are at all times glad to entertain our friends. At the same time, the privileges of the club are retained so far as possible for those who conform to a reasonable standard of good manners."

There was a sudden thumping of hands upon the table until the glasses rattled. Power's face showed not a single sign of anger. He was simply puzzled. He had come into touch with something which he could not understand. There was Bridges, earning a salary at his theatre, to be thrown out into the streets or made a star of, according to his whim; Heselton, a family man, drawing his salary, and a good one, too, also from the theatre; men whose faces were familiar to him — some of them, he knew, on newspapers in which he owned a controlling interest. The power of which he had bragged was a real enough thing. What had come to these men that they failed to recognise it? — to this slim young boy of an Englishman that he dared to defy him?

"Pretty queer crowd, you boys," he muttered.

Philip, who had been waiting by the door, came a few steps back again.

"Mr. Power," he said, "I don't know much about you, and you don't seem to know anything at all about us. I am only at present a member by courtesy of this club, but it isn't often that any one has reason to complain of lack of hospitality here. If you take my advice, you'll apologise to these gentlemen for your shockingly bad behaviour when you came in. Tell them that you weren't quite yourself, and I'll stand you a drink myself."

"That goes," Honeybrook assented gravely. "It's up to you, sir."

Mr. Sylvanus Power felt that he had wandered

into a cul-de-sac. He had found his way into one
of those branch avenues leading from the great road
of his imperial success. He was man enough to
know when to turn back.

"Gentlemen," he said, "I offer you my apologies.
I came here in a furious temper and a little drunk.
I retract all that I said. I'll drink to your club, if
you'll allow me the privilege."

Willing hands filled his tumbler, and grateful ones
forced a glass between Philip's fingers. None of
them really wanted Sylvanus Power for an enemy.

"Here's looking at you all," the latter said.
"Luck!" he muttered, glancing towards Philip.

They all drank as though it were a rite. Philip
and Sylvanus Power set their glasses down almost at
the same moment. Philip turned towards the door.

"I am at your service now, Mr. Power," he announced. "Good night, you fellows!"

There was a new ring of friendliness in the hearty
response which came from every corner of the room.

"Good night, Ware!"

"So long, old fellow!"

"Good night, old chap!"

There was a little delay in the cloakroom while the
attendant searched for Philip's hat, which had been
temporarily misplaced. Honeybrook, who had followed the two men out of the room, fumbling for a
moment in his locker and, coming over to Philip,
dropped something into the latter's overcoat pocket.

"Rather like a scene in a melodrama, isn't it,
Ware," he whispered, "but I know a little about
Sylvanus Power. It's only a last resource, mind."

CHAPTER X

Philip fetched his hat, and the two men stepped out on to the pavement. A servant in quiet grey livery held open the door of an enormous motor car. Sylvanus Power beckoned his companion to precede him.

"Home," he told the man, "unless," he added, turning to Philip, "you'd rather go to your rooms?"

"I am quite indifferent," Philip replied.

They drove off in absolute silence, a silence which remained unbroken until they passed through some elaborate iron gates and drew up before a mansion in Fifth Avenue.

"You'll wait," Sylvanus Power ordered, "and take this gentleman home. This way, sir."

The doors rolled open before them. Philip caught a vista of a wonderful hall, with a domed roof and stained glass windows, and a fountain playing from some marble statuary at the further end. A personage in black took his coat and hat. The door of a dining room stood open. A table, covered with a profusion of flowers, was laid, and places set for two. Mr. Sylvanus Power turned abruptly to a footman.

"You can have that cleared away," he directed harshly. "No supper will be required."

He swung around and led the way into a room at the rear of the hall, a room which, in comparison with

Philip's confused impressions of the rest of the place, was almost plainly furnished.   There was a small oak sideboard, upon which was set out whisky and soda and cigars; a great desk, covered with papers, before which a young man was seated; two telephone instruments and a phonograph.   The walls were lined with books.   The room itself was long and narrow.   Power turned to the young man.

"You can go to bed, George," he ordered.   "Disconnect the telephones."

The young man gathered up some papers, locked the desk in silence, bowed to his employer, and left the room without a word.   Power waited until the door was closed.   Then he stood up with his back to the fireplace and pointed to a chair.

"You can sit, if you like," he invited.   "Drink or smoke if you want to.   You're welcome."

"Thank you," Philip replied.   "I'd rather stand."

"You don't want even to take a chair in my house, I suppose," Mr. Sylvanus Power went on mockingly, "or drink my whisky or smoke my cigars, eh?"

"From the little I have seen of you," Philip confessed, "my inclinations are certainly against accepting any hospitality at your hands."

"That's a play-writing trick, I suppose," Sylvanus Power sneered, "stringing out your sentences as pat as butter.   It's not my way.   There's the truth always at the back of my head, and the words ready to fit it, but they come as they please."

"I seem to have noticed that," Philip observed.

"What sort of a man are you, anyway?" the other demanded, his heavy eyebrows suddenly lowering, his wonderful, keen eyes riveted upon Philip. " Can I buy you, I wonder, or threaten you? "

" That rather depends upon what it is you want from me? "

" I want you to leave this country and never set foot in it again. That's what I want of you. I want you to get back to your London slums and write your stuff there and have it played in your own poky little theatres. I want you out of New York, and I want you out quick."

" Then I am afraid," Philip regretted, " that we are wasting time. I haven't the least intention of leaving New York."

" Well, we'll go through the rigmarole," Power continued gruffly. " We've got to understand one another. There's my cheque book in that safe. A million dollars if you leave this country — alone — within twenty-four hours, and stay away for the rest of your life."

Philip raised his eyebrows. He was lounging slightly against the desk.

" I should have no use for a million dollars, Mr. Power," he said. " If I had, I should not take it from you, and further, the conditions you suggest are absurd."

" Bribery no good, eh? " Mr. Power observed. " What about threats? There was a man once who wrote a letter to a certain woman, which I found. I killed him a few days afterwards. There was a sort of a scuffle, but it was murder, right enough. I am nearer the door than you are, and I should say about three times as strong. How would a fight suit you? "

Ware's hand was in his overcoat pocket.

"Not particularly," he answered. "Besides, it wouldn't be fair. You see, I am armed, and you're not."

As though for curiosity, he drew from his pocket the little revolver which Honeybrook had slipped into it. Power looked at it and shrugged his shoulders.

"We'll leave that out, then, for the moment," he said. "Now listen to me. I'm off on another tack now. Eight years ago I met Elizabeth Dalstan. I was thirty-eight years old then — I am forty-six now. You young men nowadays go through your life, they tell me, with a woman on your hands most of the time, waste yourself out in a score of passions, go through the same old rigmarole once a year or something like it. I was married when I was twenty-four. I got married to lay my hands on the first ten thousand dollars I needed. My wife left me fifteen years ago. You may have read of her. She was a storekeeper's daughter then. She has a flat in Paris now, a country house in England, a villa at Monte Carlo and another at Florence. She lives her life, I live mine. She's the only woman I'd ever spoken a civil word to until I met Elizabeth Dalstan, or since."

Philip was interested despite his violent antipathy to the man.

"A singular record of fidelity," he remarked suavely.

"If you'd drop that play-acting talk and speak like a man, I'd like you better," Sylvanus Power continued. "There it is in plain words. I lived with my wife until we quarrelled and she left me, and while she lived with me I thought no more of women

than cats. When she went, I thought I'd done with
the sex. Elizabeth Dalstan happened along, and I
found I hadn't even begun. Eight years ago we met.
I offered her at once everything I could offer. Nothing doing. We don't need to tell one another that
she isn't that sort. I went off and left her, spent a
winter in Siberia, and came home by China. I suppose there were women there and in Paris. I was
there for a month. I didn't see them. Then America. Elizabeth Dalstan was still touring, not doing
much good for herself. I hung around for a time,
tried my luck once more — no go. Then I went
back to Europe, offered my wife ten million and
an income for a divorce. It didn't suit her, so
I came back again. The third time I found Elizabeth discouraged. If ever a man found a woman at
the right time, I did. She is ambitious — Lord
knows why! I hate acting and the theatres and
everything to do with them. However, I tried a new
move. I built that theatre in New York — there
isn't another place like it in the world — and offered
it to her for a birthday present. Then she began
to hesitate."

"Look here," Philip broke in, "I know all this.
I know everything you have told me, and everything
you can tell me. What about it? What have you
got to say to me?"

"This," Sylvanus Power declared, striking the
desk with his clenched fist. "I have only had one
consolation all the time I have been waiting — there
has been no other man. Elizabeth isn't that sort.
Each time I was separated and came back, I just
looked at her and I knew. That's why I have been

patient. That is why I haven't insisted upon my debt being paid. You understand that? "

" I hear what you say."

Power crossed the room, helped himself to whisky, and returned to his place with the tumbler in his hand. There was a brief silence. A little clock upon the mantelpiece struck two. The street sounds outside had ceased save for the hoot of an occasional taxicab. Philip was conscious of a burning desire to get away. This man, this great lump of power and success, standing like a colossus in his wonderful home, infuriated him. That a man should live who thought he had a right such as he claimed, was maddening.

" Well," Power proceeded, setting down the tumbler empty, " you won't be bought. How am I going to get you out of the way? "

" You can't do it," Philip asserted. " I am going to-morrow morning to Elizabeth, and I am going to pray her to marry me at once."

Power swayed for a single moment upon his feet. The teeth gleamed between his slightly parted lips. His great arm was outstretched, its bursting muscles showing against the sleeve of his dinner coat. His chest was heaving.

" If you do it," he shouted, " I'll close the theatre to-morrow and sack every one in it. I'll buy any theatre in New York where you try to present your namby-pamby play. I'll buy every manager she goes to for an engagement, every newspaper that says a word of praise of any work of yours. I tell you I'll stand behind the scenes and pull the strings which shall bring you and her to the knowledge of what failure and want mean. I'll give up the great things in life. I'll devote every dollar I have, every thought of my brain, every atom of my power, to bringing you two face to face with misery. That's if I keep my hands off you. I mayn't do that."

Philip shrugged his shoulders.

"If I put you in a play," he said, "which is where you really belong, people would find you humorous. Your threats don't affect me at all, Mr. Power. Elizabeth can choose."

Power leaned over to the switch and turned on an electric light above Philip's head.

"Blast you, let me look at you!" he thundered. "You're a white-faced, sickly creature to call yourself a man! Can't you see this thing as I see it? You're the sort that's had women, and plenty of them. Another will do for you, and, my God! she is the only one I've looked at — I, Sylvanus Power, mind — I, who have ruled fate and ruled men all my life — I want her! Don't be a fool! Get out of my path. I've crushed a hundred such men as you in my day."

Philip took up his hat.

"We are wasting time," he observed. "You are a cruder person than I thought you, Mr. Power. I am sorry for you, if that's anything."

"Sorry for me? You?"

"Very," Philip continued. "You see, you've imbibed a false view of life. You've placed yourself amongst the gods and your feet really are made of very sticky clay. . . . Shall I find my own way out?"

"You can find your way to hell!" Power roared.

" Use your toy pistol, if you want to.   You're going
where you'll never need it again! "

He took a giant stride, a stride which was more
like the spring of a maddened bull, towards Philip.
The veneer of a spurious civilisation seemed to have
fallen from him.   He was the great and splendid
animal, transformed with an overmastering passion.
There was murder in his eyes.   His great right arm,
with its long, hairy fingers and its single massive
ring, was like the limb of some prehistoric creature.
Philip's brain and his feet, however, were alike nimble.   He sprang a little on one side, and though that
first blow caught him just on the edge of the shoulder and sent him spinning round and round, he
saved himself by clutching at the desk.   Fortunately,
it was his left arm that hung helpless by his side.
His fingers groped feverishly in the cavernous folds
of his overcoat pocket.   Power, who had dashed
against the wall, smashing the glass of one of the
pictures, had already recovered his balance and
turned around.   The little revolver, with whose use
Philip was barely acquainted, flashed suddenly out
in the lamplight.   Even in that lurid moment he kept
his nerve.   He aimed at the right arm outstretched
to strike him, and pulled the trigger.   Through the
little mist of smoke he saw a spasm of pain in his
assailant's face, felt the thundering crash of his other
arm, striking him on the side of the head.   The room
spun round.   There was a second almost of uncon-
sciousness. . . . When he came to, he was lying with
his finger pressed against the electric bell.   Power
was clutching the desk for support, and gasping.
The sober person in black, with a couple of footmen

behind, were already in the room. . . . Their master turned to them.

" There has been an accident here," he groaned, " nothing serious. Take that gentleman and put him in the car. It's waiting outside for him. Telephone round for Doctor Renshaw."

For a single moment the major-domo hesitated. The weapon was still smoking in Philip's hand. Then Power's voice rang out again in furious command.

" Do as I tell you," he ordered. " If there's one of you here opens his lips about this, he leaves my service to-morrow. Not a dollar of pension, mind," he added, his voice shaking a little.

The servant bowed sombrely.

" Your orders shall be obeyed, sir," he promised.

He took up the telephone, and signed to one of the footmen, who helped Philip to the door. A moment afterwards the latter sank back amongst the cushions, a little dizzy and breathless, but revived almost instantly by the cool night air. He gave the chauffeur his address, and the car glided through the iron gates and down Fifth Avenue.

CHAPTER XI

Philip was awakened the next morning by the insistent ringing of the telephone at his elbow. He took up the receiver, conscious of a sharp pain in his left shoulder as he moved.

" Is this Mr. Merton Ware? " a man's smooth voice enquired.

" Yes ! "

" I am speaking for Mr. Sylvanus Power. Mr. Sylvanus Power regrets very much that he is unable to lunch with Mr. Ware as arranged to-day, but he is compelled to go to Philadelphia on the morning train. He will be glad to meet Mr. Ware anywhere, a week to-day, and know the result of the matter which was discussed last night."

" To whom am I speaking? " Philip demanded. " I don't know anything about lunching with Mr. Power to-day."

" I am Mr. Power's secretary, George Lunt," was the reply. " Mr. Power's message is very clear. He wishes you to know that he will not be in New York until a week to-day."

" How is Mr. Power? " Philip enquired.

" He met with a slight accident last night," the voice continued, " and is obliged to wear his arm in a sling. Except for that he is quite well. He has already left for Philadelphia by the early train. He was anxious that you should know this."

" Thank you very much," Philip murmured, a little dazed.

He sprang out of bed, dressed quickly, hurried over his coffee and rolls, boarded a cross-town car, and arrived at the Monmouth House flats just in time to meet Martha Grimes issuing into the street. She was not at all the same Martha. She was very neatly dressed, her shoes were nicely polished, her clothes well brushed, her gloves new, and she wore a bunch of fresh-looking violets in her waistband. She started in surprise as Philip accosted her.

" Whatever are you doing back in the slums? " she demanded. " Any fresh trouble? "

" Nothing particular," Philip replied, turning round and falling into step with her. " I can't see my way, that's all, and I want to talk to you. You're the most human person I know, and you understand Elizabeth."

" Gee! " she smiled. " This is the lion and the mouse, with a vengeance. You can walk with me, if you like, as far as the block before the theatre. I'm not going to arrive there with you, and I tell you so straight."

" No followers, eh? "

" There's no reason to set people talking," she declared. " Their tongues wag fast enough at the theatre, as it is. I've only been there for one day's work, and it seems to me I've heard the inside history of every one connected with the place."

" That makes what I have to say easier," he remarked. " Just what do they say about Miss Dalstan and Mr. Sylvanus Power? "

She looked at him indignantly.

" If you think you're going to worm things out of
me —"

" Don't be foolish," he interrupted, a little
wearily. " How could you know anything? You
are only the echo of a thousand voices. I could find
out, if I went where they gossip. I don't. In effect I don't care, but I am up against a queer situation. I want to know just what people think of
them. Afterwards I'll tell you the truth."

" Well, they profess to think," she said slowly,
" that the theatre belongs to Miss Dalstan, and that
she —"

" Stop, please," he interrupted. " I know you
hate saying it, and I know quite well what you mean.
Well, what about that? "

" It isn't my affair."

" It isn't true," he told her.

" Whether it's true or not, she is one of the best
women in the world," Martha declared vigorously.

" There isn't any doubt about that, either," he
assented. " This is the situation. Listen. Sylvanus Power has been in love with Elizabeth for the
best part of his life. He built that theatre for her
and offered it — at a price. She accepted his terms.
When the time came for payment, he saw her flinch.
He went away again and has just come back. She
is face to face now with a decision, a decision to
which she is partly committed. In the meantime,
during these last few months, Elizabeth and I have
become great friends. You know that I care for
her. I think that she cares for me. She has to
make up her mind. Martha, which is she to
choose? "

" How do you want me to answer that? " the girl asked, slackening her pace a little. " I'm not Miss Dalstan."

" From her point of view," he explained eagerly. " This man Power is madly and I believe truly in love with her. In his way he is great; in his way, too, he is a potenate. He can give her more than luxury, more, even, than success. You know Elizabeth," he went on. " She is one of the finest women who ever breathed, an idealist but a seeker after big things. She deserves the big things. Is she more likely to find them with me or with him? "

" Power's wife is still alive," she ruminated.

" And won't accept a divorce at present," he observed. " If ever she does, of course he will marry her. That has to be taken into account not morally but the temporal side of it. We know perfectly well that whatever Elizabeth decides, she couldn't possibly do wrong."

Martha smiled a little grimly.

" That's what it is to be born in the clouds," she said. " There is no sin for a good woman."

He looked at her appreciatively.

" I wonder how I knew that you would understand this," he sighed.

Suddenly he clutched at her arm. She glanced up in surprise. He was staring at a passer-by. Her eyes followed his. In a neat morning suit, with a black bowler hat and well-polished shoes, a cigar in his mouth and a general air of prosperity, Mr. Edward Dane was strolling along Broadway. He passed without a glance at either of them. For a moment Philip faltered. Then he set his teeth and walked on. There was an ashen shade in his face. The girl looked at him and shook her head.

"Mr. Ware," she said, "we haven't talked much about it, but there is something there behind, isn't there, something you are terrified about, something that might come, even now?"

"She knows about it," he interposed quickly.

"Would it be very bad if it came?"

"Hideous!"

"If she were your wife —?"

"She would be notorious. It would ruin her."

"Do you think, then," she asked quietly, "that you needed to come and ask my advice?"

He walked on with his head high, looking upwards with unseeing eyes. A little vista of that undisturbed supper table on the other side of the marble hall, a dim perspective of those eight years of waiting, flitted through his brain. The lord of that Fifth Avenue Mansion was in earnest, right enough, and he had so much to offer.

"It will break me if I have to give her up," he said simply. "I believe I should have gone overboard, crossing the Atlantic, but for her."

"There are some women," she sighed, "the best of all women, the joy of whose life seems to be sacrifice. That sounds queer, don't it, but it's true. They're happy in misfortune, so long as they are helping some one else. She is wonderful, Elizabeth Dalstan. She may even be one of those. You'll find that out. You'd better find out for yourself. There isn't any one can help you very much."

"I am not sure that you haven't," he said. "Now I'll go. Where did you get your violets, Martha?

Had them in water since last night, haven't you?"

She made a little grimace at him.

"A very polite young gentleman at the box office sent us each a bunch directly we started work yesterday. I've only had a few words with him yet, but Eva — that's the other girl — she's plagued to death with fellows already, so I'm going to take him out one evening."

Philip stopped short. They were approaching the theatre.

"Not a step further," he declared solemnly. "I wouldn't spoil your prospects for worlds. Run along, my little cynic, and warm your hands. Life's good at your age — better than when I found you, eh?"

"You don't think I am ungrateful?" she asked, a little wistfully.

He shook his head.

"You couldn't be that, Martha. . . . Good luck to you!"

She turned away with a little farewell wave of the hand and was lost at once in the surging stream of people. Philip summoned a taxicab, sat far back in the corner, and drove to his rooms. He hesitated for a moment before getting out, crossed the pavement quickly, hurried into the lift, and, arriving up-stairs, let down the latch of the outside door. Edward Dane was back in New York! For a moment, the memory of the great human drama in which he found himself a somewhat pathetic figure seemed swallowed up by this sudden resurrection of a grisly tragedy. He looked around his room a little helplessly. Against his will, that hideous vision

which had loomed up before him in so many moments
of depression was slowly reforming itself, this time
not in the still watches of the night but in the broad
daylight, with the spring sunshine to cheer his heart,
the roar of a friendly city in his ears.   It was no
time for dreams, this, and yet he felt the misery
sweeping in upon him, felt all the cold shivers of
his ineffective struggles.   Slowly that fateful panorama unfolded itself before his memory.   He saw
himself step out with glad relief from the uncomfortable, nauseous, third-class carriage, and, clutching his humble little present in his hand, cross the
flinty platform, climb the long, rain-swept hill, keeping his head upraised, though the very sky seemed
grimy, battling against the miserable depression of
that everlasting ugliness.   Before him, at least, there
was his one companion.   There would be kind words,
sympathy, a cheerful fireside, a little dreaming, a
little wandering into that world which they had
made for themselves with the help of such treasures
as that cheap little volume he carried.   And then
the last few steps, the open door, the room, its air
at first of wonderful comfort, and then the queer
note of luxury obtruding itself disquietingly, the
picture on the mantelpiece, her coming.   He had
never been in love with Beatrice.   He knew that now
perfectly well.   He had simply clung to her because
she was the only living being who knew and understood, because they had mingled their thoughts and
trodden the path of misery together.   Removed now
from that blaze of passion, smouldering perhaps in
him through previous years of discontent, but which
leaped into actual and effective life for the first

time in those few moments, he realised a certain justice in her point of view, a certain hard logic in the
way she had spoken of life and their relations. There
had been so little real affection between them. So
little had passed which might have constituted a
greater bond. It was his passionate outburst of revolt against life, whose drear talons seemed to have
fastened themselves into his very soul, which had
sent him out with murder in his brain to seek the
man who had robbed him of the one thing which
stood between him and despair; the pent-up fury
of a lifetime which had tingled in his blood and had
given him the strength of the navvy in those few
minutes by the canal side.

He covered his face with his hands, strode around
the room, gazing wildly out over the city, trying to
listen to the clanging of the surface cars, the rumble
of the overhead railway in the distance, the breaking of the long, ceaseless waves of human feet upon
the pavement. It was useless. No effort of his will
could keep from his brain the haunting memory of
those final moments — the man's face, handsome and
well-satisfied at first, the careless greeting, the sudden change, the surprise, the apprehension, the
ghastly fear, the agony! He heard the low, gur-
gling shriek of terror; he looked into the eyes with
the fear of hell before them! Then he heard the
splash of the black, filthy water.

There was a cry. It was several seconds before
he realised that it had broken from his lips. He
looked around him like a hunted creature. There
was another terror now — the gloomy court with
its ugly, miserable paraphernalia — the death, uglier

still, death in disgrace, a sordid, ghastly thing! And
in his brain, too, there was so much dawning, so many
wonderful ideas craving for fulfilment. These few
months had been months of marvellous development.
The power of the writer had seemed to grow, hour
by hour. His brain was full of fancies, exquisite
fancies some of them. It was a new world growing
up around him and within him, too beautiful a world
to leave. Yet, in those breathless moments, fear was
the dominant sensation. He felt a coward to his
fingertips. . . .

He walked up and down the room feverishly, as
a man might pace a prison in the first few moments
of captivity. There was no escape! If he disappeared again, it would only rivet suspicion the more
closely. There was no place to which he could fly,
no shelter save on the other side of the life which
he had just begun to love. His physical condition
began to alarm him. He felt his forehead by accident and found it damp with sweat. His heart was
beating irregularly with a spasmodic vigour which
brought pain. He caught sight of his terror-stricken
face in the looking-glass, and the craving to escape
from his frenzied solitude overcame all his other reso-
lutions. He rushed to the telephone, spoke with
Phoebe, waited breathlessly whilst she fetched his
mistress to the instrument.

"I want to see you," he begged, as soon as he was
conscious of her presence at the other end. "I want
to see you at once."

"Has anything happened?" she asked quickly.

"Yes!" he almost groaned. "I can't tell
you —"

" I will be with you in ten minutes," she promised.

He set the receiver down.   Those ten minutes were surely the longest which had ever ticked their way into Eternity!   And then she came.   He heard the lift stop and his door open.   There was a moment's breathless silence as their eyes met, then a little gathering together of the lines of her forehead, a half querulous, half sympathetic smile.   She shook her head at him.

" You've had one of those silly nervous attacks," she declared.   " Tell me at once why? "

" Dane is back — I saw him on the pavement this morning!" he exclaimed.   " He has been to England to find out! "

She made him sit down and seated herself by his side.

" Listen," she said, " Dane came back on the *Orinoco*, the day before yesterday.   I saw his name in the paper.   If his voyage to England had been a success, which it could not have been, you would have heard from him before now."

" I didn't think of that," he muttered.

" I have never asked you," she went on, " to tell me exactly what happened behind there.   I don't want to know.   Only I have a consciousness — I had from the first, when you began to talk to me about it — that your fears were exaggerated.   If you have been allowed to remain safe all this time, you will be safe always.   I feel it, and I am always right in these things.   Now use your own common sense.   Tell me truthfully, don't you think it is very improbable that anything could be discovered? "

" That anything could be proved," he admitted eagerly, " yes! "

" Then don't be silly. No one is likely to make accusations and attempt a case unless they had a definite end in view. We are safe even from the *Elletania* people. Mr. Raymond Greene has ceased to talk of your wonderful resemblance to Douglas Romilly. Phoebe — the only one who could really know — will never open her lips. Now take me for a little walk. We will look in the shops in Fifth Avenue and lunch at the Ritz-Carlton. Go and brush yourself and make yourself look respectable. I'll have a cigarette and read the paper. . . . No, I won't, I'll look over these loose sheets and see how you are getting on."

He disappeared into his room for a few minutes. When he returned she was entirely engrossed. She looked up at him with something almost of reverence in her face.

" When did you write this? " she asked.

" Yesterday, most of it," he answered. " There is more of it — I haven't finished yet. When you send me away this afternoon, I shall go on. That is only the beginning. I have a great idea dawning."

" What you have written is wonderful," she said simply. " It makes me feel almost humble, makes me feel that the very best actress in the world remains only an interpretress. Yes, I can say those words you have written, but they can never be mine. I want to be something more than an intelligent parrot, Philip. Why can't you teach me to feel and think things like that? "

"You!" he murmured, as he took her arm and led her to the door. "You could feel all the sweetest and most wonderful things in heaven. The writer's knack is only a slight gift. I put on paper what lives in your heart."

She raised her head, and he kissed her lips. For a moment he held her quite quietly. Her arms encircled him. The perfume of her clothes, her hair, her warm, gentle touch, seemed like a strong sedative. If she said that he was safe, he must be. It was queer how so often at these times their sexes seemed reversed; it was he who felt that womanly desire for shelter and protection which she so amply afforded him. She patted his cheek.

"Now for our little walk," she said. "Open the windows and let out all these bad fancies of yours. And listen," she went on, as they stepped out of the lift a moment or two later, and passed through the hall towards the pavement, "not a word about our own problem. We are going to talk nonsense. We are going to be just two light-hearted children in this wonderful city, gazing at the sights and taking all she has to offer us. I love it, you know. I love the noise of it. It isn't a distant, stifled roar like London. There's a harsh, clarion-like note about it, like metal striking upon metal. And the smell of New York — there isn't any other city like it! When we get into Fifth Avenue I am going to direct your attention to the subject of hats. Have you ever bought a woman's hat, Philip?"

"Never," he answered, truthfully enough.

"Then you are going to this morning, or rather you are going to help me to choose one," she de-

clared, " and in a very few moments, too. There
is a little place almost underground in Fifth Avenue
there, and a Frenchwoman — oh, she is so French!
— and all her assistants have black hair and wear
untidy, shapeless clothes and velvet slippers. It
isn't New York at all, but I love it, and I let them
put their name on the programme. They really
don't charge me more than twice as much as they
ought to for my hats. We go down here," she added,
descending some steps, " and if you make eyes at
any of the young women I shall bring you straight
out again."

They spent half an hour choosing a hat and nearly
two hours over lunch. It was late in the afternoon
before she dropped him at his rooms. Not a word
had they spoken of Sylvanus Power or their future,
but Philip was a different man. Only, as he turned
and said good-by, his voice trembled.

" I can't say thank you," he muttered, " but you
know!" . . .

The lift was too slow for him. He opened his
door with almost breathless haste. He only paused
to light a cigarette and change his coat and wheel
his table round so as to catch the afternoon light
more perfectly. Then, with his brain teeming with
fancies, he plunged into his work.

CHAPTER XII

Philip let the pen slip at last from his tired fingers. The light had failed. He had been writing with straining eyes, almost in the darkness. But there was something else. Had it been fancy or . . . This time there could be no mistake. He had not heard the lift stop, but some one was knocking softly at the door, softly but persistently. He turned his head. The room seemed filled with shadows. He had written for hours, and he was conscious that his limbs were stiff. The sun had gone down in a cloudy sky, and the light had faded. He could scarcely distinguish the articles of furniture at the further end of the room. For some reason or other he felt tongue-tied. Then, without any answer from him to this mysterious summons, the handle of the door slowly turned. As he sat there he saw it pushed open. A woman, wrapped in a long coat, stepped inside, closing it firmly behind her. She stood peering around the room. There was something familiar and yet unfamiliar in her height, her carriage. He waited, spellbound, for her voice.

"Douglas!" she exclaimed. "Ah, there you are!"

The words seemed to die away, unuttered, upon his lips. He suddenly thought that he was choking. He stared at her blankly. It was impossible! She came a step further into the room. Her hand was stretched out accusingly.

"So I've found you, have I, Douglas?" she cried, and there was a note of bitter triumph in her words, "found you after all these months! Aren't you terrified? Aren't you afraid? No wonder you sit there, shrinking away! Do you know what I have come for?"

He tried to speak, but his lips were as powerless to frame words as his limbs were to respond to his desire for movement. This was the one thing which he had not foreseen.

"You broke your promise," she went on, raising her voice a little in passionate reproach. "You left me there alone to face dismissal, without a penny, and slipped off yourself to America. You never even came in to wish me good-by. Why? Tell me why you went without coming near me? . . . You won't, eh? You daren't. Be a man. Out with it. I am here, and I know the truth."

For the first time some definite sound came from his lips.

"Beatrice!" he gasped.

"Ah!" she mocked. "You can remember my name, then? Douglas, I knew that you were a bad man. I knew that when you told me how you meant to cheat your creditors, how you meant to escape over here on the pretext of business, and bring all the money you could scrape together. I knew that, and yet I was willing to come with you, and I should have come. But there was one thing I didn't reckon upon. I didn't know that you had the heart or the courage to be a murderer!"

244 THE CINEMA MURDER

The little cry that broke from his lips was stifled even before it was uttered.

"I shall never forgive you!" she sobbed. "I never want to touch your bloodstained fingers! I have forgotten that I ever loved you. You're horrible — do you hear? — horrible! And yet, I don't mean to be left to starve. That's why I've followed you. You're afraid I am going to give you up to justice? Well, I don't know. It depends. . . . Turn on the lights. I want to see you. Do you hear? I want to see how you can face me. I want to see how the memory of that afternoon has dealt with you. Do as I tell you. Don't stand there glowering at me."

He crossed the room with stumbling footsteps.

"You've learnt to stoop, anyhow," she went on. "You're thinner, too. . . . My God!"

The room was suddenly flooded with light. Philip, rigid and ghastly, was looking at her from the other side of the table. She held up her hands as though to shut out the sight of him.

"Philip!" she shrieked. "Philip! . . . Oh, my God!"

Her eyes were lit with horror as she swayed upon her feet. For a moment she seemed about to collapse. Then she groped her way towards the door and stood there, clinging to the handle. Slowly she looked around over her shoulder, her face as white as death. She moistened her lips with her tongue, her eyes glared at him. Behind, her brain seemed to be working. Her first spasm of inarticulate fear passed.

"Philip — alive!" she muttered. "Alive! . . .

Speak! Can't you speak to me? Are you a ghost?"

"Of course not," he answered, with a calm which surprised him. "You can't have forgotten in less than six months what I look like."

A new expression struggled into her face. She abandoned her grasp of the handle and came back to her former position.

"Look here," she faltered, "if you are Philip Romilly, where's he — Douglas? . . . Where's Douglas?"

There was no answer. Philip simply looked at her. She began to shake once more upon her feet.

"Where's Douglas?" she demanded fiercely. "Tell me? Tell me quickly, before I go mad! If you are Philip Romilly alive, if it wasn't your body they found, where's Douglas?"

"You can guess what happened to him," Philip said slowly. "I met him on the towing-path by the side of the canal. I spoke to him — about you. He answered me with a jest. I think that all the passion of those grinding years of misery swept up at that moment from my heart. I was strong — God, how strong I was! I took him by the throat, Beatrice. I watched his face change. I watched his damned, self-satisfied complacency fade away. He lost all his smugness, and his eyes began to stare at me, and his lips grew whiter as they struggled to utter the cries for mercy which choked back. Then I flung him in — that's all. Splash! . . . God, I can hear it now! I saw his face just under the water. Then I went on."

" You went on ? " she repeated, trembling in every limb.

" I picked up the pocketbook which I had shaken out of his clothes in that first struggle. I studied its contents, and it gave me an idea. I went to Liverpool, stayed at the hotel where he had engaged rooms, dressed myself in his clothes, and went on the steamer in his place. I travelled to New York as Mr. Douglas Romilly of the Douglas Romilly Shoe Company, occupied my room at the Waldorf under that name. Then I disappeared suddenly — there were too many people waiting to see me. I took the pseudonym which he had carefully prepared for himself and hid for a time in a small tenement house. Then I rewrote the play. There you have my story."

" You — murdered him, Philip ! . . . You ! "

" It was no crime," he continued calmly, filled with a queer sense of relief at the idea of being able to talk about it. " My whole life, up till that day, had been one epitome of injustice and evil fortune. You were my one solace. His life — well, you know what it had been. Everything was made easy for him. He had a luxurious boyhood, he was sent to college, pampered and spoilt, and passed on to a dissipated manhood. He spent a great fortune, ruined a magnificent business. He lived, month by month, hour by hour, for just the voluptuous pleasures which his wealth made possible to him. That was the man I met on the canal bank that afternoon. You know the state I was in. You know very well the grievance I had against him."

" You had no right to interfere," she said dully.

"If I chose to accept what he had to give, it was my business. There never had been over-much affection between you and me. We were just waifs together. Life wouldn't give us what we wanted. I had made up my mind months before to escape whenever the opportunity came. Douglas brought it to me and I snatched at it. I am not accepting any blame."

He leaned towards her.

"Neither am I," he declared. "Do you remember we used to talk about the doctrine of responsibility? I am a pervert. I did what I had to do, and I am content."

She stood quite still for several moments. Then she took out the pins from her hat, banged it upon the table, opened her tweed coat, came round to the fireside, and threw herself into an easy-chair. Her action was portentous and significant.

"Tell me how you found me out?" he asked, after a brief pause.

"I was dismissed from Detton Magna," she told him. "I had to go and be waiting-maid to Aunt Esther at Croydon. I took the place of her maid-of-all-work. I scrubbed for my living. There wasn't anything else. I hadn't clothes to try for the bolder things, not a friend in the world, but I was only waiting. I meant, at the first chance, to rob Aunt Esther, to come to London, dress myself properly, and find a post on the stage, if possible. I wasn't particular. Then one day a man came to see me — an American. He'd travelled all the way from New York because he was interested in what he called the mysterious Romilly disappearance. He knew that I had been Douglas' friend. He asked me to come out and identify — you! He offered me my passage, a hundred pounds, and to give me a start in life here, if I needed it. So I came out with him."

"With Dane," he muttered.

She nodded.

"Yes, that was his name — Mr. Edward Dane. I came out to identify Douglas."

"You weren't going to give him away?" Philip asked curiously.

"Of course not. I should have made my bargain, and then, after I had scared Douglas for leaving me as he did, I should have said that it wasn't the man. And instead — I found you!"

He tapped the table with his fingers, restlessly. A new hope was forming in his brain. This, indeed, might be the end of all his troubles.

"Listen," he said earnestly, "Dane has always suspected me. Sometimes I have wondered whether he hadn't the truth at the back of his head. You can make me safe forever."

She made no reply. Her eyes were watching his face. She seemed to be waiting to hear what else he had to say.

"Don't you understand?" he went on impatiently. "You have only to tell Dane that I am neither Douglas nor Philip, but curiously like both, and he will chuck the thing up. He must. Then I shall be safe. You see that, don't you?"

"Yes, I see that," she admitted.

"Well?"

"Tell me exactly how much of Douglas' money you have spent?" she demanded.

"Only the loose money from the pocketbook. Not all of that. I am earning money now."

She leaned across the table.

"What about the twenty thousand pounds?"

"I haven't touched it," he assured her, "not a penny."

"On your honour?"

He rose silently and went to his desk, unlocked one of the drawers, and drew from a hidden place a thin strip of paper. He smoothed it out on the table before her.

"There's the deposit note," he said,—"*Twenty thousand pounds to the joint or separate credit of Beatrice Wenderly and Douglas Romilly, on demand.* The money's there still. I haven't touched it."

She gripped the paper in her fingers. The sight of the figures seemed to fascinate her. Then she looked around.

"How can you afford to live in a place like this, then?" she demanded suspiciously. "Where does your money come from?"

"The play," he told her.

"What, all this?" she exclaimed.

"It is a great success. The theatre is packed every night. My royalties come every week to far more than I could spend."

She looked once more around her, gripped the deposit note in her fingers, and leaned back in her chair. She laughed curiously. Her eyes had travelled back to Philip's anxious face.

"Wonderful!" she murmured. "You paid the price, but you've won. You've had something for it. I paid the price, and up till now —"

She stared at the paper in her hand. Then she looked away into the fire.

"I can't get it all into my head," she went on. "I pictured him here, living in luxury, spending the money of which he had promised me a share . . . and he's dead! That was his body — that unrecognisable thing they found in the canal. You killed him — Douglas! He was so fond of life, too."

"Fond of the things which meant life to him," Philip muttered.

"I should never have believed that you had the courage," she observed ruminatingly. "After all, then, he wasn't faithless. He wasn't the brute I thought him."

She sat thinking for what seemed to him to be an interminable time. He broke in at last upon her meditations.

"Well," he asked, "what are you going to say to Dane?"

"I shan't give you away — at least I don't think so," she promised cautiously. "I shall see. Presently I will make terms, only this time I am not going to be left. I am going to have what I want."

"But he'll be waiting to hear from you!" Philip exclaimed. "He may come here, even."

She shook her head.

"He's gone to Chicago. He can't be back for five days. I promised to wire, but I shan't. I'll wait until he's back. And in the meantime —"

Her fingers closed upon the deposit note. He nodded shortly.

"That's yours," he said. "You can have it all.

I have helped myself to a fresh start in life at his expense. That's all I wanted."

She folded up the paper and thrust it carefully into the bosom of her gown. Then she stood up.

" Well," she pronounced, " I think I am getting used to things. It's wonderful how callous one can become. The banks are closed now, I suppose? "

He nodded.

" They will be open at nine o'clock in the morning."

" First of all, then," she decided, " I'll make sure of my twenty thousand pounds, and then we'll see. I don't think you'll find me hard, Philip. I ought not to be hard on you, ought I? "

She looked at him most kindly, and he began to shiver. Curiously enough, her very kindness, when he realised the knowledge which lay behind her brain, was hateful to him. He had pleaded for her forgiveness, even her toleration, but — anything else seemed horrible! She strolled across the room and glanced at the clock, took one of his cigarettes from a box and lit it.

" Well, this is queer! " she murmured reflectively. " Now I want some dinner, and I'll see your play, Philip. You shall take me. Get ready quickly, please."

He looked at her doubtfully.

" But, Beatrice," he protested, " think! You know why you came here? You know the story you will have to tell? We are strangers, you and I. What if we are seen together? "

She snapped her fingers at him.

" Pooh! Who cares! I am a stranger in New

York, and I have taken a fancy to you.   You are a
young man of gallantry, and you are going to take
me out. . . . We often used to talk of a little excursion like this in London.   We'll have it in New York
instead."

He turned slowly towards the door of his bedroom.
She was busy looking at her own eyes in the mirror,
and she missed the little gleam of horror in his face.

"In ten minutes," he promised her.

CHAPTER XIII

Beatrice replaced the programme which she had been studying, on the ledge of the box, and turned towards Philip, who was seated in the background. There was something a little new in her manner. Her tone was subdued, her eyes curious.

"You really are a wonderful person, Philip," she declared. "It's the same play, just as you used to tell it me, word for word. And yet it isn't. What is it that you have gained, I wonder? — a sense of atmosphere, breadth, something strangely vital."

"I am glad you like it," he said simply.

"Like it? It's amazing! And what an audience! I never thought that the people were so fashionable here, Philip. I am sitting right back in the box, but ten minutes after I have cashed my draft to-morrow I shall be buying clothes. You won't be ashamed to be seen anywhere with me then."

He drew his chair up to her side, a little haggard and worn with the suspense of the evening. She laughed at him mockingly.

"What an idiot you are!" she exclaimed. "You ought to be one of the happiest men in the world, and you look like a death's-head."

"The happiest man in the world," he repeated.

" Beatrice, sometimes I think that there is only one thing in the world that makes for happiness."

" And what's that, booby? " she asked, with some of her old familiarity.

" A clear conscience."

She laid her hand upon his arm.

" Look here, Philip," she said, " the one thing I determined, when I threw up the sponge, was that whether the venture was a success or not I'd never waste a single moment in regrets. Things didn't turn out too brilliantly with me, as you know. But you — see what you've attained! Why, it's wonderful! Your play, the one thing you dreamed about, produced in one of the greatest cities in the world, and a packed house to listen to it, people applauding all the time. I didn't realise your success when we talked this evening. I am just beginning to understand. I've been reading some of these extracts from the newspapers. You're Merton Ware, the great dramatist, the coming man of letters. You've won, Philip. Can't you see that it's puling cowardice to grumble at the price? "

He, for his part, was wondering at her callousness, of which he was constantly discovering fresh evidences. The whole shock of her discovery seemed already, in these few hours, to have passed away.

" If you can forget — so soon," he muttered, " I suppose I ought to be able to."

She made a little grimace, but immediately afterwards he saw the cold tightening of her lips.

" Listen, Philip," she said. " I started life with the usual quiverful of good qualities, but there's one I've lost, and I don't want it back again. I'm a self-

ish woman, and I mean to stay a selfish woman. I
am going to live for myself. I've paid a fair price,
and I'm going to have what I've paid for. See?"

"Do you think,' he asked, "that it is possible to
make that sort of bargain with one's self and fate?"

She laughed scornfully.

"There's room for a little stiffening in you, even
now, Philip! No one but a weakling ever talks
about fate. You'd think better of me, I suppose,
if I stayed in my room and wept. Well, I could do
it if I let myself, but I won't. I should lose several
hours of the life that belongs to me. You think I
didn't care about Douglas? I am not at all sure
that I didn't care for him as much as I ever did for
you, although, of course, he wasn't worthy of it.
But he's gone, and all the shudders and morbid regrets in the world won't bring him back again. And
I am here in New York, and to-morrow I shall have
twenty thousand pounds, and to-night I am with
you, watching your play. That's life enough for me
at present — no more, no less. I hate missing the
first act, and I'm coming to see it again to-morrow.
What time is it over?"

"Soon after eleven," he told her.

She glanced at her watch.

"You shall take me out and give me some supper,"
she decided, "somewhere where there's music."

He made no remark, but she surprised again something in his face which irritated her.

"Look here, Philip," she said firmly, "I won't
have you look at me as though I were something in-
human. There are plenty of other women like me
in the world, even if they are not quite so frank

about it. I want to live, and I will live, and I grudge every moment out of which I am not extracting the fullest amount of happiness. That's because I've paid. It's the woman's bargaining instinct, you know. She wants to get value. . . . Now I want to hear about Miss Dalstan. Where did you meet her, and how did you get her to accept your play?"

"She was on the *Elletania*," he explained. "We crossed from Liverpool together. She sat at my table."

"How much does she know about you?" Beatrice asked bluntly.

"Everything," he confessed. "I don't know what I should have done without her. She has been the most wonderful friend any one could have."

Beatrice looked at him a little critically.

"You're a queer person, Philip," she exclaimed. "You're not fit to go about alone, really. Good thing I came over to take care of you, I think."

"You don't understand," he replied. "Miss Dalstan is — well, unlike anybody else. She wants to see you. I am to take you round after the next act, if you would like to go."

Beatrice smiled at him in a gratified manner.

"I've always wanted to go behind the scenes," she admitted. "I'll come with you, with pleasure. Perhaps if I decide that I'd like to go on the stage, she may be able to help me. How much is twenty thousand pounds in dollars, Philip?"

"A little over a hundred thousand," he told her.

"I don't suppose they think that much out here," she went on ruminatingly. "The hotel where Mr.

Dane sent me — it's nice enough, in its way, but very stuffy as regards the people — is twice as expensive as it would be in London. However, we shall see."

The curtain rang up on the third act, and Beatrice, seated well back in the shadows, followed the play attentively, appreciated its good points and had every appearance of both understanding and enjoying it. Afterwards, she rose promptly to her feet, still clapping.

"I'm longing to meet Miss Dalstan, Philip," she declared. "She is wonderful. And to think that you wrote it — that you created the part for her! I am really quite proud of you."

She laughed at his embarrassment, affecting to ignore the fact that it was less the author's modesty than some queer impulse of horror which seemed to come over him when any action of hers reminded him of their past familiarity. He hurried on, piloting her down the corridor to the door of Elizabeth's dressing room. In response to his knock they were bidden to enter, and Elizabeth, who was lying on a couch whilst a maid was busy preparing her costume for the next act, held out her hand with a little welcoming smile.

"I am so glad to see you, Miss Wenderley," she said cordially. "Philip, bring Miss Wenderley over here. You'll forgive my not getting up, won't you? I have to rest for just these few minutes before the next act."

Beatrice was for a moment overpowered. The luxury of the wonderful dressing room, with its perfect French furniture, its white walls hung with a few choice sketches, the thick rugs upon the polished wood floor, the exquisite toilet table with its wealth of gold and tortoiseshell appurtenances — Elizabeth herself, so beautiful and gracious — even a hurried contemplation of all these things took her breath away. She felt suddenly acutely conscious of the poverty of her travelling clothes, of her own insignificance.

"Won't you sit down for a moment?" Elizabeth begged, pointing to a chair by her side. "You and I must be friends, you know, for Philip's sake."

Beatrice recovered herself a little. She sank into the blue satin chair, with its ample cushions, and looked down at Elizabeth with something very much like awe.

"I am sure Philip must feel very grateful to you for having taken his play," she declared. "It has given him a fresh chance in life."

"After all he has gone through," Elizabeth said gently, "he certainly deserves it. It is a wonderfully clever play, you know . . . don't blush, Mr. Author!"

"I heard the story long ago," Beatrice observed, "only of course it sounded very differently then, and we never dreamed that it would really be produced."

"Philip has told me about those days," Elizabeth said. "I am afraid that you, too, have had your share of unhappiness, Miss Wenderley. I only hope that life in the future will make up to you something of what you have lost."

The girl's face hardened. Her lips came together in familiar fashion.

"I mean it to," she declared. "I am going to make a start to-morrow. I wish, Miss Dalstan, you

could get Philip to look at things a little more cheerfully.   He has been like a ghost ever since I arrived."

Elizabeth turned and smiled at him sympathetically.

"Your coming must have been rather a shock,"
she reminded Beatrice.   "You came with the idea,
did you not, that — you would find Mr. Douglas
Romilly?"

The girl nodded and glanced around for the maid,
who had disappeared, however, into an inner apartment.

"They were always alike," she confided,—"the
same figures, same shaped head and that sort of
thing.   Douglas was a little overfond of life, though,
and Philip here hasn't found out yet what it means.
It was a shock, though, Miss Dalstan.   Philip was
sitting in the dark when I arrived at his rooms this
evening, and — I thought it was Douglas."

Elizabeth shivered a little.

"Don't let us talk about it," she begged.   "You
must come and see me, won't you, Miss Wenderley?
Philip will tell you where I live.   Are you going back
to England at once?"

"I haven't made up my mind yet," the girl replied, with a slight frown.   "It just depends."

Elizabeth glanced at the little clock upon her
table, and Philip threw away his cigarette and came
forward.

"We must go, Beatrice," he announced.   "Miss
Dalstan has to change her dress for this act."

He held out his hand and Elizabeth rose lightly to
her feet.   So far, no word as to their two selves had
passed their lips.   She smiled at him and all this

sense of throbbing, almost theatrical excitement subsided. He was once more conscious of the beautiful
things beyond. Once more he felt the rest of her
presence.

"You must let me see something of you to-
morrow, Philip," she said. "Telephone, will you?
Good night, Miss Wenderley."

The maid, who had just returned, held the door
open. Philip glanced back over his shoulder. Elizabeth blew him a kiss, a gesture which curiously
enough brought a frown to Beatrice's face.

CHAPTER XIV

The close of the performance left them both curiously tongue-tied. They waited until the theatre was half empty before they left their seats. Then they joined the little throng of stragglers at the end.

"Your play!" she murmured, as they faced the soft night air. "I can't believe it, even now. We've seen it together — your play — and this is New York! That's a new ending, isn't it?"

"Absolutely," he confessed. "The ending was always what bothered me, you know."

She laughed, not quite naturally. She was unexpectedly impressed.

"So you're a genius, after all," she went on. "Sometimes I wondered — but never mind that now. Philip, do you know I am starving? We took exactly ten minutes over dinner!"

He led her to a huge restaurant a few doors away, where they found a corner table. Up in the balcony an orchestra was playing light music, and a little crowd of people were all the time streaming through the doors. Beatrice settled herself down with an air of content. Few of the people were in evening dress, and the tone of the place was essentially democratic. Philip, who had learnt a little about American dishes, gave an order, and Beatrice sipped her cocktail with an air of growing appreciation.

" Queer idea, this, but the stuff tastes all right,"
she acknowledged. " I suppose, if you were taking
your dear Miss Dalstan out, you'd go to a different
sort of place, eh? "

" We generally go further up town," he admitted
unthinkingly.

She set her glass down quickly.

" So you do take her out, do you? " she asked
coldly. " You'd have been with her to-night, perhaps, if I hadn't been here? "

" Very likely."

She was half inclined to rally him, behind it all a
little annoyed.

" You're a nice sort of person! Why, it's only a
few months ago since you pretended to be in love
with me! "

He looked at her, and her eyes fell before his.

" I don't think there was ever much question of our
being in love with one another, was there? We simply seemed to have drifted together because we
were both miserable, and then, as the time passed
on — well, you came to be my only solace against the
wretchedness of that life."

She nodded appreciatively. For a moment the
sights and sounds of the noisy restaurant passed
from her consciousness.

" Do you remember how glad I was to see you?
How we used to spend our holidays out in those
dingy fields and hope and pray for better things
some day? But it was all so hopeless, wasn't it!
You could barely keep yourself from starving, and I
— oh, the misery of that awful Detton Magna and
teaching those wretched children! There never were

such children in the world. I couldn't get their
mothers to send them clean. They seemed to have
inherited all the vice, the bad language, the ugly
sordidness with which the place reeked. They were
old men and women in wickedness before they
passed their first standard. It's a corner of the
world I never want to see again. I'd rather find
hell! Have you ordered any wine, Philip? I want
to forget."

He pointed to the bottle which stood in the pail
by their side, and summoned a waiter. She watched
it being opened and their glasses filled.

"This is like one of our fairy stories of the old
days, isn't it?" she said. "Well, I drink to you,
Philip. Here's success to our new lives!"

She raised her glass and drained it. A woman
had entered who reminded him of Elizabeth, and his
eyes had wandered away for a moment as Beatrice
pledged him. She called him back a little impatiently.

"Don't sit there as though you were looking at
ghosts, Philip! Try and remember who I am and
what we used to mean to one another. Let us try
and believe," she added, a little wistfully, "that one
of those dreams of ours which we used to set floating
like bubbles, has come true. We can wipe out all
the memories we don't want. That ought to be
easy."

"Ought it?" he answered grimly. "There are
times when I've found it difficult enough."

She laughed and looked about her. He realised
suddenly that she was still very attractive with her
rather insolent mouth, her clear eyes, her silky hair

with the little fringe. People, as they passed, paid her some attention, and she was frankly curious about everybody.

"Well," she went on presently, "thank heavens I have plenty of will power. I remember nothing, absolutely nothing, which happened before this evening. I am going to tell myself that an uncle in Australia has died and left me money, and so we are here in New York to spend it. To-morrow I am going to begin. I shall buy clothes — all sorts of clothes — and hats. You won't know me to-morrow evening, Philip."

His heart sank. To-morrow evening!

"But Beatrice," he expostulated, "you don't think of staying out here, do you? You don't know a soul. You haven't a friend in the city."

"What friends have I in England?" she retorted. "Not one! I may just as well start a new life in a new country. It seems bright enough here, and gay. I like it. I shall move to a different sort of hotel to-morrow. You must help me choose one. And as to friends," she whispered, looking up at him with a little provocative gleam in her eyes, "don't you count? Can't you do what I am going to do, Philip? Can't you draw down that curtain?"

He shivered.

"I can't!" he muttered.

A waiter brought their first course, and she at once evinced interest in her food. She returned to the subject, however, later on, after she had drunk another glass of wine.

"You're a silly old thing, you know," she declared. "You found the courage, somehow, to break away from that loathsome existence. You had more courage, even, than I, because you ran a risk I never did. But here you are, free, with the whole world before you, and your last danger disappearing with the knowledge that I am ready to be your friend and am sensible about everything that has happened. This ought to be an immense relief to you, Philip. You ought to be the happiest man on earth. And there you sit, looking like a death's-head! Look at me for a moment like a human being, can't you? Drink some more wine. There must be some strength, some manhood about you somewhere, or you couldn't have done what you have done."

He filled his glass mechanically. She leaned across the table. Her eyes were bright, her cheeks delicately pink.

" Courage, Philip," she murmured. " Remember that what you did . . . well, in a way it was for my sake, wasn't it? — for love of me? I am here now and we are both free. The old days are passed. Even their shadow cannot trouble us any longer. Don't be a sentimentalist. Listen and I'll tell you something — at the bottom of my heart I rather admire you for what you did. Don't you want your reward? "

" No," he answered firmly, " I don't! "

She shrugged her shoulders and kept time with her foot to the music. Across the table, although she kept silence for a while, she smiled at him whenever she caught his eye. She was not angry, not even hurt. Philip had always been so difficult, but in the end so easily led. She had unlimited confidence in herself.

"Don't be a goose!" she exclaimed at last. "Of course you want your reward, and of course you'll have it, some day! You've always lived with your head partly in the clouds, and it's always been my task to pull you down to earth. I suppose I shall have to do the same again, but to-night I haven't patience. I feel suddenly gay. You are so nice-looking, Philip, but you'd look ten times nicer still if you'd only smile once or twice and look as though you were glad."

The whole thing was a nightmare to him. The horror of it was in his blood, yet he did his best to obey. Plain speaking just then was impossible. He drank glass after glass of wine and called for liqueurs. She held his fingers for a moment under the table.

"Oh, Philip," she whispered, "can't you forget that you have ever been a school-teacher, dear? We are only human, and did suffer so. You know," she went on, "you were made for the things that are coming to us. You've improved already, ever so much. I like your clothes and the way you carry yourself. But you look — oh, so sad and so far away all the time! When I came to your rooms, at my first glimpse of you I knew that you were miserable. We must alter all that, dear. Tell me how it is that with all your success you haven't been happy?"

"Memories!" he answered harshly. "Only a few hours before you came, I was in hell!"

"Then you had better make up your mind," she told him firmly, "that you are going to climb up out of there, and when you're out, you're going to stay out. You can't alter the past. You can't

alter even the smallest detail of its setting. Just as
inevitably as our lives come and go, so what has
happened is finished with, unchangeable. It is only
a weak person who would spoil the present and
the future, brooding. You used not to be weak,
Philip."

"I don't think that I am, really," he said. "I am
moody, though, and that's almost as bad. The sight
of you brought it all back. And that fellow Dane
— I've been frightened of him, Beatrice."

"Well, you needn't be any longer," she declared.
"What you want is some one with you all the time
who understands you, some one to drive back those
other thoughts when they come to worry you. It is
really a very good thing for you, dear, that I came
out to New York. Mr. Dane is going to be very
disappointed when I tell him that I never saw you
before in my life. . . . Don't you love the music?
Listen to that waltz. That was written for happy
people, Philip. I adore this place. I suppose we
shall find others that we like better, as time goes on,
but I shall always think of this evening. It is the
beginning of my task, too, Philip, with you — for
you. What has really happened, dear? I can't
realise anything. I feel as though the gates of some
great prison had been thrown wide-open, and everything there was to long for in life was just there,
within reach, waiting. I am glad, so much gladder
than I should have imagined possible. It's wonderful to have you again. I didn't even feel that I
missed you so much, but I know now what it was that
made life so appalling. Tell me, am I still nice to
look at?"

" Of course you are," he assured her. " Can't you understand that by the way people notice you? "

She strummed upon the table with her fingers. Her whole body seemed to be moving to the music. She nodded several times.

" I don't want them to notice me, Philip," she murmured. " I want you to look just for a moment as though you thought me the only person in the world — as you did once, you know."

He did his best to be responsive, but he was not wholly successful. Nevertheless, she was tolerant with his shortcomings. They sat there until nearly three o'clock. It was she at last who rose reluctantly to her feet.

" I want to go whilst the memory of it all is wonderful," she declared. " Come. Here's a card with my address on. Drive me home now, please."

He paid his bill and they found a cab. She linked her arm through his, her head sank a little upon his shoulder. He made no movement. She waited for a moment, then she leaned back amongst the cushions.

" Philip," she asked quietly, " has this Elizabeth Dalstan been letting you make love to her? "

" Please don't speak of Miss Dalstan like that," he begged.

" Answer my question," she insisted.

" Miss Dalstan has been very kind to me," he admitted slowly, " wonderfully kind. If you really want to know, I do care for her."

" More than you did for me? "

" Very much more," he answered bravely, " and in a different fashion."

In the darkness of the cab it seemed to him that her face had grown whiter. Her arm remained within his but it clasped him no longer. Her body seemed to have become limp. Even her voice, firm though it was, seemed pitched in a different key.

"Listen," she said. "You will have to forget Miss Dalstan. I have made up my mind what I want in life and I am going to have it. I shall draw my money to-morrow morning and afterwards I shall come straight to your rooms. Then we will talk. I want more than just that money. I am lonely. And do you know, Philip, I believe that I must have cared for you all the time, and you — you must have cared for me a little or you would never have done that for my sake. You must and you shall care, Philip, because our time has come, and I want you, please — shall I have to say it, dear? — I want you to marry me."

He wrenched himself free from her.

"That is quite out of the question, Beatrice," he declared.

She laughed at him mockingly.

"Oh, don't say that, Philip! You might tempt me to be brutal. You might tempt me to speak horribly plain words to you."

"Speak them and have done with it," he told her roughly. "I might find a few, too."

"I am past hurting," she replied, "and I am not in the least afraid of anything you could say. You robbed me of the man who was bringing me to America — who would have married me some day, I suppose. Well, you must pay, do you see, and in my way? I have told you the way I choose."

"You want me to marry you?" he demanded — "simply marry you? You do not care whether I have any love for you or whether I loathe you now."

"You couldn't loathe me, could you?" she begged. "The thought of those long days we spent together in our prison house would rise up and forbid it. Kiss me."

"I will not!"

Her lips sought his, in vain. He pushed her away.

"Don't you understand?" he exclaimed. "There is another woman whom I have kissed — whom I am longing to kiss now."

"But we are old friends," she pleaded, "and I am lonely. Kiss me how you like. Don't be foolish."

He kissed her upon the cheek. She pulled down her veil. The cab had stopped before the door of her hotel.

"You are not to worry any more about ugly things, Philip," she whispered, holding his hand for a moment as he rang the bell for her. "You are safe, remember — quite safe. I've come to take care of you. You need it so badly. . . . Good night, dear!"

CHAPTER XV

Late though it was when Philip reached his rooms, he found on his writing table a message addressed to him from the telephone call office in the building. He tore it open:

" Kindly ring up Number 551 Avenue immediately you return, whatever the time."

He glanced at the clock, hesitated, and finally approaching the instrument called up Elizabeth's number. For a few moments he waited. The silence in the streets outside seemed somehow to have become communicated to the line, the space between them emptied of all the jarring sounds of the day. It was across a deep gulf of silence that he heard at last her voice.

" Yes? Is that you, Philip? "

" I am here," he answered. " I am sorry it is so late."

" Have you only just come in? "

" This moment."

" Has that girl kept you out till now? " she asked reprovingly.

" I couldn't help it," he replied. " It was her first night over here. I took her to Churchill's for supper."

"Is everything — all right with her? She doesn't mean to make trouble?"

The unconscious irony of the question almost forced a smile to his lips.

"I don't think so," he answered. "She is thoroughly excited at the idea of possessing the money. I believe she thought that Douglas would have drawn it all. She is going straight to the bank, early in the morning, to get hold of it."

"What about the man Dane?"

"He has gone to Chicago. He won't be back for several days."

There was a moment's pause.

"Have you anything to ask me?" she enquired.

"Nothing."

"I have had the most extraordinary letter from Sylvanus. You and he have met."

"Yes," he admitted.

"Philip, we must make up our minds."

"You mean that you must make up your mind," he answered gently.

There was another silence. Then she spoke a little abruptly.

"I wonder whether you really love me, Philip. . . . No! don't, please — don't try to answer such a foolish question. Go to bed and sleep well now. You've had a trying day. Good night, dear!"

He had barely time to say good night before he heard the ring off. He set down the receiver. Somehow, there was a sensation of relief in having been, although indirectly, in touch with her. The idea of the letter from Sylvanus Power affected him only hazily. The crowded events of the day had somehow or other dulled his power of concentrated thought. He felt a curious sense of passivity. He undressed without conscious effort, closed his eyes, and slept until he was awakened by the movements of the valet about the room.

Philip was still seated over his breakfast, reading the paper and finishing his coffee, when the door was thrown suddenly open, and Beatrice entered tumultuously. She laughed at his air of blank surprise.

"You booby!" she exclaimed. "I couldn't help coming in to wish you good morning. I have just discovered that my hotel is quite close by here. Lucky, isn't it, except that I am going to move. Good morning, Mr. Serious Face!" she went on, leaning towards him, her hands behind her, her lips held out invitingly.

He set down his paper, kissed her on the cheek, and looked inside the coffeepot.

"Have you had your breakfast?"

"Hours ago. I was too excited to sleep when I got to bed, and yet I feel so well. Philip, where's Wall Street? Won't you take me there?"

He shook his head.

"I am expecting a visitor, and I have piles of work to do."

She made a grimace.

"I know I shall be terrified when I march up to the counter of the bank and say I've come for twenty thousand pounds!"

"You must transfer it to a current account," he explained, "in your own name. Have you any papers with you — for identification, I mean?"

She nodded.

" I've thought of all that. I've a photograph and
a passport and some letters. It isn't that I'm really
afraid, but I hate being alone, and you look so nice,
Philip dear. I always loved you in blue serge, and
I adore your eyeglass. You really have been clever
in the small things you have done to change your
appearance. Perhaps you are right not to come,
though," she went on, looking in the mirror. " These
clothes are the best I could get at a minute's notice.
Mr. Dane was really quite nice, but he hadn't the
least idea how long it takes a woman to prepare for
a journey. Never mind, you wait until I get back
here this afternoon! I am going round to all the
shops, and I am going to bring the clothes I buy
away with me. Then I am going to lock myself in
my room and change everything. I am going to
have some of those funny little patent shoes, and silk
stockings — and, oh, well, all sorts of things you
wouldn't understand about. And do try and cheer
up before I get back, please, Philip. Twelve months
ago you would have thought all this Paradise. Oh,
I can't stop a moment longer!" she wound up, throwing away the cigarette she had taken from the box
and lit. " I'm off now. And, Philip, don't you dare
to go out of these rooms until I come back!"

She turned towards the door — she was half-way
there, in fact — when they were both aware of a ring
at the bell. She stopped short and looked around
enquiringly.

" Who's that?" she whispered.

Philip glanced at the clock. It was too early for
Elizabeth.

" No idea," he answered. " Come in."

The door opened and closed. Philip sat as though turned to stone. Beatrice remained in the middle of the room, her fingers clasping the back of a chair. Mr. Dane, hat in hand, had entered.

" Good morning, Miss Wenderley! " he said. " Good morning, Mr. Ware! "

Philip said nothing. He had a horrible feeling that this was some trap. Beatrice at first could only stare at the unexpected visitor. His sudden appearance had disconcerted her.

" I thought you were in Chicago, Mr. Dane! " she exclaimed at last.

" My plans were altered at the last moment," he told her. " No, I won't sit down, thanks," he added, waving away the chair towards which Philip had pointed. " As a matter of fact, I haven't been out of New York. I decided to wait and hear your news, Miss Wenderley."

" Well, you're going to be disappointed, then," she said bluntly. " I haven't any."

Mr. Dane was politely incredulous. He was also a little stern.

" You mean," he protested, " that you cannot identify this gentleman — that you don't recognise him as Mr. Douglas Romilly? "

" I cannot identify him," she repeated. " He is not Mr. Douglas Romilly."

" I have brought you all this way, then, to confront you with a stranger? "

" Absolutely," she insisted. " It wasn't my fault. I didn't want to come."

Mr. Dane's expression suddenly changed. His

276 THE CINEMA MURDER

hard knuckles were pressed upon the table, he leaned forward towards her. Even his tone was altered. His blandness had all vanished, his grey eyes were as hard as steel.

"A stranger!" he exclaimed derisively. "Yet you come here to his rooms early in the evening, you stay here, you go to the theatre with him the same night, you go on to supper at Churchill's and stay there till three o'clock in the morning, you are here with him again at nine o'clock — at breakfast time. A stranger, Miss Wenderley? Think again! A story like this might do for Scotland Yard. It won't do for us out here."

She knew at once that she had fallen into a trap, but she was not wholly dismayed. The position was one which they had half anticipated. She told herself that he was bluffing, that it was simply the outburst of a disappointed man. On the whole, she behaved extraordinarily well.

"You brought me out here," she said, "to confront me with this man — to identify him, if I could, as Mr. Douglas Romilly. Well, he isn't Mr. Douglas Romilly, and that's all there is about it. As to my going out with him last evening, I can't see that that's any concern of any one. He was kind to me, cheered me up when he saw that I was disappointed; I told him my whole story and that I didn't know a soul in New York, and we became friends. That's all there is about it."

"That so?" the detective observed, with quiet sarcasm. "You seem to have a knack of making friends pretty easily, Miss Wenderley."

"It is not your business if I have," she snapped.

"Well, we'll pass that, then," he conceded. "I haven't quite finished with you yet, though. There are just one or two more points I am going to put before you — and this gentleman who is not Mr. Douglas Romilly," he added, with a little bow to Philip. "The first is this. There is one fact which we can all three take for granted, because I know it — I can prove it a hundred times over — and you both know it; and that is that the Mr. Merton Ware of to-day travelled from Liverpool on the *Elletania* as Mr. Douglas Romilly, occupied a room at the Waldorf Astoria Hotel as Mr. Douglas Romilly, and absconded from there, leaving his luggage and his identity behind him, to blossom out in an attic of the Monmouth tenement house as Mr. Merton Ware, a young writer of plays. Now I don't think," Mr. Dane went on, leaning a little further over the table, "that the Mr. Douglas Romilly who has disappeared was ever capable of writing a play. I don't think he was a man of talent at all. I don't think he could have written, for instance, 'The House of Shams.' Let us, however, leave the subject of Douglas Romilly for a moment. Let us go a little further back — to Detton Magna, let us say. Curiously enough, there was another young man who disappeared from that little Derbyshire village about the same time, who has never been heard of since. His name, too, was Romilly. I gathered, during the course of my recent enquiries, that he was a poor relation, a cousin of Mr. Douglas Romilly."

"He was drowned in the canal," Beatrice faltered. "His body has been found."

"A body has been found," Mr. Dane corrected,

" but it was in an unrecognisable state.   It has been presumed to be the body of Philip Romilly, the poor relation, a starving young art teacher in London with literary aspirations — but I hold that that presumption is a mistake.   I believe," the detective went on, his eyes fastened upon Philip, his voice a little raised, " that it was the body of Douglas Romilly, the shoe manufacturer, which was fished out from the canal, and that you, sir, are Mr. Philip Romilly, late art-school teacher of Kensington, who murdered Douglas Romilly on the banks of the canal, stole his money and pocketbook, assumed his identity in Liverpool and on the *Elletania*, and became what you are now — Mr. Merton Ware."

Philip threw away the cigarette which he had been smoking, and, leaning over the box, carefully selected another.   He tapped it against the table and lit it.

" Mr. Dane," he said coolly, " I shall always be grateful to you for your visit this morning, for you have given me what is the most difficult thing in the whole world to stumble up against — an excellent idea for a new play.   Apart from that, you seem, for so intelligent a man, to have wasted a good deal of your time and to have come, what we should call in English, a cropper.   I will take you into my confidence so far as to admit that I am not particularly anxious to disclose my private history, but if ever the necessity should arise I shall do so without hesitation.   Until that time comes, you must forgive me if I choose to preserve a certain reticence as to my antecedents."

Mr. Dane, in the moment's breathless silence which followed, acknowledged to himself the perpetration

of a rare mistake. He had selected Philip to bear
the brunt of his attack, believing him to be possessed
of the weaker nerve.   Beatrice, who at the end of his
last speech had sunk into a chair, white and terrified,
an easy victim, had rallied now, inspired by Philip's
composure.

"You deny, then, that you are Mr. Philip Romilly?" the detective asked.

"I never heard of the fellow in my life," Philip replied pleasantly, "but don't go, Mr. Dane. You
can't imagine how interesting this is to me. You
have sent me a most charming acquaintance," he
added, bowing to Beatrice, "and you have provided
me with what I can assure you is almost pathetically
scarce in these days — a new and very dramatic idea.
Take a seat, won't you, and chat with us a little
longer? Tell us how you came to think of all this?
I have always held that the workings of a criminolo-
gist's brain must be one of the most interesting
studies in life."

Mr. Dane smiled enigmatically.

"Ah!" he protested, "you mustn't ask me to disclose all my secrets."

"You wouldn't care to tell us a little about your
future intentions?" Philip enquired.

Mr. Dane shook his head.

"It is very kind of you, Mr. Merton Ware," he
confessed, "to let me down so gently. We all make
mistakes, of course. As to my future intentions,
well, I am not quite sure about them. You see, this
isn't really my job at all. It isn't up to me to hunt
out English criminals, so long as they behave themselves in this city. If an extradition order or any-

thing of that sort came my way, it would, of course, be different."

"Why not lay this interesting theory of yours before the authorities at Scotland Yard?" Philip suggested. "I am sure they would listen with immense interest to any report from you."

"That's some idea, certainly," the detective admitted, taking up his hat from the table. "For the present I'll wish you both good morning — or shall I say au revoir?"

"We may look for the pleasure of another visit from you, then?" Philip enquired politely.

The detective faced them from the doorway.

"Sir," he said to Philip, "I admire your nerve, and I admire the nerve of your old sweetheart, Miss Wenderley. I am afraid I cannot promise you, however, that this will be my last visit."

The door closed behind him. They heard the shrill summons of the bell, the arrival of the lift, the clanging of the iron gate, and its subsequent descent. Then Beatrice turned her head. Philip was still smoking serenely, standing with his back to the mantelpiece, his hands in his pockets. She rose and threw her arms around him.

"Philip!" she cried. "Why, you are wonderful! You are marvellous! You make me ashamed. It was only for a moment that I lost my nerve, and you saved us. Oh, what idiots we were! Of course he meant to watch — that's why he told me he was going to Chicago. The beast!"

"He seems to have got hold of the idea all right, doesn't he?" Philip muttered.

"Pooh!" she exclaimed encouragingly. "I know

a little about the law — so do you. He hasn't any proof — he never can have any proof. No one will ever be able to swear that the body which they picked out of the canal was the body of Douglas Romilly. There wasn't a soul who saw you do it. I am the only person in the world who could supply the motive, and I — I shall never be any use to them. Don't you see, Philip? . . . I shall be your wife! A wife can't give evidence against her husband! You'll be safe, dear — quite safe."

He withdrew a little from her embrace.

" Beatrice," he reminded her, " there is another tragedy beyond the one with which Dane threatens us. I do not wish to marry you."

She suddenly blazed up.

" Because — ? "

" Not because of any reason in the world," he interrupted, " except that I love Elizabeth Dalstan."

" Does she want to marry you? "

He was suddenly an altered person. Some of his confidence seemed to desert him. He shook his head doubtfully.

" I am not sure. Sometimes I think that she would. Sometimes I fancy that it is only a great kindness of heart, an immense sympathy, a kind of protective sympathy, which has made her so good to me."

She looked at herself steadily for a moment in the mirror. Then she pulled down her veil.

" Philip," she said, " we find out the truth when we are up against things like this. I used to think I could live alone. I can't. Whatever you may think of me, I was fond of Douglas. It wasn't only

for the sake of the money and the comfort. He was
kind, and in his way he understood. And then, you
know, misery didn't agree with you. You were often,
even in those few hours we spent together, very hard
and cold. Anyway," she added, with a little tightening of the lips, " I am going to get my money now.
No one can stop that. You stay here and think it
over. It would be better to marry me, Philip, and
be safe, than to have the fear of that man Dane
always before you. And wait — wait till you see me
when I come back! " she went on, her spirits rapidly
rising as she moved towards the door. " You'll
change your mind then, Philip. You were always so
impressionable, weren't you? A little touch of colour, the perfume of flowers, a single soft word spoken
at the right moment — anything that took your
fancy made such a difference. Well — just wait till
I come back! "

She closed the door. Philip heard her descend in
the lift. He moved to the window and watched for
her on the pavement. She appeared there in a moment or two and waited whilst the boy whistled for a
taxicab, her face expectantly upraised, one hand
resting lightly on her bosom, just over the spot where
her pocketbook lay.

CHAPTER XVI

Philip was still gazing into vacancy and smoking cigarettes when Elizabeth arrived. She seemed conscious at once of the disturbed atmosphere. His hands, which she held firmly in hers, were as cold as ice.

"Is that girl going to be troublesome?" she demanded anxiously.

"Not in the way we feared," he replied. "All the same, the plot has thickened so far as I am concerned. That fellow Dane has been here."

"Go on," she begged.

"He laid a trap for us, and we fell into it like the veriest simpletons. He let Beatrice think that he had gone to Chicago. Of course, he did nothing of the sort. He turned her loose to come to me, and he had us watched. He knew that we spent last evening together as old friends. She was here in my rooms this morning when he arrived."

"Oh, Philip, Philip!" she murmured. "Well, what does he suspect?"

"The truth! He accused me to my face of being Philip Romilly. Beatrice did her best but, you see, the position was a little absurd. She denied strenuously that she had ever seen me before, that I was anything but a stranger to her. In the face of last evening, and his finding her here this morning, it didn't sound convincing."

"What is Dane going to do?"

"Heaven knows! It isn't his affair, really. If there were any charge against me — well, you see, there'd have to be an extradition order. I should think he will probably lay the facts before Scotland Yard and let them do what they choose."

She made him sit down and drew a low chair herself to his side. She held his hand in hers.

"Philip," she said soothingly, "they can't possibly prove anything."

"They can prove," he pointed out, "that I was in Detton Magna that afternoon. I don't think any one except Beatrice saw me start along the canal path, but they can prove that I knew all about Douglas Romilly's disappearance, because I travelled to America under his name and with his ticket, and deliberately personated him."

"They can prove all that," she agreed, "but they can't prove the crime itself. Beatrice is the only person who could do that."

"She proposes to marry me," he announced grimly. "That would prevent her giving evidence at all."

Elizabeth suddenly threw her arms around his neck and held her cheek to his.

"She shan't marry you!" she declared. "I want you myself!"

"Elizabeth!"

"Yes, I have made up my mind, Philip. It is no use. The other things are fascinating and splendid in their way, but they don't count, they don't last. They're tinsel, dear, and I don't want tinsel — I want the gold. We'll face this bravely, wherever it leads,

however far, however deep down, and then we'll start
again."

"You know what this means, Elizabeth?" he faltered.   "That man Power —"

She brushed the thought away.

"I know.   He'll close the theatre.   He'll do all he
can to harm us.   That doesn't matter.   The play is
ours.   That's worth a fortune.   And the new one
coming — why, it's wonderful, Philip.   We don't
want wealth.   Your brain and my art can win us all
that we desire in life.   We shall have something
sweeter than anything which Sylvanus Power's millions could buy.   We shall have our love — your love
for me, dear, and mine for you."

He felt her tears upon his cheek, her lips pressed
to his.   He held her there, but although his heart was
beating with renewed hope, he said nothing for a
time.   When she stepped back to look at his face,
however, the change was already there.

"You are glad, Philip!" she cried.   "You are
happy — I can see it!   You didn't ever care really
for that girl, did you?"

He almost laughed.

"Not like this!" he answered confidently.   "I
never even for a single moment pretended to care in
a great way.   We were just companions in misfortune.   The madness that came over me that day had
been growing in my brain for years.   I hated Douglas Romilly.   I had every reason to hate him.   And
then, after all he had robbed me of — my one companion —"

She stopped him.

"I know — I know," she murmured.   "You need

never try to explain anything to me. I know everything, I understand, I sympathise."

A revulsion of feeling had suddenly chilled him. He held her to him none the less tightly but there was a ring of despair in his tone.

"Elizabeth, think what it may mean!" he muttered. "How can I drag you through it all? A trial, perhaps, the suspense, and all the time that guilty knowledge behind — yours and mine!"

"Pooh!" she exclaimed lightly. "I am not a sentimentalist. I am a woman in love."

"But, Elizabeth, I am guilty!" he groaned. "That's the horror of it! I'd take the risk if I were an innocent man — I'd risk everything. But I am afraid to stand there and know that every word they say against me will be true, and every word of the men who speak in my defence will be false. Can't you realise the black, abominable horror of it? I couldn't drag you into such a plight, Elizabeth! I was weak to think of it. I couldn't!"

"You'll drag me nowhere," she answered, holding him tightly. "Where I go my feet will lead me, and my love for you. You can't help that. We'll play the game — play it magnificently, Philip. My faith in you will count for something."

"But, dear," he protested, "don't you see? If the case ever comes into court, even if I get off, every one will know that it is through a technicality. The evidence is too strong. Half the world at least will believe me guilty."

"It shan't come into court," she proclaimed confidently. "I shall talk to Dane. I have some influence with the police authorities here. I shall point

out how ridiculous it all is. What's the use of formu-
lating a charge that they can never, never prove? "

"Unless," he reminded her hesitatingly, "Beatrice —"

"Beatrice! You're not afraid of her? "

"I am afraid of no one or anything," he declared,
"when you are here! But Beatrice has been behav-
ing strangely ever since she arrived. She has a sudden fancy for remembering that in a sense we were
once engaged."

"Beatrice," Elizabeth announced, "must be satisfied with her twenty thousand pounds. I know what
you are trying to say — she wants you. She shan't
have you, Philip! We'll find her some one else.
We'll be kind to her — I don't mind that. Very soon
we'll find her plenty of friends. But as for you,
Philip — well, she just shan't have you, and that's
all there is about it."

He took her suddenly into his arms. In that moment he was the lover she had craved for — strong,
passionate, and reckless.

"All the love that my heart has ever known," he
cried, "is yours, Elizabeth! Every thought and
every hope is yours. You are my life. You saved
me — you made me what I am. The play is yours,
my brain is yours, there isn't a thought or a dream
or a wish that isn't for you — of you — yours!"

He kissed her as he had never dreamed of kissing
any woman. It was the one supreme moment of their
life and their love. Time passed uncounted. . . .

Then interruption came, suddenly and tragically.
Without knock or ring, the door was flung open and
slammed again. Beatrice stood there, still in her

shabby clothes, her veil pushed back, gloveless and breathless. Her clenched hand flew out towards Philip as though she would have struck him.

"You liar!" she shrieked. "You've had my money! You've spent it! You've stolen it! Thief! Murderer!"

She paused, struggling for breath, tore her hat from her head and threw it on the table. Her face was like the face of a virago, her eyes blazed, her cheeks were as pale as death save for one hectic spot of colour.

"You are talking nonsense, Beatrice," he expostulated.

"Don't lie to me!" she shouted. "You can lie in the dock when you stand there and tell them you never murdered Douglas Romilly! That makes you cringe, doesn't it? I don't want to make a scene, but the woman you're in love with had better hear what I have to say. Are you going to give me back my money, Philip?"

"As I stand here," he declared solemnly, "I have not touched that money or been near the bank where it was deposited. I swear it. Every penny I have spent since I moved into this apartment, I have spent from my earnings. My own royalties come to over a hundred pounds a week — more than sufficient to keep me in luxury. I never meant to touch that money. I have not touched it."

His words carried conviction with them. She stood there for several seconds, absolutely rigid, her eyes growing larger and rounder, her lips a little parted. Bewilderment was now struggling with her passion.

"Who in God's name, then," she asked hoarsely,

" could have known about the money and forged his signature! I tell you that I've seen it with my own eyes, a few minutes ago, in the bank. They showed me into a little cupboard, a place without any roof, and laid it there before me on the desk — his cheque and signature for the whole amount."

Philip looked at her earnestly, oppressed by a sense of coming trouble.

" Beatrice," he said, " I wouldn't deceive you. I should be a fool to try, shouldn't I? I can only repeat what I have said. I have never been near the bank. I have never touched that money."

She shivered a little where she stood. It was obvious that she was convinced, but her sense of personal injustice remained unabated.

" Then there is some one else," she declared, " who knows everything — some one else, my man," she added, leaning across the table and shaking her head with a sudden fierceness, " who can step into the witness box and tell the truth about you. You must find out who it is. You must find out who has stolen that money and get it back. I tell you I won't have everything snatched away from me like this!" she cried, her voice breaking hysterically. " I won't be robbed of life and happiness and everything that counts! I want my money. Are you going to get it back for me? "

" Beatrice, don't be absurd," he protested. " You know very well that I can't do that. I am not in a position to go about making enquiries. I shall be watched from now, day and night, if nothing worse happens. A single step on my part in that direction would mean disaster."

" Then take me straight to the town hall, or the registry office, or wherever you go here, and marry me," she demanded. " A hundred pounds a week royalty, eh? Well, that's good enough. I'll marry you, Philip — do you hear ? — at once. That'll save your skin if it won't get me back my twenty thousand pounds. You needn't flatter yourself overmuch, either. I'd rather have had Douglas. He's more of a man than you, after all. You are too self-conscious. You think about yourself too much. You're too intellectual, too. I don't want those things. I want to live! Any way, you've got to marry me — to-day. Now give me some money, do you hear? "

He took out his pocketbook and threw it towards her. She smoothed out the wad of notes which it contained and counted them with glistening eyes.

" Well, there's enough here for a start," she decided, slipping them into her bosom. " No one shall rob me of these before I get to the shops. Better come with me, Philip. I'm not going to leave you alone with her."

Elizabeth would have intervened, but Philip laid his hand upon her arm.

" Beatrice," he said sternly, " you are a little beside yourself. Listen. I don't understand what has happened. I must think about it. Apparently that twenty thousand pounds has gone, but so far as regards money I recognise your claim. You shall have half my earnings. I'll write more. I'll make it up somehow. But for the rest, this morning has cleared away many misunderstandings. Let this be the last

word. Miss Dalstan has promised to be my wife.
She is the only woman I could ever love."

"Then you'll have to marry me without loving
me," Beatrice declared thickly. "I won't be left
alone in this beastly city! I want some one to take
care of me. I am getting frightened. It's uncanny
—horrible! I—oh! I am so miserable — so miserable!"

She sank into a chair and fell forward across the
table, sobbing hysterically.

"I hate every one!" she moaned. "Philip, why
can't you be kind to me! Why doesn't some one
care!"

CHAPTER XVII

And, after all, nothing happened. Dane's barely
veiled threats seemed to vanish like the man himself
into thin air. Beatrice, after the breakdown of her
one passionate outburst, had become wonderfully
meek and tractable. Sylvanus Power, who had received from Elizabeth the message for which he had
waited, showed no sign either of disappointment or
anger. After the storm which had seemed to be
breaking in upon him from every quarter, the days
which followed possessed for Philip almost the calm
of an Indian summer. He had found something in
life at last stronger than his turbulent fears. His
whole nature was engrossed by one great atmosphere
of deep and wonderful affection. He spent a part
of every day with Elizabeth, and the remainder of
his time was completely engrossed by the work over
which she, too, the presiding genius, pored eagerly.
Together they humoured many of Beatrice's whims,
treating her very much as an unexpected protégée, a
position with which she seemed entirely content. She
made friends with the utmost facility. She wore new
clothes with frank and obvious joy. She preened
herself before the looking-glass of life, developed a
capacity for living and enjoying herself which, under the circumstances, was nothing less than remarkable.

And then came the climax of Philip's new-found

happiness. His earnest protests had long since been overruled, and certainly no one could have accused him of posing for a single moment as the reluctant bridegroom. The happiness which shone from their two faces seemed to brighten the strangely unecclesiastical looking apartment, in which a cheerful and exceedingly pleasant looking American divine completed the formalities of their marriage. It was a queer little company who hurried back to Elizabeth's room for tea — Elizabeth and Philip themselves, and Martha Grimes and Beatrice sharing the attentions of Noel Bridges. For an event of such stupendous importance, it was amazing how perfectly matter-of-fact the two persons chiefly concerned were. There was only one moment, just before they started for the theatre, when Elizabeth betrayed the slightest signs of uneasiness.

" I sent a telegram, Philip," she said, " to Sylvanus Power. I thought I had better. This is his answer."

Philip read the few typewritten words on the little slip of paper:

" You will hear from me within twenty-four hours."

Philip frowned a little as he handed it back. It was dated from Washington.

" I think," Elizabeth faltered, " he might have sent his good wishes, at any rate."

Philip laughed confidently.

" We have nothing to fear," he declared confidently, " from Sylvanus Power."

" Nor from any one else in the world," Elizabeth murmured fervently.

Then followed the wonderful evening. Philip found Beatrice alone in the stage box when he returned from taking Elizabeth to her dressing-room.

" Where's Martha? " he asked.

" Faithless," Beatrice replied. " She is in the stalls down there with a young man from the box office. She said you'd understand."

" A serious affair? " Philip ventured.

Beatrice nodded.

" They are engaged. I had tea with them yesterday."

" We shall have to do something for you, Beatrice, soon," he remarked cheerfully.

A very rare gravity settled for a moment upon her face.

" I wonder, Philip," she said simply. " I thought, a little time ago, it would be easy enough to care for the right sort of person. Perhaps I am not really quite so rotten as I thought I was. Here comes Elizabeth. Let's watch her."

They both leaned a little forward in the box, Philip in a state of beatific wonder, which turned soon to amazement when, at Elizabeth's first appearance, the house suddenly rose, and a torrent of applause broke out from the floor to the ceiling. Elizabeth for a moment seemed dumbfounded. The fact that the news of what had happened that afternoon could so soon have become public property had not occurred to either her or Philip. Then a sudden smile of comprehension broke across her face. With understanding, however, came a momentary embarrassment. She looked a little pathetically at the great audience, then laughed and glanced at Philip,

seated now well back in the box. Many of them followed her gaze, and the applause broke out again.
Then there was silence. She paused before she
spoke the first words of her part.

"Thank you so much," she said quietly.

It was a queer little episode. Beatrice gripped
Philip's hand as she drew her chair back to his.
There were tears in her eyes.

"How they love her, these people! And fancy
their knowing about it, Philip, already! You ought
to have shown yourself as the happy bridegroom.
They were all looking up here. I wonder why men
are so shy. I'm glad I have my new frock on. . . .
Fancy being married only a few hours ago! Tell
me how you are feeling, can't you, Philip? You sit
there looking like a sphinx. You are happy, aren't
you?"

"Happier, I think, than any man has a right to
be," he answered, his eyes watching Elizabeth's every
movement.

As the play proceeded, his silence only deepened.
He went behind at the end of each act and spent a
few stolen moments with Elizabeth. Life was a marvellous thing, indeed. Every pulse and nerve in his
body was tingling with happiness. And yet, as he
lingered for a moment in the vestibule of the theatre,
before going back to his box at the commencement
of the last act, he felt once more that terrible
wave of depression, the ghostly uprising of his old
terrors even in this supreme moment. He looked
down from the panorama of flaring sky-signs into
the faces of the passers-by along the crowded pavement. He had a sudden fancy that Dane was there,

watching. His heart beat fiercely as he stood, almost transfixed, scanning eagerly every strange face. Then the bell rang behind him. He set his teeth and turned away. In less than half an hour the play would be over. They would be on their way home.

He found the box door open and the box itself, to his surprise, empty. There was no sign anywhere of Beatrice. He waited for a little time. Then he rang the bell for the attendant but could hear no news of her. His uneasiness increased as the curtain at last fell and she had not returned. He hurried round to the back, but Elizabeth, when he told her, only smiled.

"Why, there's nothing to worry about, dear," she said. "Beatrice can take care of herself. Perhaps she thought it more tactful to hurry on home tonight. She is really just as kind-hearted as she can be, you know, Philip, underneath all that pent-up, passionate desire for just a small share of the good things of life. She has wasted so much of herself in longings. Poor child! I sometimes wonder that she is as level-headed as she seems to be. Now I am ready."

They passed down the corridor amidst a little chorus of good nights, and stepped into the automobile which was waiting. As it glided off she suddenly came closer to him.

"Philip," she whispered, "it's true, isn't it? Put your arms around me. You are driving me home — say it's true!"

Elizabeth sat up presently, a little dazed. Her fingers were still gripping Philip's almost fiercely. The automobile had stopped.

" I haven't the least idea where we are," she murmured.

" And I forgot to tell you," he laughed, as he
helped her out. " I took the suite below mine by
the week. There are two or three rooms, and an
extra one for Beatrice. Of course, it's small, but
then with this London idea before us —"

" Such extravagance! " she interrupted. " Your
own rooms would have done quite nicely, only it is
a luxury to have a place for Phoebe. I hope Beatrice won't have gone to bed."

" I am sure she won't," he replied. " She has done
all the arranging for me — she and Phoebe together."

They crossed the pavement and entered the lift.
The attendant grinned broadly as he stopped at the
eighth floor, and held out his hand for the tip for
which Philip had been fumbling. The door of the
suite was opened before they could reach the bell.
Elizabeth's maid, Phoebe, came forward to take her
mistress' cloak, and the floor valet was there to re-
lieve Philip of his overcoat. A waiter was hovering
in the background.

" Supper is served in the dining room, sir," he
announced. " Shall I open the wine? "

Philip nodded and showed Elizabeth over the little
flat, finally ushering her into the small, round dining
room.

" It's perfectly delightful," she declared, " but we
don't need nearly so much room, Philip. What a
dear little dining table and what a delicious supper!
Everything I like best in the world, from pâté de foie
gras to cold asparagus. You are a dear."

The waiter disappeared with a little bow. They

were alone at last. She held his hands tightly. She was trembling. The forced composure of the last few minutes seemed to have left her.

"I am silly," she faltered, "but the servants and everything — they won't come back, will they?"

He laughed as he patted her hand.

"We shan't see another soul, dear," he assured her.

She laid her cheek against his.

"How hot your face feels," she exclaimed. "Throw open the window, do. I shan't feel it."

He obeyed her at once. The roar of the city, all its harshness muffled, came to them in a sombre, almost melodious undernote. She rested her hands upon his shoulder.

"What children we are!" she murmured. "Now it's you who are trembling! Sit down, please. You've been so brave these last few days."

"It was just for a moment," he told her. "It seems too wonderful. I had a sudden impulse of terror lest it should all be snatched away."

She laughed easily.

"I don't think there's any fear of that, dear," she said. "Perhaps —"

There was a little knock at the door. Philip, who had been holding Elizabeth's chair, stood as though transfixed. Elizabeth gripped at the side of the table. It was some few seconds before either of them spoke.

"It's perhaps — Beatrice," Elizabeth faltered.

The knock was repeated. Philip drew a little breath.

"Come in," he invited.

The door opened slowly towards them and closed again. It was Mr. Dane who had entered. From outside they caught a momentary glimpse of another man, waiting. Mr. Dane took off his hat. For a man with so expressionless a countenance, he was looking considerably perturbed.

"Miss Dalstan," he said, "I am very sorry, believe me, to intrude. I only heard of your marriage an hour ago. I wish I could have prevented it."

"Prevented it?" Elizabeth repeated. "What do you mean?"

"I think that Mr. Philip Romilly could explain," Dane continued, turning towards Philip. "I am sorry, but I have received an imperative cable from Scotland Yard, and it is my duty to arrest you, Philip Romilly, and to hold you, pending the arrival of a special police mission from England. I am bound to take note of anything you may say, so I beg of you not to ask me any particulars as to the charge."

The colour slowly faded from Elizabeth's cheeks. She had risen to her feet and was gripping the mantelpiece for support. Philip, however, was perfectly calm. He poured out a glass of water and held it to her lips.

"Drink this, dear," he begged, "and don't be alarmed. It sounds very terrible, but believe me there is nothing to be feared."

He swung suddenly round to Dane. His voice shook with passion.

"You've kept me under observation," he cried, "all this time. I haven't attempted to escape. I haven't moved from New York. I haven't the slightest intention of doing so until this thing is cleared up. Can't you take my parole? Can't you leave me alone until they come from England?"

Mr. Dane shook his head slowly. He was a hard man, but there was an unaccustomed look of distress in his face.

"Sorry, Mr. Romilly," he said regretfully. "I did suggest something of the sort, but they wouldn't hear of it at headquarters. If we let you slip through our fingers, we should never hear the last of it from London."

Then there came another and a still more unexpected interruption. From outside they heard Beatrice's voice raised in excitement. Mr. Dane stood on one side as the door was thrown open. Beatrice suddenly flung herself into the room, dragging after her a man who was almost breathless.

"I say, Beatrice, steady!" the latter began good-naturedly.

There followed the most wonderful silence in the world, a silence which was filled with throbbing, indescribable emotions, a silence which meant something different for every one of them. Beatrice, gripping her captive by the wrist, was looking around, striving to understand. Elizabeth was filled with blank wonder. Mr. Dane was puzzled. But Philip, who a moment before had seemed perfectly composed, was the one who seemed torn by indescribable, by horrible emotions. He was livid almost to the lips. His hands were stretched out as though to keep from him some awful and ghastly vision. His eyes, filled with the anguished light of supreme terror, were fastened upon the newcomer. His lips shook as he tried to speak.

"Take him away!" he shrieked. "Oh, my God!"

Beatrice, more coherent than any of them, scoffed at him.

"Don't be a fool!" she cried. "Take him away, indeed! He's the most wonderful thing that ever happened. He's the one man in life you want to see! So you've come for him, eh?" she went on, turning almost like a wild-cat on Dane. "You beast! You chose to-night, did you? Now get on with it, then, and I'll give you the surprise of your life. What are you here for?"

"I am here to arrest that man, Philip Romilly, for the murder of his cousin, Douglas Romilly, Miss Wenderley," Dane announced gravely. "I am sorry."

Beatrice threw her head back and laughed hysterically.

"You'll never write a play like it, Philip!" she exclaimed. "There never was anything like it before. Now, Mr. Dane, what is it you say in America when you want to introduce anybody? — shake hands with Mr. Douglas Romilly — that's it. Shake hands with the dead man here and then get on with your arresting. He must be dead if you say so, but he doesn't look it, does he?"

Philip's face had become a more natural colour. His eyes had never left the other man's. He swayed a little on his feet and his voice seemed to him to come from a long way off.

"Douglas! It isn't you, Douglas! . . . It isn't you really?"

" I wish you'd all leave off staring at me as though
I were a ghost," the other man answered, almost pet-
tishly. " I'm Douglas Romilly, right enough. You
needn't look in such a blue funk, Philip," he went on,
his fingers mechanically rearranging his collar and
tie, which Beatrice had disarranged. " I served you
a beastly trick and you went for me. I should have
done the same if I'd been in your place. On the other
hand, I rather turned the tables on you by keeping
quiet. Perhaps it's up to me to explain."

Elizabeth, feeling her way by the mantelpiece, came
to Philip's side. His arm supported her, holding her
as though in a vise.

" Is that your cousin? " she whispered hoarsely.
" Is that Douglas Romilly? Is he alive, after
all? "

Philip had no words, but his face spoke for him.
Then they both turned to listen. The newcomer had
dragged a chair towards him and was leaning over the
back of it. He addressed Philip.

" We met, as you know, on the canal path that
beastly afternoon," he began. " I was jolly well
ashamed of myself for having made love to Beatrice,
and all the rest of it, and you were mad with rage.
We had a sort of tussle and you threw me into the
canal. It was a nasty dark spot just underneath
the bridge. I expect I was stunned for a moment,
but it was only for a moment. I came to long before
I choked, and when I remembered your grip upon my
throat, I decided I was safer where I was. I could
swim like a duck, you know, and though it was filthy
water I took a long dive. When I came up again —
gad, what disgusting water it was ! — you were tear-

ing off like a creature possessed. That's the true
history of our little fracas."

"But afterwards?" Philip asked wonderingly.
"What happened afterwards?"

"You just tell them all about it," Beatrice ordered
him sternly. "Go on, Douglas."

"Well, you see," Douglas Romilly continued, "I
was just going to scramble out on to the bank when
my brain began to work, and I swam slowly along
instead. You see, just then I was in a devil of a
mess. I'd spent a lot of money, and though I'd kept
the credit of the firm good, I knew that the business
was bust, and the one thing I was anxious about was
to get off to America without being stopped. I've
explained this all to Beatrice, and why I didn't send
for her before. Anyway, I swam along until I met
with an old barge. I climbed in and got two of the
choicest blackguards you ever saw to let me spend
an hour or two in their filthy cabin and to keep their
mouths closed about it. Fortunately, I had another
pocketbook, with sufficient to satisfy them and keep
me going. Then I borrowed some clothes and came
out to America, steerage. I had no difficulty in getting my money, as I had a couple of pals in Lynn
whom I had fixed things up with before I started.
They came and identified me as Merton Ware, and
we all three started in business together as the Ford
Boot and Shoe Manufacturing Company at Lynn in
Massachusetts. Incidentally, we've done all right.
Heaps more, of course, but that's the pith of it. As
for the body that was fished out of the canal, if you
make enquiries, you'll find there was a tramp missing,
a month or so before."

Elizabeth had begun to sob quietly. Philip, who was holding her tenderly in his arms, whispered unheard things into her ears. It was Beatrice who remained in charge of the situation.

"So now, Mr. Dane," she jeered, "what about your little errand? I hope this will be a lesson to you not to come meddling in other people's affairs."

Dane turned to the man who had brought this bombshell into their midst.

"Do you swear that you are Douglas Romilly?" he asked.

"I not only swear it but I can prove it, if you'll come along with me to Murray's," he answered. "My partner's there, waiting supper, and another man who has known me all his life."

The detective glanced interrogatively towards Philip.

"That is my cousin, Douglas Romilly," the latter pronounced.

Dane took up his hat.

"Mr. Merton Ware," he said, "or Mr. Philip Romilly, whichever you may in future elect to call yourself, you may not believe it, but the end of this affairs is an immense relief to me. I offer you my heartiest congratulations. You need fear no more annoyance. Good night!"

He passed out. They heard the sound of his footsteps and his companion's, as they crossed the corridor and rang for the lift. Speech was a little difficult. It was still Beatrice who imposed conviction upon them.

"I was seated in the box," she explained, "when Philip went round to see you, Elizabeth. I had been looking down into the stalls to find Martha, and all of a sudden I saw Douglas there. He, too, was staring at me. Of course, I thought it was some extraordinary likeness, but, whilst I was clutching at the curtain, he stood up and waved his hand. You should have seen me tear from the box! You know, ever since they showed me that signature at the bank I have had a queer idea at the back of my head. Luckily for him," she went, patting his arm, " he sent home for me a fortnight ago, and sent a draft for my expenses out. You won't mind, will you, if I take him off now? " she concluded, turning to Elizabeth. " They are waiting supper for us, but I wasn't going to let Philip —"

" Did you know that Dane was going to be here? " Elizabeth asked.

" Not an idea," Beatrice declared. " I simply dragged Douglas along here, as soon as we'd talked things out, because I knew that it would be the one thing wanting to complete Philip's happiness. We'll leave you now. Douglas will bring me back, and we are going to be married in a few days."

Philip held out his hand a little diffidently.

" You wouldn't —"

" My dear fellow," Douglas interrupted, grasping it, " wouldn't I! I'm thundering sorry for all you've been through. I suppose I ought to have let you know that I was still in the land of the living, but I was waiting until things blew over in England. That's all right now, though," he went on. " I've turned over a new leaf and I am making money — making it after a style they don't understand in England. I am going to pay my creditors twenty shillings in the pound before a couple of years have gone, and do pretty well for Beatrice and myself as well. You wouldn't care, I suppose," he added, as they stood there with locked hands, " to offer us just a glass of wine before we start out? Beatrice has been riddling me with questions and dragging me through the streets till I scarcely know whether I am on my head or my heels."

Philip emptied the contents of the champagne bottle into the glasses. Never was wine poured out more gladly.

" Douglas," he explained, " this is Miss Elizabeth Dalstan, whom you saw act this evening. We were married this afternoon. You can understand, can't you, just what your coming has meant for us? "

Douglas shook Elizabeth by the hand. Then he held up his glass.

" Here's the best of luck to you both! " he said heartily. " Very soon Beatrice and I will ask you to wish us the same. Philip, old chap," he added, as he set his glass down and without the slightest protest watched it replenished, " that's a thundering good play of yours I've seen this evening, but you'll never write one to beat this! "

Soon Beatrice and Douglas also took their departure. Elizabeth held out her arms almost as the door closed. The tear-stains were still on her cheeks. Her lips quivered a little, but her voice was clear and sweet and passionate.

" Philip," she cried, " it's all over — it's all finished with — the dread, the awful days! I am not going to be hysterical any more, and you — you are just going to remember that we have everything we want in the world. Sit down opposite to me, if you please, and fill my glass. I have only one emotion left. I am hungry — desperately hungry. Move your chair nearer so that I can reach your hand. There! Now you and I will drink our little toast."

It was an hour before they thought of leaving the table. A very perplexed waiter brought them coffee and watched them light cigarettes. Then the telephone bell rang. They both stared at the instrument. Philip would have taken off the receiver, but Elizabeth held out her hand.

"I have an idea," she said. "I believe it is from Sylvanus Power. Let me answer it."

She held the receiver to her ear and listened.

"Yes?" she murmured. "Yes? . . . At what time?"

Her face grew more puzzled. She listened for a moment longer.

"But, Sylvanus," she expostulated, "what do you mean? . . . Sylvanus? . . . Mr. Power?"

The telephone had become a dumb thing. She replaced the receiver.

"I don't understand," she told Philip. "All that he said was —' You will receive my present at five o'clock this morning!'"

"Does he think we are going to sit up for it?" Philip asked.

"He is the strangest man," she sighed. . . .

After all, some queer fancy awoke Philip at a little before five that morning and drew him to the window. He sat looking out over the still sleeping

city. All sound now was hushed. It was the brief
breathing space before the dawn. In the clear
morning spring light, the buildings of the city seemed
to stand out with a new and marvellous distinctness. Now and then from the harbour came the
shriek of a siren. A few pale lights were still burning along the river way. From one of the city
clocks the hour was slowly tolled. Philip counted
the strokes — one, two, three, four, five. Then, almost as he was preparing to leave his post, there
came a terrific roar. The window against which he
leaned shook. Some of the buildings in the distance
trembled. One, with its familiar white cupola,
seemed for a moment to be lifted from the ground
and then split through by some unseen hand. The
roar of the explosion was followed by the crashing
of falling masonry. Long fingers of fire suddenly
leapt up into the quiet, cool air. Fragments of masonry, a portion, even, of that wonderful cupola,
came crashing down into the street. He heard Elizabeth's voice behind him, felt her fingers upon his
shoulder.

"What is it? Philip, what is it?"

He pointed with steady finger. The truth seemed
to come to him by inspiration.

"It is Sylvanus Power's message to you," he replied. "The theatre!"

There were flames now, leaping up to the sky.
Together they watched them and listened to the
shrieking of sirens and whistles as the fire engines
galloped by from every section of the city. There
was a strange look in Elizabeth's face as she watched
the curling flames.

"Philip," she whispered, "thank God! There it goes, all his great offering to me! It's like the man and his motto —'A man may do what he will with his own.' Only last night I felt as though I would give anything in the world never to stand upon the stage of that theatre again. He doesn't know it, Philip, but his is a precious gift."

He passed his arm around her and drew her from the window.

"'A man may do what he will with his own,'" he repeated. "Well, it isn't such a bad motto. Sylvanus Power may destroy a million-dollar theatre for a whim, but so far as you and I are concerned —"

She sighed with content.

"We do both need a holiday," she murmured. "Somewhere in Europe, I think."

THE END

www.ingramcontent.com/pod-product-compliance
Lightning Source LLC
Chambersburg PA
CBHW020645030726
47498CB00002B/373